The Last Hybrid

Bloodline of Angels

The Last
HYBRID
Bloodline of Angels

Lee Wilson

William and Keats Publishing™
www.williamandkeats.com

Visit Lee Wilson's choice publishing company at
www.WilliamAndKeats.com
Published by WilliamandKeats, Fyffe, Nashville. PO Box 2, Fyffe,
Alabama 35971

WILLIAMANDKEATS is a registered trademark of William and
Keats Publishing.

Cover photo by Linda Russell-Walton.
Back author photo by Kat Slatery.
Cover design by Linda Russell-Walton and Rosamond Grupp,
edited by James Russell Lingerfelt and Cerian Griffiths.

Library of Congress Cataloging-in-Publication Data
Wilson, Lee.
The Last Hybrid: Bloodline of Angels. -1st ed.
2013935132

ISBN-13: 978-0-9844766-6-4
ISBN-10: 0-9844766-6-0

PRINTED IN THE UNITED STATES OF AMERICA.

For Joanna (of course)

CONTENTS

They say the best men are molded out
of faults and, for the most, become much
the better for being a little bad.

– William Shakespeare

PROLOGUE

RACHEL'S FIRST STEP on the ice gave her the confidence to walk the rest of the way to the oak tree growing in the lake. She planted her foot on a low branch and climbed until she overlooked the surrounding woods.

After a few minutes of peering up at the stars, she scooted onto the middle of the high branch to get a better view of the ice covering the deepest part of the lake.

She called to her mother, Cynthia, who was searching for her along the shore. "Here I am, Mommy. Up here!"

Though horrified, Cynthia found the will to remain calm so she wouldn't startle her young daughter. "Sweetie, I need you to carefully climb down, *right now*."

"No, Mommy, it's okay. Watch!" She moved out on the limb, stopping only when it creaked ominously beneath her. The weight tilted it down, sliding her a few inches further. *Crack!* The limb snapped and Rachel fell helplessly, crashing through the thin ice. When she floated up, her head struck the underside of the ice several feet from the hole.

Screaming, Cynthia rushed onto the lake, but the ice began to split beneath her feet. She yelled in vain for her husband and turned in desperation searching for a stick, rock, or anything at all that might be useful.

Racing footsteps sounded from the dark and a man leapt just beside Cynthia and hung above the lake, suspended in air, then dove through the ice.

Frantic seconds passed as the two remained under the lake. "God please!" Cynthia yelled into the black air. And then the stranger rammed his way up through the ice, holding the child under his arm. He hurried to the shore and laid her down beside Cynthia. Calmly opening the girl's mouth, the man sealed his lips against hers. His air filled her chest and he lifted her head as she coughed up water.

When Rachel had stopped spluttering, and was breathing well, Cynthia pulled her close.

"Hurry, get her inside and warm," the stranger said.

Cynthia looked up at his face. Moonlight revealed his blond hair, and the contrast of the moon and snow caused his blue eyes to glow. She nodded briskly, bundled her shivering daughter up, and carried the girl a few steps toward the pier. She turned back to look for him. "Thank you!" she yelled.

The man watched from the edge of the nearby woods before turning away into the trees.

Hiding in the woods, watching, stood a man with graying-brown hair and a scar on his right cheek. He smirked and lifted a large stick from the ground. His fingers squeezed the end of the stick and it surged into flames. "Well, now do you believe I know how to track wonder boy to his guardian subjects?"

Leaves crunched under the feet of a massive figure

who had been leaning against a tree. He pushed his long brown hair out of his face, revealing his strong jaw line and high cheek bones. He spoke solemnly. "It certainly seems you have the formula. But I'm going to withhold judgment until our little immortal friend is spitting on the graves of the Council."

Saying no more, they walked away into the cold woods.

Chapter 1

RETREAT

HANNAH SAWYER FOCUSED on breathing as she stared up through low-hanging tree branches into the starry black sky. She reached, in spite of the pain, to dig her cell phone from her pocket and noted the time on its cracked screen. She was five minutes late for the night shift.

With the temperature below freezing, she knew that what she felt trickling down the side of her face couldn't be sweat; it had to be blood. A couple more deep breaths gave her the strength to turn and see her car. Its front end was wrapped around a tree trunk, and the one headlight with power left to continue shining revealed smoke rising from the engine. She shuddered.

Red and blue lights strobed against the climbing smoke.

"I'm over here! Please…" Hannah called out.

A police officer kneeled beside her. "Can you hear me? Ma'am?"

Her vision blurred and all went black.

✳

"Hey there!" Hannah's mother was the first to see her eyes flicker open following hours of unconsciousness. "The doctor said you should be waking up soon. Thank goodness." She smiled. "How do you feel?"

"I'm not sure yet, Mom—shaken up at least. Where's Dad?"

"He went to get a snack from the vending machine. He'll be right back."

"I wrecked the car."

"You hit a patch of ice. There was nothing you could've done." She pushed Hannah's merlot red hair off of her forehead and brushed her pale face with the back of her hand.

"Am I okay? I mean… anything serious?"

"You have a concussion and some bruises, but the doctor says you'll be fine. You were thrown through the windshield. We're extremely lucky, blessed even." Her brown eyes welled up with tears and Hannah felt a twinge of guilt for worrying her parents so. She cleared her throat and changed the subject. "When do you think I can go home?"

"They said probably the day after tomorrow if everything goes well. Don't worry, I called Amber and she said you can take as much time off work as you need."

Five days later, Hannah walked swiftly across the Waffle Shack parking lot. She wore jeans, a thick jacket, and a woolen cap from which her long red curls always managed to escape. Aside from a dull ache in her temple, she felt fine.

As Hannah approached, Amber was visible through the glass front door: her brown hair neatly stacked in braids cascading down her neck. She opened the door for Hannah and hugged her. "Welcome back! How do you feel?"

"I'm fine as long as I don't touch my bruises." Taking her jacket off, Hannah rolled up her shirtsleeve to display the dark patches mottling the ivory of her slender forearm.

"Oh, that's not good," Amber shrugged. "Still, it could've been worse. Make sure you take care of yourself. Now, do you know what today is?"

Hannah smiled, raising her eyebrows. "Tuesday?"

"Yeah, but it's also your fifth year working at Waffle Shack today. Happy Anniversary!"

Hannah's smile faded. Amber went on. "You, me and Tony are working the night. Should be fun!"

The girls were interrupted as a middle-aged man in glasses, black slacks and a solid tan tie pushed open the door and paused in front of Hannah and Amber.

Amber stepped forward and spoke through her smile. "Hi there, feel free to sit anywhere you like."

The man nodded and walked to a table. Amber grinned at Hannah. "You know who that is?" she whispered.

Hannah studied the man and slowly shook her head. Amber's mouth gaped. "It's Mr. Howard."

Hannah stared back blankly.

Amber rolled her eyes. "From eleventh grade algebra!"

"Oh. I'd never have recognized him. He taught when

you were in eleventh grade too?" Hannah smirked, green eyes sparkling.

"Oh stop, I only graduated three years ahead of you."

"I'm just messing with you. Geez, the years fly." Hannah walked to Mr. Howard's table. "Hi. Do you know what you'd like, or do you need some more time?"

He tapped the menu with the back of his hand. "I'll have a cheese omelet with green peppers please."

"Sure thing. By the way, Mr. Howard, do you remember me from algebra class about nine years ago? I'm—"

"Hannah Sawyer. Of course I remember my students, especially the good ones. You had an 'A' on every assignment I gave that semester if I remember correctly. How long have you been working here?"

Hannah barely managed a fake grin. "I just started my fifth year." Mr. Howard looked back in silence, so Hannah continued. "I haven't finished college yet, but I plan to start back this semester." Her eyes drifted as though her own words surprised her.

"That's good. It's usually best to finish what you start. Best of luck to you. And I'll have some black coffee please." His glance down at the newspaper ended his side of the conversation.

"It's great to see you, Mr. Howard. I'll get your order in right away."

Hannah got to the counter in time to see Tony tying his apron. She waited until he looked up. "Hey, good to see you. I need a cheese omelet with green peppers."

"Sure thing, girl." Tony, a short, cheery man of Italian descent, put his Waffle Shack hat over his black hair and began pouring eggs onto the grill.

Hannah turned toward the coffee pots to find Amber standing with her arms crossed, looking indignant. "I heard you tell Mr. Howard you're going back to college this semester. Don't you know classes start in like two weeks? Were you even going to tell me?"

Hannah flushed and bit her lip. "I'm sorry, I don't know. It only just hit me that I wanted to go back while I was talking to him. It's weird, the accident made me think differently or something. I'm as surprised as you."

Hannah finished the nightshift and made it home just before sunrise. She collapsed on her bed and slipped into deep, warm sleep.

She dreamed of falling into blackness, grasping in desperation at empty air. A man suddenly grabbed hold of her arm, fingers digging into her flesh, and she dangled in his grip above the black abyss. She could make out an outline of his upper body and a flash of lightning intensified his sapphire-blue eyes.

The phone shrilled from her nightstand. Hannah flung her arm at it, and after missing a couple of times, opened her eyes and snatched it up.

"Hello?" she mumbled groggily.

"Hey it's Amber. Did I wake you?"

"Umm…"

"I know I did. Sorry."

"Don't worry about it. I was in the middle of the same dream I've been having for months."

"I wanted to talk to you about going back to college.

Do you still feel that way now that you've slept on it? Obviously we'll need to hire someone to replace you."

Hannah glanced out her window at a leafless tree shaking in the wind. "I haven't had a chance to think about it much more, but I'm pretty sure."

"I thought so. I knew it was just a matter of time."

"You did?"

"Yeah. I mean I'm content with this job and my life. Phillip and I'll probably get married in the next couple of years and I'm happy with everything. But I knew you wouldn't be. You want something more, right?"

"I guess so. I've just felt like I've been trapped for the last couple of years. Like I've been numb and didn't deserve anything else, because I blew it at college last time. But when I saw Mr. Howard, it reminded me of how I used to have a future. I wanted that again. I feel like something is waiting for me." Hannah smiled, realizing that was really how she felt.

"Well, I'm excited for you. Just promise me you'll keep in touch, okay?"

"Of course."

"Will you be back to work before you leave?"

"Yeah, you need me, right?"

"If you need to finish work earlier, I'll try and get someone to cover your shifts, and I'll look for a replacement in the meantime. If you can just do the shifts I can't get covered."

"Of course, Amber, thanks. I'm glad we're friends."

"We'll talk soon. Good luck."

Hannah hung up the phone and fell back in bed, still tired. Following minutes of insomnia, she sighed, sat up and looked at the clock. Two-thirty. Her dad would be home soon and she'd need to tell her parents about her plans. Getting up, she showered in the family bathroom, washed her unruly hair, and dressed in her favorite skinny jeans.

"It's about time!" Hannah's father grinned down at her with his arms crossed, when she told them. "I guess you want us to pay for it again?" His thinning gray hair and short beard, much like everything else about him, had gone mostly unchanged since Hannah's days of junior high.

Hannah glanced away, avoiding eye contact. "I've got a lot saved up from working. I think I can handle it."

"Well I guess with you not paying rent for five years, that makes sense. What do you think, Regina?"

Hannah's mother looked back at the two of them from the couch. She had a maroon sleep mask on top of her red hair from an earlier nap. Today had been one of her migraine days. "Marty, she's twenty-six years old. It's not like we have any right to make her decisions."

Marty tapped a finger on his upper lip, his eyes drifting away from the two of them. "I never said we did. I just don't want a repeat of last time."

"I'm past all that," Hannah said softly, "I really am. The spring semester starts in a couple of weeks. I called today and they said I could still get in. They have my transcripts."

Ten days later, an excited Hannah drove out of the garage; the secondhand silver Fiesta she had bought only days before, packed with a TV, laptop, clothes and boxes.

The route to her old college traversed a wide sampling of Tennessee landscapes: tin roofs, ivy covered arbors, rusted cars resting in knee-high grass yards, faded gray barns, corn fields, barbed-wire fences and wild flowers. Then, without warning, they converted to rock walls where roads were carved into mountains, small water-falls, gravel road ramps for runaway trucks, dark forests, mists of fog and small caves.

Hannah's stomach fluttered nervously as she took in the surrounding tree-covered mountains while passing a sign welcoming her to the town of Spring Hill. She searched the radio for local stations, but weak signals from distant towns dominated until she happened on a local news report.

"… and last night, eight-year-old Rachel Long nearly lost her life when she fell from a tree branch overhanging frozen Plunkett Lake. She fell through the ice and did not resurface until an unknown rescuer dove in and pulled her to safety. We spoke to Rachel's mother earlier today.

'She had climbed up that tree by the lake and I told her to come down, but the limb broke and she fell right through! Then out of nowhere, a man dove through and came up with her. He did CPR until she started breathing again, but he took off before I could thank him properly! So whoever you are, thank you so much, you have my eternal gratitude. Please let me meet you so I can thank you in person!'

The anchor's voice returned. "If anyone has any information on this mystery hero, please contact this station."

"Mystery hero?" Hannah repeated. She hadn't spoken since before starting the three-hour trip and it felt good to wonder out loud. "Huh, maybe real men do still exist." She turned the radio volume down as she drove through the entrance to campus. Little had changed. The dorms topped several hills and the class buildings stood mostly in valleys between them. The entire campus was tucked beyond a large wooded area that separated it from the rest of Spring Hill.

Hannah checked her paperwork again for the name of her dorm; McGee Hall. She lived in a different one last time. Since the college had a relatively small student body, the dorms were also small, so the school required several of them.

She pulled into the full parking lot at McGee Hall and parked in the nearest spot she could find, far from the entrance. Many of the other girls had returned from first-semester break the day the dorms reopened, in order to get a jump on their social lives, and Hannah wouldn't know anyone. She bit her lip anxiously.

She flipped down the visor and opened the mirror, checked she had nothing in her teeth and knotted her hair into a loose ponytail. Taking a deep breath, Hannah opened the car door to a chilling wind and her exhalation turned to wispy clouds in front of her.

In the dorm lobby, a girl of around twenty sat at a table with stacks of boxes, clipboards and papers. Her shoulder-length wavy brown hair matched her eyes perfectly and her shirt was buttoned up to her collar. The moment she saw Hannah she began her routine. "Hi, I'm Erika! Welcome back from semester break!"

"Actually, my break has probably been longer than most of the girls here," Hannah said as she looked around the empty lobby.

"Oh. Well this is my first time being a resident assistant. Did you take the semester off?"

"Yeah and then some. Are these for me?" Hannah motioned to items on the table.

"Sure are. Write your name and info on this sheet, then sign here stating you've arrived. And here that you agree to dorm policy. And this is for you." She held a booklet and key out to Hannah.

"Thanks." Hannah smiled briefly, took the key and turned back toward the front door, not relishing unloading her car.

Erika noticed her hesitance. "Um, do you have a boyfriend in one of the guys' dorms or someone who could help you bring in your stuff?"

Hannah chuckled. "I don't think there would be a guy here I even knew the last time I was on campus."

Erika looked slightly puzzled, but turned toward the hall behind her and grinned. "Hey, Anthony!"

Seconds passed and then a voice returned, "Yeah? What?"

"We need you, please."

Footsteps creaked on the old wooden floor of the hall. The sounds stopped when a large, burly young man, a little older than Erika, stepped onto the carpeted lobby floor. His hair was a slightly darker shade than Erika's, and he had tried to cover his boyish face with a beard that hadn't quite filled out.

Erika smiled at Anthony. "Babe, Hannah here needs those strong arms to help bring in some of her stuff."

Anthony grinned as though he had solved a minor mystery. "Ah… so when you need my help is when I have strong arms, huh?"

She flirted back, "No, it's because you *have* strong arms that I know you can help."

The two were mismatched in size, with Anthony towering over the petite Erika. They looked at each other a second too long, inhabiting their own private world, and Hannah looked away, embarrassed, until they finally remembered she was standing in front of them.

She wasn't only embarrassed as she thought of her anemic love life; she was also somewhat envious. She hadn't had a boyfriend since her first college stint, though she had gone out on a few dates. On one occasion she went to a movie with the son of her mother's close friend and, to her mother's great frustration, Hannah didn't find him at all attractive. His obsession with snakes and lizards didn't help matters.

"Hi, I'm Anthony. You okay?" he asked, fighting an amused grin.

"Yeah, I was just… thinking about something." Hannah quickly flipped open the booklet Erika had given her.

"I can follow you to your car and help with what I can, if you like."

Hannah raised her green eyes from the booklet that she had been holding upside-down. "Right. Thanks." She led the way, pushing through the double doors and into the chilled air of the parking lot. "All I could get was a spot in the back."

Anthony put his hands in his pockets. "No problem."

The crunching of ice beneath their feet thwarted any attempt at conversation. The remains of a recent ice storm surrounded most of the cars and the concrete dividers in the parking lot. The refrozen gashes from a snowplow made walking progressively difficult as Hannah and Anthony neared the outside of the lot, where less of the ice had been trampled.

Hannah unlocked her car and opened a back door. She pushed the button to open the trunk while Anthony picked up two boxes from out of the back seat. "I'll take this load and be back."

"Okay, thanks." Hannah laid some clothes on hangers over a box and carried it toward the dorm. As she walked, the cold air suddenly seemed difficult to breathe, her vision went fuzzy, and the box dropped from her hands. She braced against a car as her ears rung. Then blackness. She fell to the ground, hitting her head, her blood streaming onto the ice.

Chapter 2

NONTRADITIONAL STUDENT

HANNAH OPENED HER eyes, looking up at stained ceiling tiles.

"She's awake!" Erika yelled.

Anthony hurried into the lobby and kneeled on the floor beside the couch.

Hannah's head throbbed and fear tightened her chest. "How long have I been out?"

"I'd say about ten minutes. The blood made it look a lot worse than it was, I think," replied Anthony, his brown eyes filled with concern. "We were going to call an ambulance, but Erika called the campus nurse instead. She's on her way now. What happened?"

Hannah put her hand to her scalp and found the sore spot. "I just blacked out."

Erika dabbed Hannah's head with a cold wash-cloth. "Do you remember where you are?"

"Yeah, I'm at summer camp."

Erika and Anthony slowly met each other's eyes. Hannah snickered. "Yeah guys, I'm fine. I'm Hannah

Sawyer. I'm in McGee Hall. You're Anthony and you're Erika."

Anthony shrugged. "Sounds good."

"Thanks for carrying me in, Anthony."

Erika smiled at Hannah. "Daniel carried you in actually. Just like you were a baby. He was passing by."

"Oh. Who's Daniel?"

Before Erika could reply, the doors to the dorm lobby opened and Hannah felt the cold draft surround her. She glanced toward the entrance and saw a tall young man with blond hair and an unzipped black jacket, holding the door open for an older woman carrying a worn leather bag. She had slightly darker hair than him, cropped fairly short, a wiry frame, and bright, intelligent eyes.

Erika leaned near Hannah's ear. "That's Daniel. He went to hurry the nurse. She's his mother."

Daniel and his mother walked toward Hannah, Erika and Anthony. Hannah shivered involuntarily as Daniel's gaze briefly met hers.

"Hi there. I'm Marie, the campus nurse," she began as she knelt to the floor next to Hannah.

"Hi, I'm Hannah."

"I'm glad you remember who you are. I'm told it seems that you hit your head pretty hard."

As Marie lightly gripped Hannah's wrist to take her pulse, Hannah couldn't help but trace the contours of Daniel's muscular chest with her eyes. She flushed as she realized he was staring at her, but when she looked back at him, she quickly lost herself in his intense blue eyes. They seemed to shine on her like lights, and she couldn't tear her gaze away.

"Hannah, this is my son, Daniel."

Daniel smiled politely at Hannah who continued to stare back without saying a word, until Erika cleared her throat.

"I'm Hannah, sorry. It's nice to meet you."

"Nice to meet you too. I'm sorry about your fall."

"Oh, it's nothing," Hannah sputtered as she touched her head and reacted to the pain with an audible *ouch*. Her face was so burning red that she wished the floor would open up and swallow her.

"Well, there's nothing wrong with your pulse, at least." Marie smiled and gently pushed Hannah's hair to the side to inspect the sore spot. "There's definitely some swelling, though. Have you had another recent head injury?"

Hannah swallowed. "A few weeks ago. I was in a car accident. But the doctor discharged me a couple days later."

"Follow my finger please, Hannah." Marie slowly moved her finger side to side as she flashed a light in Hannah's right eye and then the left.

"In the coming few days you'll need to pay close attention to how you feel. If you feel nauseous, dizzy, have trouble concentrating, or feel unusually tired, you need to see a doctor."

Hannah nodded, hoping the concussion would not recur.

"Anthony, would you please bring Hannah an ice pack?"

"Yeah, sure." Anthony walked into a room off of the lobby and opened the freezer. Coming back in, he handed the ice pack to Marie who pressed it gently to Hannah's head. "Keep this on for ten minutes and then take a ten minute break. Do that for an hour or so."

"Thank you very much," Hannah said as she held the ice pack against her head and turned to Daniel. "And thank you for carrying me in."

"You're welcome."

Anthony smiled. "Thanks for coming, Miss Marie."

"Call anytime you need me, hun."

The five were quiet as Marie put her things back in the bag and Daniel picked it up. Anthony went toward the doors when Daniel and Marie were ready to leave.

"You coming to The Fireside tomorrow night, Daniel?" asked Anthony, clapping Daniel on the shoulder.

"Yeah, I'll see you there."

"What's 'The Fireside'?" Hannah asked Erika, sitting up.

Erika leaned over. "It's a pool hall where a bunch of the guys go. They always have a pool tournament soon after dorms open. Good food too. You should come. I mean, if you can, if you're okay."

Hannah looked to Marie. "I might, if I feel up to it."

Marie looked over her shoulder, having heard the girls, and cautioned, "Just don't drive unless you're sure you have none of the symptoms I mentioned."

Erika nodded. "She can ride with us. Daniel, you wanna ride too?"

Daniel glanced at Marie before speaking. "Yeah, that sounds good."

"Well, I've got to get back to the clinic. We always have students with stomach trouble the first few days back to campus." Marie hugged Daniel, took her bag from him and went out the door.

Daniel turned to Hannah. "I'll help Anthony unload your stuff if you feel like going to your room to show us where things go."

Hannah smiled, glad to have the help. "That would be great, thanks."

As Daniel and Anthony left the dorm lobby, Erika helped Hannah up, and walked with her to her room. Girls darted across the halls, doors slammed and music pounded through the painted cinder-block walls.

"You didn't exactly luck out by getting a room on the third floor. But at least we have elevators in this dorm now."

"Yeah, they only had stairs when I was here before."

When they got to her room, Hannah held the ice pack in one hand, fished the key from her pocket with the other, and opened the door.

"The girl who had this room before you went back home to her parents," said Erika. "She made bad grades and lost her scholarship. Too much partying, I think."

"Sounds familiar," said Hannah wryly. *Not this time*, she thought.

The girls walked into Hannah's room and looked around. The room contained a bed, two desks with shelves to hold more books than one student could read in a year, a wooden dresser, a closet, and an open door to the bathroom, which was shared with the room next door.

Erika couldn't contain her curiosity. "So, I saw you looking at Daniel. You think he's cute?"

"What? What do you mean?" Hannah flustered.

"Aw, come on Hannah, it was pretty obvious."

Hannah chuckled, looking sheepish. "Okay, so yeah, kind of. I was trying to figure out what to say. I mean, I was just passed out on the ice bleeding everywhere and he carried me inside. I should have apologized for the blood on his shirt. I should've been more grateful. He must've thought I was some kind of nut."

Erika giggled. "I'm sure he wasn't worried about his shirt. Or thought you were some kind of nut. I mean look at you!"

"What, covered in blood with a big lump on my head? Yeah, very attractive." The two girls laughed. "Do you know him pretty well?" Hannah continued.

"Yeah, I've known him since we were little kids. Anthony's good friends with him too, so I've been around him a lot. He's not dating anyone and he lives off campus… just in case you want to know." Her hazel eyes gleamed mischievously.

Hannah smiled at Erika's attempt to promote Daniel to her, as if it were necessary. As the girls heard Anthony and Daniel talking in the hall, they hushed their conversation.

Erika stepped through the open door. "Down here!" She walked toward Anthony and caught a small box from the top of the pile in his arms just before it slid off.

Hannah began to go out to help too, when her ears began ringing again and the room spun around her. She sat down on the bed, feeling nauseous, and watched as the other three walked in with the boxes.

"Hannah, are you okay?" Erika hurried over and sat by her. "You look even paler than before."

"I just still feel kind of lightheaded."

Erika shot a concerned look to Daniel and tilted her head toward Hannah, suggesting he do something to help. "Daniel, your mom's the nurse."

"You need to put that ice on your head again." Daniel got the ice pack off the dresser where Hannah had left it. He sat down on the bed beside her and gently held the pack to her matted waves of hair. "Swelling is the enemy here." He smiled and looked into her eyes.

Hannah froze, and it wasn't from the ice pack. It was weird; as though she was looking back at someone she'd known long ago. Or maybe known forever. She was riveted… lost.

Erika watched with fascination for a moment. "I'll just go help Anthony with the rest of the boxes, and you can stay here and look after Hannah." She left before he could respond.

Erika put her hands against Anthony's big chest and pushed him out into the hall with her.

"What's the hurry?" Anthony asked with his arms raised as they walked toward the elevator.

"Just watch and let me do my job."

"Dang girl, she just got here!"

"So? No sense in leaving her to waste her time with some of the immature jerks in Beck Hall. I mean look at her, she's gorgeous, and they're *all* going to hit on her."

Anthony cocked an eyebrow.

"I'm not talking about anybody you know! Well, not many anyway." Erika laughed and Anthony rolled his eyes.

"*You're* gorgeous," he said softly to her.

"Oh come here." Erika pulled Anthony's face to hers and they kissed as the elevator doors closed.

Daniel watched Hannah for signs of a concussion as the two made small talk. "Are you a freshman?"

Hannah laughed awkwardly and glanced down. "Let's just say I'm a 'nontraditional' student. What year are you?"

"I guess I'm considered a sophomore. I'm probably even less traditional than you are." Daniel smiled. She noticed his teeth were perfect: white and straight. His eyes seemed to switch from a deep crystal blue, to an icy mirror. He was lean, though clearly muscular, and near six feet tall. Although he looked young, there were small lines at the corner of his eyes, which made him appear slightly older, or wiser, than the others.

Her curiosity was piqued. "How much less?"

Daniel fixed his eyes on hers and slowly inhaled. "Well... I started college about nine years later than most, for one thing. I did some odd jobs, and travelled a bit, but lately I've been around campus a lot working with my mom at the health clinic."

"Are you in pre-med or something?"

"No, I'm just getting the basics right now. Still figuring out what I want to do and if I need a degree to do it. Have you declared a major yet?"

"I got most of my basics out of the way last time I was here. I'll probably be able to declare something soon. I'm thinking something in the area of social work or psychology."

Daniel removed the ice pack and looked at the bump on Hannah's hairline. "Are you still feeling lightheaded?"

He sat so close that Hannah felt the heat radiating from his body. As he spoke, she was transfixed on his lips, even to the point of briefly imagining cupping his face in her hands and pressing her mouth to his.

"Hannah?"

"No. I feel a lot better," she said, shaking the vision from her head. "Thanks."

"So, I notice there's only one bed in here. No roommate?"

"I asked for a private room so I could concentrate. I really need to hit the books. Last time I got pretty distracted," she replied ruefully.

Erika and Anthony walked in carrying boxes and clothes. "Hey guys, I think we got it all."

Erika pulled clothes from a box and hung them in the closet while Anthony sat other boxes on a desk.

Daniel stood. "I've gotta get going. I need to run some errands."

"We're picking you up to go to The Fireside tomorrow, right?" Erika placed her hands on her hips waiting for Daniel's answer, as though she thought he'd try to cancel.

"Yeah, I'll be ready."

The room next to Hannah's was empty and those across the hall seemed quiet. Only the adjoining room separated her from the stairway at the end of the hall. An occasional closing door was the only noise that could be heard outside the room while Erika helped Hannah finish the final bits of unpacking late the next day, before heading out for the evening.

"Why does Daniel live off campus?" Hannah asked as she stuffed her underwear in her drawer.

"Well he's over twenty-one so he's allowed of course. Besides, he lives with his mom. You do remember this school is way strict, right?"

"Yeah, that's one of the reasons my parents sent me here the first time. But after I left, I kind of missed the quaintness and the structure, if that makes sense."

Erika tilted her head back and forth as though she could see a little of Hannah's point. "I like it here and all; I just thought I'd be done with curfews once I graduated high school."

"At least we don't have uniforms."

Erika grimaced. "I hear rumors they want to do that."

"Those rumors were around when I was here too. Don't worry about it," Hannah smiled. "Um... back on the subject of Daniel. Am I imagining it, or do you want to get us together, or something? Kind of soon to try to set us up, isn't it? You don't really even know anything about me." *It is kind of weird*, Hannah thought, but refrained from saying so aloud.

"Yeah, I guess you're right. Sorry about that," Erika chuckled. "It's just that he goes through these dark phases. I don't even know how he passed his classes last semester because he sometimes missed weeks at a time. It seems like he isolates himself. Anthony and I've talked about it, too."

Hannah looked at the floor, squinting her eyes. "And so how would that make us good for each other?"

Erika laughed again. "That's not what I meant. I just think a girlfriend could do him some good, and I saw you looking at him and all." Erika glanced at her phone and her eyes widened. "We're late!"

Anthony sat in the dorm lobby repeatedly tapping on his phone. He stood and shook his head as Erika and Hannah ran into the lobby, struggling into their jackets. They both wore jeans and boots, as did Anthony.

Hannah twisted a dark green scarf around her neck, as Erika preempted Anthony's complaints. "I know, I know. We were talking and I just lost track of time."

"Sorry," Hannah added as the three walked toward the door.

Anthony held the door open for them. "Let's just hurry."

Hannah sat in the back seat of Anthony's beat up old SUV and rummaged in her purse for lip-gloss, which she applied dexterously without need for a mirror.

Anthony turned the key in the ignition. "If we can get to Daniel's house in ten minutes we should be fine."

Erika sighed. "Well, that should be easy."

"It should, but the roads are icy and it's dark." Anthony sounded more determined than annoyed.

The way to Daniel's house took them down the back roads behind the university. Hannah had only been that way once, years prior, and remembered very little. The isolated roads seemed to be mostly clear of ice. Anthony saw occasional patches and simply dodged them. He turned into a gravel driveway that went up a steep hill before revealing an old timber-framed house in the distance. As the SUV pulled up to the house, the front door opened and Daniel emerged wearing a black leather jacket. He walked down and reached for the rear car door opposite Hannah.

"Hello, fellow students. Everyone enjoying the heater?" Daniel talked loudly and wore a silly expression as he held the door open, letting in the cold.

Anthony turned up the heater. "Dude, get in. It's freezing!"

Daniel sat down and closed the door. Warmth slowly filled the car again as Anthony drove down the driveway toward the road.

"So how far is this place from here?"

Erika glanced back at Hannah. "Only about five minutes. When you were here before it was just a restaurant called Manny's, I think."

Daniel cleared his throat. "Yeah, somebody else bought it and added the pool tables. When were you here before?"

Erika answered for her. "Hannah was here a few years ago and went home for a while. She's back now."

"I noticed," Daniel said, teasingly.

Hannah smiled and joined in, "Yeah, I went to Manny's some. You know, before I came back."

Erika smirked. "Yeah, yeah. You try to help people out... Geez."

Daniel leaned forward and rubbed Erika's shoulders. "Oh come on, we're just messing with you."

Hannah saw the sign for 'The Fireside' in the middle of a gravel parking lot that was almost full.

"Good thing the gang got a table for us," Anthony said as he shoved the gear stick into park.

Hannah leaned over to Daniel and asked, "Who's 'the gang'?"

"Just some guys from school who play pool a lot here. They can be a little rowdy."

The four walked inside the low-ceiling, hole-in-a-wall joint to shouts greeting them. Little could be heard over the sounds of laughter, music, yelling, scooting tables and pool balls slamming together. What was once a casual restaurant was now more of a pool hall and bar. The decor was dated, but cheerful, and the atmosphere buzzing. Radiohead sounded from the iPod dock behind the timber-topped bar.

Anthony waved across the room to some of his friends, and led the others over to a table with three empty chairs.

"Sorry, we didn't know there'd be four of you," a dark-headed man said to Anthony.

Anthony shouted back over the noise. "No problem, Chris. Erika can sit in my lap until it's my turn." He motioned toward the other two. "This is Hannah. And you know Daniel."

Chris nodded his head and said "Hey" to Hannah and Daniel. Anthony sat down and Daniel and Hannah took the remaining chairs, hanging jackets and scarves on the backs of their chairs. Erika grinned as she sat in Anthony's lap. He leaned forward and whispered something in her ear that made her laugh. Daniel smirked at Hannah and she smiled shyly.

Chris tapped Anthony's shoulder. "You and Daniel are up."

Hannah put her hand on Daniel's arm as he stood. "How does the game work?"

"Pool?" Daniel laughed.

"Well, *team* pool," she grinned, reddening slightly.

"We're playing 'Scotch Doubles'. Basically one team alternates turns between the two members when one of them sinks a ball. So when I make one, it's Anthony's turn and when he makes one it's my turn. When one of us misses, it's the other team's turn. Other than that, it's basically just like regular pool."

Hannah looked at Daniel. "Regular pool... of course."

His eyes widened slightly. "You don't know how to play?"

Hannah shook her head, feeling awkward. Her hair swung freely, shimmering in the low lighting.

Daniel resisted the temptation to reach out and brush a stray wisp from her bottom lip. "Well, I'll show you sometime."

Hannah smiled as Daniel turned to Anthony and they walked to the table.

Anthony spoke near Daniel's ear. "We can win this thing."

Daniel nodded.

Erika bought a pitcher of sweet tea for the four and she and Hannah talked as Daniel and Anthony passed several teams to advance to the final game. During a break, they came over for a drink and Anthony stole a good luck kiss from Erika.

"Having fun?" Daniel asked Hannah.

"Sure. You two are really good. Have you played together a lot?"

"Quite a bit."

Hannah leaned in to keep from shouting. "I hope you win."

Daniel nodded. "Thanks."

She kept her eyes on him as he walked back over to the pool table. *Nice view,* Hannah sighed to herself.

Anthony joined Daniel, and Chris picked up a microphone. "Attention honors students!"

The crowd responded with laughter and shouts.

"We're down to the final round! It's Anthony and Daniel against Wes and Justin. Gentlemen, begin when ready."

The raven-black-haired bartender, a girl, hopped the bar and approached the two teams. She held out a quarter and asked them to call heads or tails to see who would break. Daniel called heads and she flipped the coin. It landed on heads and half the crowd cheered.

Chris racked the balls and lifted the triangle. Daniel leaned over the table preparing to break. He held the stick still and paused. Someone in the crowd yelled, "Break it!" but Daniel didn't look away. Seconds passed. He pulled the stick back and smashed it into the waiting cue ball.

The ball rocketed off the table and flew across the room, crashing through a large window-pane and shattering into dust on the brick wall across the street.

The entire room fell silent. A few guys clapped and hollered, but the rest of the crowd remained quiet. Nearly all eyes were on Daniel. He dragged his darkening gaze from the broken window to some of the faces staring at him. His pool stick fell from his hand and made a loud clattering noise as it struck the floor. Daniel walked to the front door of the restaurant. Anthony followed and stopped him just outside the door, with Erika a few steps behind. After seconds of increasing stares from the people around her, Hannah followed and opened the door to hear Anthony's voice.

"Bro, I don't know what just happened in there, but you haven't told me why you're leaving."

Daniel nearly shouted. "Why should I stay? To give the crowd more of the one-man freak show?"

"What are you talking about? Everything was fine before that happened and it was probably just adrenaline or something. Don't worry about it. Besides, how would you get home?"

Daniel met Hannah's gaze for a second, and she looked away in bewilderment. He paled, anger glinting in his cold blue eyes. He lowered his chin before speaking. "I'll walk."

Daniel crossed the street, passing the powder of what was once a cue ball on the sidewalk.

"But it's freezing out here!" Anthony yelled after him.

Hannah turned and saw a restaurant employee putting a large piece of cardboard in place of where the glass had been.

"Daniel!" Erika yelled into the darkness. But he was gone.

Chapter 3

DONATING PLASMA

On the way back, Anthony drove slowly and the three peered out of the windows. The moonlight flickered off the snow patches as they passed the trees.

Anthony broke several minutes of silence. "It's like a six mile walk back and it's below freezing. He could get hypothermia!"

"Okay, I don't understand what happened back there. Was it a trick ball or something?" Hannah asked.

"Now that's something I hadn't thought of," Anthony began. "Maybe one of the guys pranked us."

"A rocket ball? *Really,* Anthony?" Erika's voice quivered with sarcasm and anger.

"Who are you mad at? Me?" Anthony locked eyes with Erika before returning his gaze to the road.

"No, I'm mad that he just walked out like that and now we're driving in the dark looking for him!"

Anthony thought quietly for a few seconds and then chuckled. "I don't think a prank like that is even possible."

"Then what happened?" Hannah's voice urged from the back seat.

"I don't know," Anthony finally mumbled. He pulled

his phone from his pocket and dialed, but sighed almost right away. "Straight to voicemail. Hey, man, call me as soon you get this."

Anthony pulled into the McGee Hall parking lot under the awning near the door.

"Well, Hannah, sorry for the weirdness," Anthony said.

Erika spun to Hannah. "Yeah, how's that for a first date?"

"I don't know if it could be considered a date. But I just hope Daniel's okay. Keep me posted."

"We will," Erika promised.

Hannah walked into the dorm lobby and turned, expecting to see Erika following her inside, but instead she watched the car drive away with the two of them.

She walked down the hall and up the stairs to her room. This would be her first night back on campus and something about that made her heart race, especially after the peculiar events of the evening.

Pulling the door closed, Hannah turned the deadbolt. She stepped into the bathroom and brushed her teeth before changing into her pajamas and slipping under her bed sheets. Just before she fell asleep, Hannah thought of Daniel's blazing blue eyes, and the flash of anger in them, and wondered again what had happened.

Her dreams were chaotic and disturbing. Scenes of windows shattering, walls crashing down and other havoc, all at the hands of Daniel, dominated her sleep. Near the end of one dream, Daniel walked into a patch of woods as he had done earlier that night. She woke suddenly when he turned and looked at her with glowing eyes. Hannah gasped as the early sun shone through the window. Rising, she looked out at the fresh layer of snow blanketing the campus. Students were making their way toward the student center for breakfast.

Hannah's phone rang and she dug it out of her brown leather purse.

"Hello?"

"Hey, it's Erika."

"Oh, hey. How'd you get my number?"

"I saw you write it on some of your dorm papers and I have a really good memory with numbers. Plus, I'm looking right at the papers," Erika laughed.

Hannah spoke quickly, "Did you two go looking for Daniel last night after you dropped me off?"

"Yeah, we drove to his house and waited until he got there. Anthony calmed him down some."

Hannah poured water into her old, dented stainless steel percolator. "It was so weird. It seems like a dream now. Was he okay?"

"Yeah, he seemed fine. Didn't even seem like the cold fazed him."

"That's good." Hannah was glad, though she thought Erika must have been exaggerating. It had been *freezing*.

"Anthony and I were going to hang around campus today, maybe walk to the new place for lunch. You want to go? I could see if Daniel wants to come."

Hannah smiled; relieved it wasn't her who had to suggest Daniel coming along. "Yeah, that's great. That way I won't be a third wheel."

"Even if he doesn't come, you're not a third wheel. We've had a few days alone so time with other people is good. So," she continued, "you want to meet us for breakfast too?"

"Yeah, sure. When?"

"Well, it's 8:30 now, how's 9:30?"

"9:30's good, I'll meet you there."

"Okay, see ya soon."

Hannah tossed the phone on her bed and walked to the bathroom. She turned on the shower and dug in her faded pink bathroom bag until she found her shampoo, conditioner, and a razor. She locked the suite door before undressing and stepping into the falling warm water.

She shampooed her hair and slid the razor up her soapy right shin. A thud from inside the bathroom caused her to nick herself with the blade and red trickled down to her toes. Unable to see through the fogged glass of the shower door, her breath escaped her. She felt her heart beating in her throat.

"Is someone there?"

Stepping back, Hannah looked over the shower glass. The suite door stood wide open. "Who's there?"

She anxiously looked around for something in the shower to use as a weapon, but had only the razor in her hand. Covering her chest with one arm, she pushed the shower door open slightly with the other. It wasn't enough for her to see anyone, so Hannah pulled the towel down from the top of the shower wall and wrapped it around her before shoving the door completely open and stepping out. As soon as her feet touched the floor she held up the razor, hoping to appear threatening to whomever she saw.

The intruder stared at Hannah, before bending his head to pick up a tennis ball with his mouth. The dog turned and walked through the open door to the other suite, tail wagging happily.

Hannah exhaled the breath she'd been holding and gasped for more. "Hello? Whose dog is this?" The running shower water was the only sound that could be heard. She walked to the open suite door. The dog lay in the middle of the room, surrounded by opened boxes and full laundry baskets. He chewed on his ball, paused, cocked his head to one side, and looked at her, seemingly puzzled at the shampoo still in her hair.

The main door to the room stood open with the key still in the lock. Hannah heard footsteps creaking down the hall so she backed into the frame of the bathroom door. A tall girl with mid-length, straight blond hair walked into the room carrying a suitcase with one arm and a pillow under the other.

"Good boy, Zeb! Mommy forgot to shut the door, but you stayed 'cause you're a good boy." The girl continued her baby talk to the dog until she noticed Hannah standing in the bathroom doorway. She flinched.

"Oh, I'm sorry," Hannah stammered, "I didn't mean to scare you. The dog opened the door and came into the bathroom."

"No problem. I just didn't see you there. I'm Natalie."

"I'm Hannah. Nice to meet you."

Natalie gestured to Hannah's towel turned robe. "Did you run out of hot water or something?"

Hannah looked down at herself. "No, I was in the shower and I kind of freaked out when I heard a thud, I guess… I didn't know it was a dog that came in."

Natalie snickered. "Totally my fault. I'm used to that

room being empty, so I got in the habit of unlocking the bathroom door from my side whenever I walk in. The thud was probably Zeb's head. That's how he pushes doors open. Sorry."

Hannah watched Zeb. The white and brown boxer examined the two girls, deciphering whether the meeting was friendly or not.

"No problem. Nice meeting you." Hannah started to walk back into the bathroom, but turned to Natalie again. "I'm just curious, do you keep Zeb here?"

"I sure do. He's real quiet at night so don't worry about him keeping you awake."

"I just thought pets weren't allowed."

"I'm careful and he's well behaved. Besides, the dorm mom here is really lax. She doesn't worship the rules."

"Really?"

"Yeah. But you're not going to rat me out are you?"

Hannah smiled. "Of course not. It's none of my business."

Natalie turned away. "I think you're going to like it here," she said as she started pulling clothes out of the boxes.

Hannah walked back into the bathroom and shut the door. She turned the lock again and let out a sigh, finally relieved from the nerves that erupted when Zeb played peeping Tom.

She finished washing her hair, wrapped it in a towel and went into her room. Opening her closet, she fingered through her jeans, selecting a black pair of straight legs, and a burgundy sweater to match. After she dried her hair, she applied clear lip-gloss. Having a good complexion, she rarely wore other makeup, just a touch of mascara now and then.

Hannah slipped her feet into a pair of black flats, picked up her purse, and grabbed her phone. Glancing at the screen before dumping it into her bag, she noticed a voicemail and tapped the icon to listen.

"Hey Hannah, it's Erika again. I'd totally forgotten I have an errand to run today. A few of us do, actually. Anthony and Daniel are going, and another friend. We'd love for you to come, but it's not exactly a fun trip. I mean, we think it's kind of fun in a dark kind of... okay I'm really talking a lot so if you want to go, call me."

"Go where?" Hannah asked the empty room. She pressed 'return call' and Erika answered.

"You never said where you're going," Hannah said.

"Oh, right. We're going to donate plasma."

Hannah's jaw dropped. "Plasma?"

"We do it to earn some extra money. I make about forty dollars a week. Some of the guys make fifty because they're bigger."

"What? How?"

"It's like giving blood, except it takes longer and they put some of it back."

"What do you mean?"

"Yeah, the blood from your arm goes into a machine and they take out the plasma and put the red blood cells back in you."

Hannah swallowed hard. "And that's *fun*?"

"Well, once you get used to it, it's fun for some of us... kind of. So you in?"

Hannah leaned her head back and closed her eyes. She took a deep breath. "Yeah, I'm in."

Hannah waited in the lobby as girls walked in and out parading bags from trendy stores and talking about their class schedules.

Finally, Anthony's SUV pulled up with Erika in the passenger seat. Hannah pushed open the clear double doors and walked to the rear car door. She opened it to find Daniel and Natalie.

"Oh. Hi guys," she said, trying to cover her surprise as she slid in beside her. Natalie wore pink lipstick and lots of perfume. Hannah sneezed. "So you guys know each other, huh?"

Erika piped in from the front seat. "Yeah, we've known Natalie for years. Well, except for Anthony. He's known her for like a year now, I guess. She grew up about four miles from here, so she's a townie."

"Oh, right. Did you know she's my suitemate?" Hannah asked and then turned to Natalie, smiled, and said, "I'm sorry, we're talking about you like you're not here."

Erika laughed and answered before Natalie could open her mouth. "Yeah, we know she's your suitemate. It's a small campus."

As they drove away, Hannah smiled across at Daniel.

He grinned back. "Hey Hannah, you ready for a needle?"

"Let's not get ahead of ourselves," she laughed. "Right now I'm just along for the ride."

"It's by appointment anyway, so I don't think you could donate today, even if you wanted to," Daniel reassured.

"Yeah, I don't think I would've wanted to. So, you've *all* got appointments?" Hannah asked.

Daniel squirmed in his seat. "They do. I don't."

Erika wore a thick winter coat and scarf, with a braid sneaking out from beneath it. She turned to the back seat, her brown eyes sparkling with amusement as she looked at Hannah. "Daniel says he can't handle the needle thing. I couldn't either, until I needed the cash."

Daniel rubbed his arm. "It's not the needles, really. It's more the blood part I'm not thrilled about."

Hannah shuddered. "So, why are you going?"

"I'm the designated driver."

Hannah laughed. "Really? Why?"

"The blood letters here get a little dizzy after they have their fluids changed," Daniel chuckled.

Hannah nodded. "Ah, I see."

"When Anthony first went to donate," said Natalie, "he was as white as a sheet before they even stuck him. When it was over, he stood and passed out on the nurse. She went down and couldn't move with him on top of her. It was great!"

Everyone laughed as Anthony tried to talk over them.

"No, it wasn't like that! She reached her arm out to me like she was offering to hold me up, and then she wasn't strong enough." The group laughed again. "Well she was real small, like probably a hundred pounds or something."

"Then he threw up the orange juice they gave him," Daniel snickered.

The remainder of the trip consisted of stories of horror and humor from the plasma clinic. As Anthony parked the car, Natalie rested her head on the back of the seat in front of her and sighed. "I hate this."

"You don't think it's fun then? Is it that bad?" Hannah asked.

"No, it's not fun," she glanced at Hannah. "I just need not to think about it."

She reached across Hannah and opened the door. Hannah got out and waited as Natalie walked by her toward the clinic entrance.

The group found seats in the waiting room while a woman in scrubs sat behind a counter and spoke with Erika.

"Assuming her blood pressure checks out and she does the paper work, yes."

Erika walked over to Hannah. "You're in."

"What? No. I don't want to be in." Hannah objected, horrified.

"So is that three or four?" asked the woman behind the counter.

Erika's gaze guilted Hannah.

"Okay, geez. I guess I could use the money."

Hannah sat in the chair between Daniel and Natalie and started filling out the papers with slightly trembling fingers, while Anthony went to the donation room with Erika.

Hannah glanced at Daniel. "Why didn't they pressure you to do this?"

Daniel smiled, blue eyes glinting. "They tried a while back, but figured out pretty quick it wasn't happening."

"So how does this work? Do they just take us back one at a time?" Hannah asked.

Natalie stared at the floor. "No, they get one of us started and then bring the next person back. We all sit by each other in the recliners. It takes about forty-five minutes unless you have a really fattening diet. Then it's longer."

The counter woman called Natalie's name and she cut her eyes toward Daniel. He held her gaze for a couple of seconds before looking away as though he didn't approve.

She looked down again as she walked past.

"Am I missing something?" Hannah asked Daniel.

"What do you mean?"

"It seems like there's some tension between you two. Or something's going on that I don't understand. Sorry," she quickly added, "it's really none of my business."

Daniel's quick glance at Hannah added fuel to her suspicions that something strange was happening. "No, it's okay. I mean, we're kind of like brother and sister. So sometimes maybe we have a little friction."

Hannah felt Daniel was hiding something, but figured that since she was the newbie of the group, no one owed her transparency.

"Right. You've known Natalie for a long time then?"

"Since we were kids."

"Did she take a more relaxed route to finishing college too?"

Daniel turned toward Hannah, brushing a strong hand swiftly through his blond hair, and looked a little irritated with her. "Yeah, something like that," he said.

He didn't want to talk and Hannah wondered why he seemed annoyed. *Maybe I'm being too nosy asking so many questions about Natalie,* she thought.

Daniel shot up from his chair, tense, staring at the door to the donating area. Hannah looked around, but didn't hear or see anything out of the ordinary. He walked over and opened the door to find Erika standing on the other side reaching toward the knob. She nearly shouted, "It's Natalie, they can't wake her up!"

Daniel brushed past her and disappeared around the corner with Erika following. Hannah caught the door before it closed and rounded the corner to find reclining chairs with white machines beside them. Two nurses, along with Daniel and Erika, stood over Natalie.

Erika spoke frantically to Daniel. "She was on the machine and everything seemed fine, then she passed out!"

One nurse checked her pulse while the other gently patted her face.

Hannah watched Natalie's chest slowly rise and fall. Then, seconds of stillness. "She's not breathing!" Hannah yelled.

The nurses looked at Natalie's chest. "I will now administer CPR," one of them said, officiously.

Daniel pushed the nurse aside. "Oh for God's sake, get out of my way."

He put his ear over Natalie's face. After hearing nothing he opened her mouth and breathed into her.

One of the nurses turned to Erika. "Is he a doctor?"

"No," Erika said without taking her eyes from Daniel.

Suddenly, Natalie sat up gasping and coughing as

though she were strangling. She laid her forehead on Daniel's shoulder and breathed in gulps.

"That's it," Daniel whispered.

Anthony turned to a nurse. "Don't you have a protocol or something for times like that?"

"Yes, I was about to begin," she snapped.

The other nurse hurried away and returned in a few seconds with a cup of orange juice. She handed it to Natalie who coughed a "Thank you" and laid back on the recliner. The first nurse checked her pulse, but Natalie pulled away as she reached for Daniel and hugged him for a few seconds.

Daniel gently moved away and went back toward the waiting room, as Hannah followed. She sat down, turned to him and attempted to lighten things up. "Your group of friends is pretty high drama, you know?"

"Tell me about it."

Hannah picked up the papers from the seat beside her and let them fall in her lap. She suddenly had a weird hunch. "When I drove in a few days ago, I heard a story on the radio about a local guy saving a little girl who'd fallen into a frozen lake."

Daniel looked at her expressionless before giving a slight smile and nodding his head. "Oh yeah, I heard about that too."

"You wouldn't know anything about it, would you?"

"What do you mean?" His eyes bored into her, and she looked away, momentarily. But she knew she was right.

"Well, you happened to be there when I passed out, and carried me inside. And you just now revived Natalie. So I'm wondering if it was you who saved that little girl, too. You seem to have a knack for being in the right place at the right time."

Daniel's eyes flashed with an emotion she couldn't define. "I guess I do." He grinned, shaking off her words, and tried to change the subject. "My timing isn't half bad in other areas," he said, leaning slowly toward Hannah, tucking a lock of her hair behind her ear. He gently lifted her chin with his hand.

She felt his breath on her face and unconsciously moistened her lips with the tip of her tongue. Her body shivered as his hand brushed the inside of her arm, and the distance between their mouths diminished.

The sound of a throat clearing startled Hannah and Daniel and they pulled back with a jump. Anthony stood at the door, smirking. Hannah's skin flushed red and she turned away.

"Well, maybe not so good after all," chuckled Daniel under his breath.

Chapter 4

COMING CLEAN

"Excuse me, didn't mean to interrupt." Anthony crossed his arms and snickered.

What's wrong with me? thought Hannah, *I barely know Daniel.* Still, she couldn't help feeling irritated with Anthony.

Daniel glanced at him and then grinned at Hannah. He didn't seem bothered by someone walking in.

Erika appeared, helping Natalie to the doorway, but she stopped behind Anthony. "What is it? What'd I miss?"

Anthony winked at Hannah and Daniel. "Nothing, we were just waiting on you two. Let's get going."

Hannah occupied herself with handing her paperwork to the woman behind the desk. "I'll donate another time. I think we've all had enough for one day."

Once in the car, Natalie filled everyone in. "I've always had kind of low blood pressure. That's why I passed out like that."

Anthony eyed her in the rearview mirror. "You shouldn't really be donating then. How come it's never happened before?"

"Just lucky I guess. They always check it first, and it's been okay in the past. But when blood is taken the pressure can drop, and I guess that's what happened."

The rest of the ride back was accompanied by helpful suggestions from Erika on how Natalie could be healthier overall. Anthony joked about eating a pizza and hamburger diet like his to raise her blood pressure. Daniel was completely quiet and other than a few courtesy laughs, so was Natalie. When the discussion turned from health to other topics, Hannah chimed in enough to feel like part of the group.

As the car pulled into the parking lot, everyone took turns revealing their first class for the following day, and shared how they planned to spend their final night of freedom.

Natalie was first to excuse herself to errands and rest. She left the car with a general, "Bye," to the entire group.

Erika turned around in her seat. "So anyway, Anthony and I are going to the Gentry's farm to walk around the corn maze tonight around six. "Then we were going to grab something to eat after if you two want to come. The farm is open to the public and really pretty after sunset… and a little spooky."

"I remember," Hannah nodded.

"Would you two like to join us?"

Daniel had been far away in thought, but Erika's words reined him in. Hannah answered too eagerly. "I can do that."

She and Erika both watched Daniel for an answer. He looked back and forth at the two of them and chuckled. "Okay, I won't be the stick in the mud."

Daniel smiled at Hannah. "I can pick you up around ten to six, if you like?"

"Thanks. I'll be ready." A wave of anticipation passed over her. *He* was going to pick her up.

Daniel patted Anthony's shoulder, opened the door and walked to his truck.

Hannah was tired of sitting. "Okay, see you two tonight."

Erika nodded. "It'll be fun."

Hannah hurried to the solitude of her room. Living with her parents for the previous several years hadn't given her much time alone, and she was relishing having her own space again. She opened the door and fell into bed. After several minutes of trying to sleep, she sat up and flipped through TV channels before finally settling on music videos.

Just as a 'Florence and the Machine' song she liked came on, a knock sounded from the other suite door. She walked through the bathroom and opened it to find Natalie standing there with a half-smile.

"You're going to that farm with Daniel?"

Hannah was caught off guard by the question and the lack of a greeting of any kind.

"Yeah. Anthony and Erika are going, too. You coming?"

Natalie walked through the door into Hannah's room. She looked around scrutinizing Hannah's belongings. "No, I wasn't invited."

Hannah leaned against the door-frame and bit the inside of her cheek, uncertain how to handle this. "You're more than welcome to come."

"So you speak for them now?" Natalie almost snapped.

"I only speak for me, but I'm sure they'd be fine with it. I was just trying to be nice."

Natalie spun and faced Hannah. "Well, I can certainly see you've been trying to be nice to Daniel."

Hannah felt the sting of her face turning red. "Look I'm new here, sort of, so you've got to cut me some slack. I don't really know what you mean, but if you think I'm stepping in, and you've got something with Daniel, I didn't know."

Natalie brushed by Hannah toward the bathroom door. "Hannah, I don't know about cutting you any slack, but you're right about one thing. There's a lot you don't know."

Hannah didn't turn around to watch her leave, but heard the door close and lock. After a deep breath, she pulled a sweater from her drawer, grabbed her keys and pulled on her jacket.

She wandered around the historic campus discovering several new faces and beautiful winter scenery, but couldn't shake the idea that Natalie was right. Aside from all the normal little things that you don't know when you meet new people, she had the feeling there was something major… something that somehow centered on Daniel. But as much as she felt that getting closer to him could mix her up in something perhaps even worse than what had revoked her scholarship years ago, all she could think about was that almost kiss. A thrill went through her as she relived the moment. *Thanks a lot Anthony!*

Hannah had experience with jealous girls like Natalie. *It would just take perseverance,* she thought.

After grabbing a cup of dark roast at a campus coffee shop, Hannah headed back to her room to get ready for the farm.

She sifted through her clothes for something else to wear. After looking through her closet twice she lamented out loud, "How am I supposed to dress sexy to go to a farm in January?"

After leaving the others, Daniel drove to his house and hung black sheets over his window shades. He slept peacefully for an hour until he dreamed of a chase through a wooded area. A teenage girl yelled, "What do you want?" just before she tripped over a tree root and slid across the ground. Her attacker threw himself on top of her and began a succession of fierce punches. Daniel's body jolted and shook until the violent images shocked him awake.

He sat up in bed, panting and holding his face in his hands as he tried to reclaim his grip on reality. He punched the bed in frustration and lay face down on his pillow. After a few seconds of catching his breath, he glanced at the clock on his nightstand and walked to his closet to dress for the night out.

Hannah decided on the same black jeans and a thin long-sleeved shirt over a couple of layers. She glanced at the clock, grabbed her jacket and headed to the lobby.

Several other girls were there waiting on boyfriends and friends. Every car that pulled up to the double doors was met with a few raised heads and sighs of frustration from some of the girls left waiting.

Luckily, Hannah didn't have to wait long before Daniel's faded red truck pulled up and he pushed open the dorm door. Most of the girls watched as Hannah walked to him. "You know anybody in here?"

Daniel, dressed in blue jeans, boots, and a black bomber jacket, scanned the room. "Not exactly."

Hannah smiled and clinched Daniel's arm. "I guess they're all just wishing you were here to pick them up." She giggled and then bit her tongue, suddenly feeling like an idiot.

Daniel grinned and the two started to walk out, but a loud voice stopped them. "Everyone be quiet and look at the TV!"

The dorm mom, who was a plump, motherly type with curly brown hair and affectionately referred to as Momma Anne, watched as every eye in the room turned to her. She flipped the TV volume up as high as it would go as a local news anchor spoke.

"... The body was first discovered this afternoon. Authorities are asking viewers and those in the area who might have information to come forward, so that the killer can be found."

Momma Anne muted the TV as it showed a still picture of the victim, a teenage girl. "I want everyone to be cautious because this happened just a couple of counties away."

Hannah put her hand on Daniel's arm and turned to leave, but he pulled back, his eyes fixed on the TV.

"Someone you knew?" she asked.

Daniel turned his head slightly, but kept his eyes on the TV for a moment. "No. Let's go."

They left the lobby and headed to the truck. Daniel opened the passenger door for Hannah and walked around to the driver's side.

The trip reminded Hannah of the last time she saw the farm, a trip that required a drive past a state park engulfed by forest. It was near the end of the spring semester her sophomore year and the trees were blooming. But now, in winter, the trees were scrawny skeletons allowing visibility into a wilderness that held rumors of hikers who never returned. Bear attacks, hypothermia, wolves, and even Sasquatch were the villains of choice for juniors and seniors trying to frighten underclassmen.

Hannah turned toward Daniel and with the side of her eye saw chopped wood in the bed of the truck. "Where did that come from? Did you chop all that wood today?"

Daniel admired his work in the rearview. "Yep. I have to deliver that tomorrow on my way to chop more. The cold is good for business."

Daniel turned into the farm entrance as the sun gave way to dusk. An old guard shack stood as a source of authority that had long been abandoned. A run-down co-op building sat in the middle of a small parking lot for customers wanting fresh eggs and other farm products. Gone were the days of the farm being anything more than a business, as the owners and employees lived in subdivisions and carpooled in to manage the machines that monetized the animals. The connecting state park made it a popular place for college students looking for somewhere to make out.

Three cars were in the parking area, but all appeared to be empty. Daniel pulled up beside one of them and honked the horn. Anthony sprang up on his hands and knees in the back seat and glared through the fogged window. Daniel smirked at Hannah as he got out of the truck. He walked over to the car and Anthony rolled down the window. "Alright, you caught us. We got here early for a little fun, but we'll be out in a minute, okay? Just back off."

Daniel laughed, turned his back to the car and leaned against it. "Take your time. Hey, nice shirt Erika!"

Hannah couldn't decide if the situation was embarrassing or funny, but finally opened her door and stepped into the cold. "Did they have any clothes on?" asked Hannah.

Daniel's smirk spread into a smile. "Some."

Hannah watched steam rise from Daniel's lips. Images spun in her mind of the two of them in their own backseat, warmed from the winter chill by their bodies meshed together. She blinked, trying to dismiss the pictures, but Daniel guessed her struggle. His smile fell. "You know that moment at the clinic?" He waited until Hannah mumbled, "Yes."

"You were mouthwatering."

Hannah teetered on the knife's edge, feeling her body tremble as she inhaled.

Daniel took one step toward her. "Did you want it too?"

Hannah nodded, beyond speech.

Daniel didn't need clarification. He moved toward her with a confidence and focus she hadn't seen before this moment. His eyes flashed with power and intensity as he pulled her in and pressed his lips to hers.

Hannah's body surged with sensuality and her legs wobbled. Daniel lowered his hands and clinched her butt, pulling her tighter against him.

Despite their coats, Hannah felt Daniel's heart pound in his chest and ricochet off the drumming of her own. Kissing him was hypnotic, as though she existed only to return the fluid pressing of his lips. She unbuttoned one section of his coat and put her hands on his chest, then moved down to his abs, feeling his strength. Reaching out to wrap her arms around him, she suddenly felt an intense jolt of nervousness in her chest at the sound of Anthony's slamming car door. She gasped and pulled back from Daniel, realizing just how lost she had been in his kiss.

"Oops." Anthony yelled, his sarcasm over the top. He kicked leaves as he stomped away, his huge shoulders hanging and hands shoved deep in his pockets. "Nice shirt, Hannah!" he called back.

Hannah laughed with Daniel. "This is a new side of him," she whispered.

Daniel shook his head. "Ah, he's fine. He'll walk it off."

Erika opened the door and stood with a smile. Daniel looked her over. "It's nice to see you all bundled up!"

"It was really warm in the car. Who needs extra clothes when it's that warm?" She didn't even blush.

Daniel brandished his smirk again. "I couldn't agree more."

Pressing his hand to the small of Hannah's back, the three followed in Anthony's general direction. They crossed a bush-hogged field that ended with acres of corn stalks. Daniel's flashlight lit a path in front of them as they neared the entrance to the corn maze, marked by a sign that read, "Corn Maze $5. Do not throw corn at people or animals."

"Where's the corn?" asked Erika.

Daniel pulled part of a stalk down, snapping it in two at the middle. "Most of it's already fallen off or been picked by now. They don't use the machines to pick this field because they need the stalks standing for the maze. They also need all the word of mouth they can get."

The tall stalks shadowed the moon's light, leaving the maze path a black murk in contrast. Daniel walked into the darkness with Hannah holding one arm and Erika the other. A dried corn stalk crunched under his foot as he came to a stop and looked around for Anthony. "Now what kind of a boyfriend walks away from his girlfriend in the dark?"

A sudden burst of light from straight ahead startled both girls off of their feet, and they shrieked.

"The kind of boyfriend who is frustrated because he was interrupted on the one night he's looked forward to for weeks!" Anthony held the flashlight under his chin with one hand and pulled Erika from Daniel's side to his with the other.

Anthony nodded to Daniel before he and Erika turned to continue into the maze.

As they walked, Hannah put both arms around one of Daniel's. "I've never gotten to the end of this. I've either been out here with a girlfriend and gotten too creeped out or—"

"It's not that hard. Every year they cut it in the shape of something. This year it's a tractor. So you just walk like you're tracing a tractor and don't fall for the obvious wrong ways."

Anthony and Erika walked ahead to give themselves privacy. Daniel occasionally held the flashlight on Anthony or Erika's feet to keep up with them.

Coyotes yelped and barked in the distance, as if laughing. Hannah peered into the blackness between the stalks in the field surrounding them. "It's really spooky out here."

"I'll keep you safe." The soft words had just left Daniel's mouth when he seized Hannah and pressed his body to hers again. His hands moved down her back, and traced past her belt, cupping her behind while she trembled in his arms. She melded her body against his and opened her mouth for more. Daniel mirrored her movement and their tongues twined slowly together.

A cold wind swirled through the field, carrying the sound of someone shouting, "Shut up!"

Daniel peeled away from Hannah and took a few quick steps ahead to find Anthony around the next bend in the maze. His eyes were wide, so Daniel swung the light in the direction of his stare just as Hannah rounded the bend and stopped beside him.

Three men stood facing them. One of them held a knife to the neck of another man with long brown hair. Everyone froze.

The shorter man with his hands free stepped toward the students. His graying hair receded to the middle of his head and his neck was patterned in tattoos. He shone his flashlight at one face, and then another, until he had seen everyone in the group.

He put the light back on Daniel and sneered as he spoke. "It looks like you folks are in the wrong place at the wrong time." He pulled a gun and stepped closer.

The man stopped upon hearing Daniel's voice. "Funny, I was just thinking the same thing about your sorry ass."

The man bolted to Daniel and put the gun to his head. "What did you say to me?"

"You heard me, I didn't stutter."

The man's eyes widened with rage. "That was just the last thing you said on this Earth."

Daniel shook his head. "Not even close." He grabbed the man's arm and turned the gun away. He thrust the palm of his other hand into the man's straightened elbow and the joint fractured with an audible crack, sending the man into agonized screams.

The gun fell to the ground as the blubbering attacker dropped to his knees, cradling his lifeless arm.

Anthony hurried to where the gun fell and searched for it with his flashlight.

Daniel turned away from the fallen attacker and toward the man holding the knife. "Drop it."

The white-headed man watched Anthony rummaging for the gun and then looked back at Daniel. "You think because you broke his arm you can tell me what to do?"

Daniel slowly walked forward. "No. It's because I can tear that piece of crap you call a head off your shoulders."

From his knees, the broken-armed man yelled, "Kill him, Barry!"

Anthony leapt to his feet with the gun in hand. "Got it!" His voice wavered. He alternated the gun's aim between Barry and his accomplice.

"I'm coming to ya, Nate!" Barry walked with his hostage toward his hurt friend. Anthony followed them with the aim of the gun.

Suddenly, Barry shoved the hostage toward Anthony and ran with Nate into the darkness of the corn maze.

No one spoke while Anthony held the gun on the remaining stranger, who quickly put his hands in the air. He had a thick brown beard and his long hair hung in a slumping ponytail. After a minute of soundless stares, he broke the silence. "I guess the crickets are frozen, 'cause it's dang quiet out here."

He laughed to himself before speaking again. "Thanks for saving me, guys. You did real good. Especially you." He pointed to Daniel.

Daniel's expression remained unmoved. "Why were those guys about to kill you?"

"I saw a major drug deal going down at an empty car lot nearby. Those types sometimes come into the country to do deals. They were selling to someone and I walked up on it. Next thing I knew, I got hit in the head and woke up in the back seat of a car. They took me out here and were gonna cut my throat. You could tell the rest."

Daniel walked closer to him. "What were you doing walking through a car lot at night in this cold?"

The stranger looked at the ground for a moment and then again at Daniel. "Well normally I'd say it's none of your business, but since your boy's got a gun pointed at me, I guess I'll answer. I met a buddy at a truck stop and he drove us to a bar. We both had too much to drink, but he had way too much. He wouldn't give me the keys, so I was walking back to my car, since it was only a couple of miles away."

Daniel searched the area with his eyes before speaking again. "What's your name?"

"Zachery."

Daniel nodded his head. "Zac?"

"No, I said Zachery." His expression remained serious for a few seconds and then he grinned.

Hannah's teeth chattered. "Daniel, it's freezing. I've got to get warm and I'm pretty freaked out right now."

Erika huddled near her. "Yeah, we need to leave. Those guys could come back any minute!"

Anthony stared at the pistol in his hand, turning it on its side and examining his palm. "Wait a minute. This thing's got my finger prints on it now. So whatever those guys did, the police could blame on me!"

Zachery chuckled. "Nah, my friend. Let me have that."

Hannah held her breath as Anthony slowly handed Zachery the gun, wondering if that was the best course of action. But he took it and released the magazine, dumping the bullets into his hand. He looked up at the group. "Four of 'em!"

Anthony shrugged. "So how is that going to help?"

Zachery frowned. "Patience, my new friend. Follow me." He walked back to the maze entrance and through the field leading away from the parking lot. After a couple minutes of walking, the moon illuminated the lake shore. The group followed Zachery onto the wood bridge that crossed the lake, and he pulled a keychain from his pocket, flicking out a tool that he used to quickly disassemble the gun. He raised the magazine in the air and stepped as he threw it. "This goes in on that side of the bridge." Then he spit on the handle piece of the gun and wiped it clean of prints with the shirt under his coat, before throwing it in as well. "This goes in that side. And the rest goes in my pocket to be dumped somewhere else."

Anthony seemed moderately relieved. "Thanks. You're sure that'll take care of it?"

Zachery pulled a phone from his pocket. "It's a deep lake. Trust me. I'll call the police and give them a description of the bad guys."

Anthony again analyzed the details. "But you just hid evidence. Are you going to tell them about us being witnesses?"

"Nah, it wouldn't help them find those two and it'd give them a reason to think you're involved. Don't worry, I'll take care of it. I'll just call in an anonymous tip about the kind of car a drug dealer is driving and that's about all they'd get out of this anyway."

Anthony crossed his arms. "I guess trusting a complete stranger makes total sense."

Daniel put his arm around Hannah and started toward the truck. "Let's get some coffee."

Erika pulled on Anthony's arm and the two followed Daniel and Hannah, while Zachery lagged behind, talking to the police on his phone.

Hannah and Daniel followed the wood bridge to the lake shore and she spoke softly, "Don't you think we need to talk to the police? I mean, those men were going to kill us. You broke that guy's arm! I don't think we're taking this as seriously as we should."

Daniel didn't look concerned. "We don't have anything to worry about unless he wants a twin to that ruined arm."

Hannah smiled dubiously, unconvinced.

"Zachery, we'll take you to your car," said Daniel when they reached the parking area.

Hannah sat between the two of them in the truck as Anthony's car followed. The heater didn't take long to warm and fog covered the windows. The ride was quiet for several minutes, until Daniel cleared his throat. "So where you from?"

"About ten miles north. Near Franklin." Zachery's voice contained no worry or nerves. No one could have guessed he had just been rescued from two men who were about to slit his throat. A short time later, he pointed to the right. "Here's where I parked."

Daniel turned into the parking lot of the truck stop. "Which one's yours?"

Zachery indicated a four-door blue car and Daniel parked next to it. Zachery opened the door and stood facing them. "Since you're gonna get some coffee anyway,

I'd love to buy ya'll a cup just to say thanks. This place has got some really good brews."

Daniel nodded. "Sounds good to me."

The five walked from the icy parking lot into the truck stop. The inside walls were smooth timber resembling a log cabin, and the front area had trinkets and snacks for truckers breaking from the road. Zachery went to the front of the group and motioned toward the back. "This way, folks."

They went through the store until it opened to a country café where checkered tablecloths covered tables that stood on a dark wooden floor. A bearded man in a hat sitting at a corner table was the only other customer.

Zachery inhaled loudly. "Smell that coffee? Back when I drove trucks I couldn't wait to cross the Tennessee line so I could stop here and warm up with one of these." He pointed to a display of paper cups demonstrating size options.

Anthony went to the counter and looked at the dozens of clear drawers holding different kinds of coffee beans. "What makes the coffee so good?"

"Well, the woman who owns this place is wonderful at blending different coffee beans together. She's done it for over thirty years."

Daniel glanced up at the selection of blends. "So how do we know what blend we'll like?"

Zachery cleared his throat. "You just pick one and try 'em till you find your favorite. I've tried most of 'em. A good starter blend is the Pine Needle. Don't worry, it doesn't taste like a pine needle."

Daniel nodded his head. "Okay, that's what I'll take then."

Erika pointed up at the menu. "I'll try the Four Leaf Clover. 'Cause I like the name."

Anthony squinted his eyes at the options. "The Four Leaf Clover for me too, I guess."

The rest of the group looked at Hannah for the final choice. "I guess I'll try the Pine Needle since it's already been recommended."

Zachery raised his chin toward the barista who walked up behind the counter in time to hear the requests. "It's all on me, Caroline. And I'll take a Pine Needle also. A big one."

Caroline began blending the various beans contained in the clear drawers. While the others watched, Zachery pulled Daniel to the side.

"We need to talk. It'll take ten minutes for her to get it ready."

Daniel signaled to Hannah to stay put. The two walked into the store area of the building to be alone.

Zachery picked up an umbrella and looked it over as Daniel watched impatiently. "So what's up?"

Zachery continued to inspect the umbrella. "I'm here with a message for you."

Daniel raised his eyebrows. "I'm sorry, what?"

Zachery looked up. "I was sent to deliver you a message."

Daniel sighed. "What are you talking about?"

"You were called and you showed up. Now it's time for me to do what was asked of me."

Daniel leaned back onto his heels, observing Zachery

as though he questioned his mental grasp on reality. "You really lost me on this one. What do you mean I was called?"

Zachery blinked. "Maybe I've said too much." He put the umbrella back and crossed his arms. "The bottom line is, the Council wishes to meet with you."

Daniel snickered. "Who?"

Zachery continued. "Tomorrow night, eight o'clock. The lake." He turned and walked back toward the café.

Daniel gathered himself and followed. Zachery snatched his cup of coffee off the counter and turned to the others. "Well folks, thanks again. I'm gonna take mine to go. Take care."

He walked past Daniel, through the shop and out the door. After watching him drive away, Daniel went back into the café and slipped into the seat by Hannah. He sipped his coffee quietly while the others talked.

Chapter 5

THE COUNCIL

THE NEXT MORNING Hannah met Erika and Anthony for breakfast in the cafeteria. Hannah and Daniel had planned on comparing course schedules to see if they had classes together, but he never showed. "So I guess we'll just find out as we go," she said. "At least I have two classes with you guys." Hannah alternated her eyes between the couple. "Are you mad at Daniel for walking up on you guys last night?"

Erika held a goofy smile as she waited for Anthony to answer. He sniffled and looked around attempting to disguise the embarrassment swelling inside him.

"I don't think it's crazy for me to be a little annoyed at him."

Erika jumped in. "Oh, it's not a big deal. He probably didn't even know." She smirked.

Anthony turned red. "Well, that's why he should of freaking called or something!"

Erika tried not to laugh. "Easy, big fella. What are you going to do? Beat him up? I love you and all but come on, this is Daniel. I've seen him with his shirt off. He's like a Spartan or something. And he's our friend, so just get over it."

Anthony turned to Erika. "I'm over it. It's not a big deal. I just didn't like it."

"Besides, it's not like he saw my boobs this time."

Anthony swallowed his drink down the wrong pipe and started coughing and gasping for air. Finally he managed a strained hiss. "This time?!"

Erika tried to help by patting him on the back. "Well, by accident he walked in on me one time when I was changing. Are you okay?"

Hannah looked at her phone and saw that her first class started in five minutes. "Oh crap, I've got to go. I don't even know where this building is."

Erika turned from a wheezing Anthony back to Hannah. "What building?"

Hannah handed her the schedule with the locations.

"Laymond Center. Okay, yeah I guess that one is new since you were here last. Just go out of the caf and turn left. Follow the sidewalk until you see that historic oak tree and it's just beyond that. You'll see the sign."

Hannah took a last gulp of her orange juice. "Okay, thanks. See you later in English."

She followed Erika's directions until she got to the historic oak tree that she hadn't seen since her last time as a student. It was over one hundred years old and as wide as her bed. Unlike the other trees around, its bark split and curled due to its age. Looking up through its limbs, she encircled it, and after a few steps, someone put two hands around her waist and said, 'Gotcha!' Hannah jumped and screamed, pulling the stares of nearby students.

"You should've seen your face!" Daniel said, laughing.

Hannah started walking, breathing deeply to calm herself. "I think you scared me enough last night to last for a while, don't you?"

Daniel squinted. "I saved your life last night."

"Yes I know and I'm grateful, it was all just... I still can't believe it happened." Hannah stopped to look at Daniel who looked back at her as though her fear intrigued him; as though the concept of fear was foreign to him.

She stepped toward him, inches away from his mouth before continuing. "But what scared me most was that kiss. You hardly know me."

She held her cross expression until she couldn't any longer and exhaled with a flirty smile. Daniel grinned and she kissed him, putting her hands on his face. "I'm so glad we don't have to waste all that time getting to know each other, when instead I can just kiss you whenever I want."

Daniel laughed and put his hands around her waist. "You're late."

"Right. See you soon." Hannah kissed her finger and pushed it to his cheek. She walked away and pulled her phone out of her pocket, starting a text to Erika.

I'm acting like a slut around him or something. I'm coming on too strong. I can't help it. But some guys like that, right?

Self-doubt drowned out the words of her professor as she struggled to focus. Her thoughts lectured her far more thoroughly. *I've got to apply myself this time. I can't get caught up in a guy to the point that I mess up again.*

The next class was more of the same. Her mind

drifted back to that kiss, his sapphire-blue eyes and Erika saying he had the body of a Spartan. A tingle ran down her spine. Another class passed and she couldn't recall anything the professor said. She convinced herself that the first class of a semester was mostly a preview and rarely covered anything a student truly needed to know.

As she sat through the mental fog of her fourth class, her phone vibrated in her bag with a text from Daniel.

You going to lunch next? I'll be there.

When the professor dismissed class, Hannah was the first person out of the room. Erika walked out of another room as Hannah flashed by her in the hall.

"Hey, speed walker!"

Hannah turned around. "Oh, hey. Walk with me."

Erika dodged bodies in the hall. "If I can keep up!"

Hannah led the way and saved a spot for Erika in line at the cafeteria. When Erika got there she went toward Hannah holding a shrug. "Where's the fire?" she asked, chuckling.

"I'm just so hungry. I've been hungry ever since breakfast."

Erika rolled her eyes. "Okay, so anyway, I saw you and Daniel at the old tree this morning."

Hannah picked up a tray. "Yeah?"

"Yeah, and I got your text. You two seem pretty full on for the first week of a relationship."

"We're just having fun. He's a nice guy."

Erika smirked at her as though she had just walked out of a cheesy after-school special. "A nice guy?"

Hannah played dumb again. "What?"

Erika pointed to the woman behind the food trays.

"You need to tell her what you want. Two veggies and a meat."

After they filled their plates Hannah scanned the dining area for Daniel. She spotted him in a back corner sitting with a burr-headed guy.

Hannah stood beside the table until Daniel saw her, and he slid over so she could sit down.

Erika put her tray on the opposite side of the table. "Hey, Jeff. I didn't know you knew Daniel."

Jeff smiled at her. "I didn't until today. We needed an extra on our intramural football team and he filled in."

Daniel moved his drink out of Hannah's way. "Yeah, and he hasn't been off my case about joining their team since."

Jeff straightened his back. "He's freaking amazing. We were playing tackle and he lit up Carl Mitchell. I've never seen a hit that brutal. Carl had to be helped off the field and couldn't remember where he was. Heck, you should forget intramurals and play for the college team. You've got the upper body strength of a freaking bear!"

Daniel smiled faintly. "I don't have time for football. Or any sports really."

Jeff persisted. "But dude, you'd be awesome. At least think about it."

"Alright, I'll think about it. Do you know Hannah?"

Jeff turned toward Hannah. "Well, since I already know Erika, I guess you're the one he's talking about." He reached across the table and shook Hannah's hand. "Nice to meet you."

Hannah smiled politely, "Nice to meet you, too." *Though I'd rather be alone with Daniel.*

Jeff sat back and cut his eyes between Hannah and Daniel with one eyebrow raised. "So… is Hannah your—"

"Whoa, we haven't even known each other a week," Daniel chuckled.

Jeff rested his chin on his palm. "I wasn't asking how long you've known each other, but I gotta run. I'll see ya'll later."

He nodded toward them as he stood and then walked away leaving the table in the midst of awkwardness. Hannah's eyes fell to her arm that was interlinked with Daniel's. She had hardly noticed.

Erika was giddy. "You're welcome," she said in Daniel and Hannah's direction.

Daniel pushed his tray forward. "For what?"

"Oh, you know." She alternated pointing her finger at each of them twice. "The hook up."

Hannah's jaw dropped. "Erika, we met because my head was bleeding all over the parking lot and he carried me inside."

"Yeah, yeah." She grinned as she rolled her eyes. "Anyway, do you two have plans for tonight? Surely there's no homework on the first day. There wasn't last semester."

"I don't think I have any homework, and no plans." Hannah's curls flicked across her shoulder as she turned to look at Daniel.

Daniel shook his head. "I have plans."

Hannah's breath quickened. "Oh? What kind of plans?"

"I'm meeting with some people Zachery told me about."

"Zachery? The weirdo from last night?"

"Yep."

Erika cocked an eyebrow. "He was kind of creepy."

Daniel sipped his drink. "Maybe, but he wants me to meet some people, some kind of council or something. It's just something I think I need to do. It's probably a fraternity thing."

"Council?" Hannah looked at him, but he just shrugged and swept a hand through his hair.

Erika reached in her backpack and pulled out her phone. "Sounds weird. You're taking Anthony with you, right?"

"No, I'm going by myself." The firmness of his voice didn't invite their opinions. "Maybe we can meet for breakfast in the morning."

"Yeah, we missed you this morning," said Erika. "Did you oversleep?"

"I didn't sleep well. Kept having bad dreams."

Erika looked at him with pity. "Oh Daniel, not again."

Hannah felt left out of the conversation, but remembered Erika talking about Daniel missing classes last semester because he went through what she called 'dark phases.'

Without a word, Daniel slid to the edge of the booth, stood and walked to the coffee pot at the buffet, but saw that it was empty. He glanced at Hannah and pointed toward the other side of the building.

As he went, Hannah leaned toward Erika and spoke softly. "The bad dreams, did those happen last semester, too?"

Erika looked at Hannah quietly for a few seconds

before answering. "He's had them for years now. Even when we were kids. They seem to come and go." Erika's eyes focused on a watermark on the table as she remembered. "When we were kids, he spent the night at my house once because his mom left town for a nursing requirement. He slept on the top bunk where my older brother had slept until he got his own room. I remember he had a nightmare. He was yelling and his body was jolting like he was being hit. I woke him and he hugged me and cried for so long. I can't imagine him crying now though."

"Has he ever told you what the dreams were about?"

Erika thought for a few seconds, looking puzzled. "No, never actually."

Daniel rounded the corner and came back to the table. His mood seemed to have lifted and he smiled as he sat his coffee cup on the table.

"They made a fresh pot while I waited. It's a beautiful thing." He sat down by Hannah.

Erika and Hannah exchanged glances as Daniel sipped his coffee. His phone vibrated and Hannah strained her eyes to see the caller ID flash *Natalie*.

Daniel put the phone to his ear. "Hey." Hannah tried to hear her words, but it was no use.

"Sure, I'll have the truck on campus tomorrow so we can pick it up. See you then."

Daniel put his phone down and sipped his coffee. Hannah caught Erika's eyes and pointedly cut hers at Daniel.

Erika got the message. "So what was Natalie up to?"

"She bought a dresser and I'm gonna help her haul it

back to her room tomorrow." Daniel looked at the time on his phone and gulped down his last bit of coffee. "I've got to get to work."

Hannah finished chewing a bite of macaroni. "Work? You mean with the firewood?"

"Yeah, I chop it for folks around town. More people around here are going back to wood heaters, but don't like chopping the wood, or don't have time. So every few days during the winter I chop wood, and deliver it. It pays for some things."

He leaned over and kissed Hannah briefly on the lips. "I'll call you later or tomorrow. I don't know what time I'll get in tonight."

She thrilled at his kiss, and flushed, wishing it had been longer. Daniel smiled, knowing exactly what he had just done.

Hannah glanced at Erika and back at Daniel. "What?"

Daniel leaned toward her, pushed her hair over her shoulder, and trailed a finger over her cheek. "Well, I want to take the most beautiful girl on campus to the Valentine's dance this year. And I figure that since we kiss a lot and—"

Hannah cleared her throat, green eyes widening, and her face matching the color of her hair.

Daniel's grin widened. "Well, will you go to the dance with me?"

Hannah couldn't hold back a full, toothy grin. "Something tells me you knew my answer before you asked, but yes, I will."

Daniel pulled Hannah to him and whispered in her

ear, "I'm looking forward to it." He stood and lifted his tray. "I'll talk to you soon."

"Okay, be safe." She watched Daniel walk away before looking back to Erika.

Erika sat up straight. "This is so exciting!" She observed Hannah and raised an eyebrow. "What's wrong?"

"What do you mean?"

"I can tell something's wrong so just tell me."

Hannah took a moment to take another bite of macaroni and to compose her thoughts.

"It's hard to say. I guess I'm wondering if I'm being silly going after a guy who's got some issues. Am I getting mixed up in—"

"Just take it one day at a time. He's a good guy. He's just had a rough life with his dad leaving him so young. He started cutting firewood when he was like, twelve, to help with expenses. I think he's handled it well actually."

"I didn't know his dad left. I guess 'Why did you grow up with a single mother?' was on my list of things I figured I'd know eventually, but didn't want to ask. I wouldn't want to look like I was interviewing him for the position of 'boyfriend.'"

Erika laughed.

Hannah glanced at the time on her phone. She rushed through a few more bites from her plate and took a drink. "I've got to go. We'll talk later."

"I'm done with classes for today," Erika said. "Anthony's coming by for lunch any minute, so I'm here for a while. I'll call."

Hannah walked out of the cafeteria to her next class, a

frown creasing her brow as she wondered about Daniel's time with Zachery that evening.

Daniel drove his truck down a gravel drive to a house hidden in the woods. No vehicles were in the driveway since the older couple who owned the property were vacationing in a warmer climate until the following week, when they expected to return to ready-chopped firewood.

Daniel lifted an axe from the bed of his truck and laid it over his shoulder as he walked to the tree stump he used as his chopping block. Logs were in a pile ready to be split into sizes that would fit into a wood stove. Taking off his black jacket, he rolled up his sweater sleeves. Daniel picked up a log near the top of the pile and noticed a piece of paper wedged between it and the one beneath it. The paper had something written on it so he picked it up.

Don't forget tonight.

Daniel dropped the paper and looked around, turning to see every angle. The woods were quiet and seemed empty of everything but trees and brush. After several seconds of surveying the space among the trees, Daniel put the log on the stump and split it with a mighty chop.

Hannah finished her last class of the day. It only lasted fifteen minutes as the professor simply handed out a syllabus for the semester. It didn't seem like he wanted to be there.

Back in her room, she dropped her backpack beside her bed and started brewing a pot of coffee. A card had come in the mail from her mother congratulating her on returning to college. Hannah looked it over and smiled at the thoughtfulness. She noticed a P.S. line reading, "Your dad is proud, too."

Her phone buzzed a text from Erika.

Anthony and I r going 2 supper in caf at 7 if u want 2 join.

Hannah dropped the phone on her desk and fell back on her bed. She closed her eyes for a moment, but opened them after a few seconds to the sound of the coffee pot beeping. She got up and poured herself a cup. She breathed in the aroma and slowly exhaled, but the peace was interrupted by loud knocks on the bathroom door.

Hannah jumped, but calmed herself and opened the door to find Natalie standing with a blank expression. Before Hannah could speak, Natalie walked past her into the room. "So I see you're making yourself at home."

Anger bubbled up in Hannah's stomach, but she swallowed it before speaking. "I guess so. I like it at least."

Natalie turned toward her with a fake smile. "Well, what you think is all that matters." She held Hannah's gaze for a few seconds until Hannah looked away, then she spoke again. "Where's Daniel going tonight?"

Hannah's first thought was *none of your business* and that if Daniel wanted her to know, he would have told her. But Hannah wanted to be careful with her words.

"Um, I really don't know."

Natalie took a step toward Hannah, thickening the awkward air. "Well, what did he say?"

Hannah replayed what Daniel said in her head before speaking out loud. "He just said he was meeting some people tonight."

Natalie's expression darkened. Her eyes narrowed to slits and locked onto Hannah's as though she thought that's where Hannah hid the answers. She spoke through clinched teeth, "*What* people?"

"I don't know, Natalie," Hannah answered, then paused, wondering how much she should say. "Something about a council, or something."

Natalie's eyes widened, but quickly retracted. She took a step backwards, analyzing Hannah. "That's all he said? Did he give a time?" Her voice was intense and urgent.

Hannah shook her head. "That's all he said."

Natalie squinted again and walked uncomfortably close to Hannah who was able to feel Natalie's breath on her cheek. Natalie smiled in fake appreciation. "Thanks so much." She raised her hand and tucked Hannah's hair behind her ear. "It's nice when you can depend on someone." Her sarcasm was insulting but Hannah wanted the weirdness over too much to say anything. Natalie went through the bathroom and back into her room, slamming the door behind her.

Hannah took her cell phone and dialed Erika.

"Hey, Hannah."

"What's wrong with Natalie? She's psycho or something!"

Erika snickered. "What happened?"

"She's got to be the creepiest person I've ever met by a mile. I don't know what her problem is with me except that I'm dating Daniel, but is she really that immature?"

"She's always been close to Daniel. And you're right; she can be crazy strange sometimes. I've noticed she seems really slow to accept new people. If you and Daniel keep moving forward she'll just have to deal with it. But we all know she's been in love with him since they were kids so I guess you just need to be the bigger person."

Hannah grimaced, but felt a bit better. "Well, that shouldn't be too hard."

Erika laughed into the phone. "So, are you coming out with me and Anthony tonight?"

"Yeah, I'll be there."

Hannah heard Natalie's front door open and close, so she ran to the peep-hole and watched her walk by.

"Psycho girl has gone so I'm going to get back to my coffee and quiet."

"Okay, bye."

Hannah took a sip of coffee and again tried to relax, but her stomach felt residual nervousness from Natalie's visit and she shook her head in frustration.

Daniel's truck turned into the farm entrance. He stood and shut the door, carrying a flashlight in the dark. He walked past the corn maze to the lake and stepped onto the bridge. He pointed the light down the shore, looking for anyone. His sigh steamed into the cold as he ambled forward on the bridge toward the middle of the water. After a few seconds he pointed the light to the other side, but saw no one.

"I'm here," Daniel yelled into the darkness. He looked back toward his truck, barely visible under the single light standing over it in the parking lot. He laughed at himself for taking the word of an odd stranger and started walking off the bridge, back toward his truck.

Daniel heard a splash and turned to see a man leaping up from the water. Without warning, the man grabbed Daniel by his shirt collar and pulled him into the lake. When Daniel hit the water, he struggled to escape the man's arms, but his clothing was an obstacle, keeping Daniel from getting a grip on the man, and pinning him so that he could only hit him in the back. The man pulled him deeper into the freezing water as Daniel struggled to get free or get hold of him. He opened his eyes, but saw only darkness through the water. He couldn't tell which way the man pulled him, and desperately tried to free himself.

As Daniel's legs kicked, he hit something solid and in an instant was slammed to dry ground. He opened his eyes and through dim lighting could see what looked like the inside of a cave. Fire flickered shadows against the water and Daniel rolled over in its direction to see a dripping wet bald man standing in front of a torch hanging on the wall. Daniel leapt to his feet, fists clenched and blue eyes flashing.

The man held up his hands. "Settle down. You're alright."

Daniel swung at him, but he dodged the punch. The man did not hit back and pointed behind Daniel, stopping him from throwing another fist. Daniel continued to face him, but backed up so he could also see in the direction the man had pointed. Several others walked toward him and he braced for a fight, turning back and forth between the man and the group. They stopped ten feet from Daniel, and the man who pulled him into the water walked to the back of the group.

The leader, identified by the one who stood at the front, turned toward the bald man. "Thank you, Jonathan."

He turned back. "Hello, Daniel."

Daniel, fists still clenched, regarded the man who spoke: his dark skin contrasted against the light skin of most of the other men, and like Jonathan, he had a smooth scalp. He wore a brown linen shirt as long as a tunic over black pants.

"What do you want?" Daniel barked.

"We just want to talk. There are some things you need to know."

Daniel shook his head and threw his hands into the air. "Did you have to pull me into the freezing water and nearly drown me? A simple, 'Can we talk?' would've been just fine!"

"You wouldn't have drowned, Daniel. And we both know the cold doesn't bother you. It was important that no one saw this meeting. That's why we brought you here."

"Well, you told Zachery."

The man stepped closer to Daniel and smiled. "Zachery is a friend. We needed you to find him, so we arranged the right situation."

"You arranged the right situation? What the..." Daniel stopped himself from yelling, figuring he didn't want to fight the other dozen.

"My name is Uri. And yes, we arranged the situation that would get you to Zachery."

Daniel laughed wildly. "What does that even mean?"

Uri paced closer. "Daniel, did your mom ever tell you that you were unique?"

"Doesn't every mom tell her son that?"

"Your mom has never taken you to a doctor. She wouldn't let you play sports growing up and—"

"Why are you telling me things I already know?"

Uri glanced at one of the men behind him and then back at Daniel. "Has anyone explained your dreams?"

Daniel released a stunned laugh. "Look, I don't appreciate the eavesdropping or calling my friends, or whatever you did. And I don't have time for some wannabe psychic crap right now." Despite his confident words, he bit his lip anxiously.

Uri continued, "Do you know why you're strong enough to rip doors off hinges, and why your blood is white like milk?"

Daniel gasped and searched for the right words.

Uri smiled. "Now do I have your attention?"

Daniel nodded, eyes widening.

"Then let's have a seat and talk like civilized creatures."

The men behind Uri turned and walked deeper into the cave. They rounded a corner and Uri gestured for Daniel to walk with him. Daniel took a few wary steps forward but waited until the dark-skinned man started walking. Then Daniel followed behind.

Once around the corner, the cave opened to a large area with dozens of wooden tables, chairs and several fire pits. Uri went toward two large chairs seated in front of a fireplace. "Please have a seat, Daniel."

Daniel looked around for the others, but most had

left the room through doorways lining the walls of the cave. He sat down and Uri sat in the chair beside him.

Uri smiled. "Beautiful fire, don't you think?"

Daniel didn't look back at Uri. "You were going to tell me about the dreams?"

"Yes. What interests you about them?"

"Why am I having them? And why have I had them all my life?"

"You want to know why you're dreaming about people being murdered?"

"How do you know that?"

"You'll find I know a lot about you, Daniel."

"Then tell me how I dreamed about a girl being murdered and then saw her face on TV an hour later." Daniel's voice rose slightly.

Uri stood and took a metal poker leaning against the fire pit. He moved some coals around under the logs and the fire grew noticeably stronger. He sat back in his chair. "Daniel what did your mom tell you?"

Daniel swallowed and watched the fire. "When I was little, she used to tell me... that I was half angel. That my father was an angel. Mom's a little religious, so I think she was really just trying to make me feel better about not having a dad. She didn't talk about it when I got older. But what does that have to do with the dreams?"

"Everything. Your mom told you the truth. That's why you're having the dreams."

"Yeah, *right*. So I'm half an angel like my mom said." Daniel's voice dripped with sarcasm. "Come on, get real."

"It *is* real. Think about it, Daniel. Think about all the

things you have done, your strength, why you are so often in the right place at the right time… your good heart."

Daniel squeezed his eyes shut, and rubbed his temples. Hannah's matching words ran through his mind, and memories of rescues, and strange things happening bubbled to the surface. He recalled pulling someone from a wrecked car once, right before it exploded. And then there was his spirituality… he wasn't overly religious, but had always felt a closeness to God in some way.

Daniel looked up to find Uri studying him intently. The truth stared back from the older man's eyes.

"This has to be some sort of prank. Why would I be having nightmares about murders as they happen? I don't get it."

Uri turned to the fire. "Daniel, this isn't a prank. I realize you are having trouble believing this, but it's all real. The reason you're having these dreams is because your father was a Shomera angel."

"Shomera?"

"They guard humans."

"So he was a guardian angel?"

"Yes," Uri said. "Something like that. And some of his gifts were passed to you. The guardian part of you knows when certain people are in danger. Certain people that you're compatible to based on your guardian traits. Other half-angels whose fathers were guardians have the kind of dreams you're having. That's how we knew you would be having them."

Daniel, overwhelmed, gripped the arm of Uri's chair. "Okay, and who *exactly,* is my father?"

Uri exhaled slowly. "The Council hasn't made a decision on telling you yet."

"The 'Council'? What is that anyway?"

Uri looked around. "Many of the members are here."

"No, I mean who *are* you? Who are you to tell me who I am, but keep my father a secret from me?"

Uri stood and turned to Daniel, his dark eyes flashing. "Know your place, boy."

Power and authority riveted from Uri's stature.

"I just want to know who you are. Why are you part of this council, and how do you know these things?"

Uri crossed his arms, and smiled slightly. "Haven't you worked it out yet? 'Uri' is short for Uriel. I'm an angel. We're a council of angels."

Daniel looked up at Uri and then slowly surveyed the large room. "Uriel," he repeated slowly. "Sure. I'm half an angel, because that's what my mom told me, so why can't I believe you're a full-blooded angel, since you had me drug through a freezing lake into an underwater cave? Just like angels *would* do."

Daniel stood and walked back toward the water. Uriel followed behind him. "Daniel, you're important to all of this," his speech quickened. "There are others who've been trying to find you."

Daniel stopped and turned back toward Uriel. "What do you mean 'others'?"

"I mean that there are other angels. Rebels. Some call them 'fallen ones.' If you had let me finish, I'd have told you that the reason you've been having so many of the dreams lately, is because the others are killing people they think your guardian instincts will try to protect. Like when Zachery was in danger. You managed to be in the right place at the right time. We got it right. Eventually they will too."

Daniel ran his fingers through his hair. "So there're dark angels now? Next are you going to tell me there're vampires, too?"

"If you want to use that name for them, that's fine, but folklore's perception of them is not what they truly are. They're hybrids like you, but they follow the fallen ones."

"Are you saying that half angels become *vampires* if they follow dark angels?" Daniel peered into the dim light, incredulous.

Uriel nodded his head. "It's more complicated than that, but yes."

"And they have the teeth and stuff?"

Uriel glanced at the ground before answering. "Would it surprise you that followers of the dark one would have fangs like a serpent?"

Daniel pressed his lips together in thought. "What about the blood, why do they drink it?"

Uriel crossed his arms. "Dark hybrids, or 'vampires' as you call them, drink blood because the darkness is killing off their human half. They no longer have access to the life force provided by the Creator. They need living human blood to satisfy the deficiency."

Daniel closed his eyes, and shook his head, his blond hair glowing slightly in the torchlight. He hoped that when he opened them again, perhaps he would be in his bed, just waking from yet another dream. But no, Uriel still stood before him. Daniel sighed. "What do you want with me?"

Uriel paced away while choosing his words. He walked to a dead torch on the cave wall and squeezed the wick with his thumb and index finger. The wick caught fire and the torch glowed with full intensity.

Daniel's eyes widened. "That's impressive."

Uriel smiled faintly. "My goal isn't to impress you, Daniel. But you asked what we want with you and I can answer that question to an extent. A war has begun. You're important to it. The rebel angels can't read your thoughts because of your unique physical and spiritual composition. We can't either. You have the special strengths of both an angel and a human. You are a combination of two creatures and you aren't aware of all your capabilities, yet."

Daniel smiled. "That's one good pep talk!" He chuckled to himself while Uriel remained solemn and walked past Daniel to the edge of the water passage. "They want you on their side."

Daniel's eyes scanned the water, still unsure what to believe. "Why?"

"It's complex, but they want you as our enemy, and they want to use your rare guardian abilities for their purposes."

"So I just stick with the good guys, right?"

"They're very successful at what they do. They'll use people you love. They'll confuse you from the inside out. That's why you must control the rage you sometimes feel. They can use that to turn you into something you wouldn't even recognize."

"Will I see them coming?"

Uriel looked away from Daniel's eyes. "Even *we* can't do that consistently. But they are coming for you and they won't be the gracious hosts that we've been." He turned and went back toward the cave's depths. "Come back when you want to talk, Daniel. We'll be in touch." He rounded the corner, leaving Daniel alone.

Daniel took one final glance around and then dove into the frigid water. He surfaced at the top of the lake and swam toward the bridge.

Uriel returned to the chair where he and Daniel were minutes before. A man with graying brown hair and a scar on his right cheek sat down by him.

"He's not one of us, Uriel. I can feel his rage. He shouldn't have been brought here because he's not an angel and—"

Uriel silenced him with his raised hand. "The Council and I decided that we would reach out to him. And that's what we did, Lucas."

Lucas stood and left without another word.

Daniel pulled himself onto the bridge and walked toward the lakeshore. As he opened his truck door, leaves crunched near him and he jerked his head around. Nothing. He sat down, started his truck, and left.

A figure emerged from the shadows of the oaks surrounding the parking lot and the single dim light glowed above Natalie's head as she passed by. She had followed Daniel on foot.

Chapter 6

COLD BLOOD

NATALIE WALKED OUT of the farm and onto the highway. She stayed in the darkness on the shoulder of the road as Daniel's truck drove out of sight.

Snow fell and stuck to the frozen ground. Large flakes landed on Natalie's jacket and hair. Like Daniel, the cold didn't bother her as she quickened her steps into a run. Her speed increased to an unthinkable pace, putting her beside Daniel's truck within seconds. She looked at him through the window. He had the phone to his ear and Natalie saw his lips mouth Hannah's name. She slowed to a standstill.

Natalie stood as the snow fell, her teeth clinched in hate. She walked as she watched Daniel's truck disappear in the distance. The frustration on her face transformed into a wicked grin, and two fangs lengthened from her mouth. She laughed as she walked, focusing on some point in the distance.

Daniel's truck rolled up the drive to his house. He turned the engine off and continued talking to Hannah.

"It was all kind of weird. I'll tell you about it another time. I'm still processing it."

"Well, since you got in earlier than you thought, does that mean I'll see you at breakfast tomorrow?"

Although he would've liked nothing better than breakfast with Hannah, Daniel had to think through his schedule for the following day. "I'm helping Natalie in the morning. Catch up with you later in the day?"

"Okay, I'll see you then."

"Sleep tight."

"You too."

Daniel pressed "end" on his phone. He closed the truck door and walked inside to find his mother sitting at the dining room table.

"Hi Danny. Did you have a good night?"

"Yeah, it was fun."

"Where'd you go?"

Daniel knew she wasn't asking to pry or in attempt to control the details of his life. She asked because she sensed something. Her intuition had always been uniquely accurate. Once, when Daniel was young, he woke in the night because of one of his nightmares. He hadn't screamed or made any kind of noise, yet his mother came to his room to comfort him only seconds after he had awakened. Daniel selected his words carefully. "I went to the farm to meet up with some friends."

Marie looked into his eyes, suspicious. "And you said you had fun?"

Daniel knew he needed to get away before she pulled the truth from him. He walked behind her toward his room as he responded. "More or less. It was just really cold."

Marie turned her head to the side. "The cold has never bothered you before."

Daniel stood still, regretting his words. "Well, I mean that it bothered my friends and so that kind of put a damper on the evening. You know?"

"Oh. Well if they couldn't handle it today, it's only going to get colder tonight with the snow storm and all."

Daniel nodded. "Yeah, it's already here."

"Is that why your clothes are wet?"

Daniel hesitated. "I guess so. Good night, Mom. Love you." Daniel walked into his room and closed the door.

Hannah sat on her bed in her pajamas. Erika had come to hang out and a music video played from the TV on Hannah's dresser.

Erika finished opening a package from her mom. "Sweet! Chocolate chip." She held the box out to Hannah.

Hannah took a cookie. "Thanks."

Erika bit into one. "Oh these are perfect. I love how she adds, like, double the butter."

Hannah nodded as she chewed. "They're wonderful! I'm gonna warm one up." Hannah walked to the microwave and put the cookie in for a few seconds. The timer beeped, she removed it and took a bite. "Oh, good grief."

"Even better?"

Hannah rolled her head back and closed her eyes. "There's a word for this, I'm sure, but I don't know what it is. I probably wasn't allowed to say it growing up."

Erika grinned.

Three quick knocks hit the suite door and startled the girls. Hannah knew it was Natalie and didn't want to answer. She glanced at Erika hesitantly – glad that at least she was present – walked into the bathroom, and opened the connecting suite door. Natalie smiled.

"Hi there."

Hannah didn't expect such a polite greeting, so she stood quietly for a few awkward seconds. "Hi Natalie, what can I do for you?"

"I heard you talking. Do you have company?"

"Yeah, Erika's here."

Natalie brushed by her into the room. Hannah had gotten used to Natalie's bizarre displays of rudeness, and scowled as she followed. Natalie stood in the center of the room in front of Erika, with an expressionless stare.

Erika had to say something. "Hey, how's it going?"

Natalie blinked as though she were rearranging plans in her head. "Just thought I'd see what you two were up to."

Erika raised her eyebrows. "Well we were just trying some chocolate chip cookies my mom sent. Want one?"

Natalie again seemed to overthink the situation and waited several seconds before taking a cookie. "Thanks." She took a bite and eyed Hannah as she chewed.

Erika's skin crawled, finding the whole atmosphere eerie. "So, how is it?"

Natalie nodded her head and swallowed. "Your mom makes good cookies." She didn't take her eyes off Hannah.

Hannah forced politeness. "Would you like something to drink?"

Natalie smiled. "No thanks. I think I'm going to go on to bed. Just wanted to check on you. Make sure you weren't out meeting strangers with Daniel."

"Nope, safe and sound." Hannah shook her head, really wondering if this girl had a mental problem. "Daniel called me a while ago and was already home."

"Well, it's good to know everyone is out of the cold."

Hannah nodded, managing a "Yeah."

Natalie's smile fell. "I'm going to get some sleep and let you two get back to… whatever. So goodnight." She glanced at Erika and then back at Hannah before walking back to her room.

The door shut and Hannah shook her head again. "I don't mean to be offensive because I know she's your friend, but—"

"I know; she's beyond unique. To be honest with you, she's gotten quite a bit weirder since you came."

Hannah rubbed her forehead. "Oh, that's just great."

"At least she seemed like she was trying to be nice. Or something close to it."

"Yeah, she did. I think. I'll just keep trying to be polite I guess."

✳

The ringing phone on the nightstand blared and Daniel put his hand over it. The caller I.D. said *Natalie*. Daniel pressed talk. "Hey."

"Hey, it's me. Just giving you a wakeup call so we're not late."

"Yeah, no problem."

"I wanted to sleep late too, sorry my schedule sucks."

"It's fine, really. I'll get ready and be right over."

"Okay. See you soon," Natalie's voice carried a hint of glee.

Daniel dressed and drove to pick her up. Hannah had an early class and had already left the dorm. He walked into the lobby to find Natalie waiting. The drive to the store didn't take long. Loading the dresser was easy for Daniel, though he pretended he needed someone else to carry the other side of it, like any normal man would. Once back at the dorm, Daniel let Natalie help carry the dresser to her room, though she bore little of the bulk. They sat it down by the wall next to the bathroom.

"Is here good?"

"Sure. If it's not, I'll just move it myself."

Daniel smiled, not entirely sure if she was joking. "Yeah, you probably could, too."

"Or I'll get you to come back. There's an idea." Natalie walked close to Daniel, stopping inches from his face. She ran her finger in a slow circle across his cheek. "You're not really dating that girl, are you?"

"Natalie, come on."

"What? I was hoping we could maybe start things up again."

Daniel looked away.

"Dan, it's me. We've always been different from everyone else, together."

"Natalie…"

Natalie's lips were almost touching his. "Come on, Daniel. It can be like when we were teenagers and we just had to know what it was like." She compressed Daniel's bottom lip with hers and then traced it with her tongue. She used her arms to pull her body tight against his.

"Daniel, it's me." She pushed her lips to his again and they kissed intensely for several seconds until Daniel pulled away.

He looked at the floor briefly before saying, "I know." He walked out of the door leaving Natalie alone.

The door closed and a glass shattered against it as Natalie shrieked in frustration. Zeb whimpered.

The days passed and classes became more complex and demanding. Hannah had only one class with Daniel and she settled into a weekly routine based on the schedules for Daniel and her friends. Hannah even began to work Natalie into an occasional breakfast or lunch as she had seemed to warm up to her, and the two began to spend more time together. In the class they shared, they even started sitting by each other. "Maybe it's because classes have started and the structure has helped her move on," Hannah had suggested to Erika. Natalie actually invited Hannah to watch a movie with her in her room, and would sometimes stop in and ask if she needed anything while she was out.

The Valentine's dance was a week away. Sororities had decorated the campus with paper hearts with arrows through them and cardboard cupids announcing the dance.

Hannah had just walked into her room from class when Erika's knock rattled the door. Hannah turned the knob and Erika stomped inside. "Anthony still hasn't asked me to the Valentine's dance!"

Hannah thought carefully before she spoke. "Don't you think he just assumes you two will go together?"

"I know he does! That's the problem! If he's gotten so casual with our relationship that he just assumes I'll go with him without even being asked, then he's about to—"

"Whoa girl, settle down. Maybe he's just planning to ask you at a special time. You really don't need to jump to conclusions."

Erika flicked her brown hair over her shoulder and considered Hannah's words. "Yeah, that makes sense for now, I guess. I'll give him the benefit of the doubt for two more days. Two more days and if he still hasn't asked me then he's gonna be dealing with one angry chick!"

Hannah's phone rang and she pulled it from her pocket. She glanced at the caller ID and then up at Erika. "It's Daniel."

Erika turned to walk out of the room. "Alright, you two are in that stage where I need to leave when you talk."

Hannah rolled her eyes and closed the door. "Hey."

"Hey beautiful, how's your day been?"

"Other than a little Erika drama, it's been fine. How about you?"

"It's been alright, two classes and chopping firewood. Let's go to a movie tonight. Maybe grab something to eat first."

"I think that's called, 'dinner and a movie.'"

Daniel took a deep breath and sighed. "There you go, making it a date. I guess I'll have to bring flowers now."

Hannah laughed. "Flowers or diamonds; either is fine."

Daniel didn't respond and the silence lasted several seconds.

"Dan, I was just joking around."

"No, it's fine. I'm driving and I just saw somebody I know walking on the side of the road. I was turning around to see if he needed a ride."

"He?"

"Remember Zachery?"

"Yeah. Okay, so you need to go?"

"Yeah, I'll pick you up tonight." The phone beeped as Daniel ended the call.

"Well bye to you, too," Hannah said to the empty room. She pocketed the phone and opened the door. Erika stood sideways in the hall with her ear close to the door where she had been listening in on the conversation. Hannah smirked. "Anything interesting?"

Erika walked away and started to text on her phone. "Not nearly enough." She grinned back at Hannah. "I was just making sure things were going smoothly with my two seeds."

"Your two *what*?"

"Seeds. You know, like I planted two seeds of love or something."

Hannah smirked.

Erika sent the text. "Yeah, that was cheesy, sorry. I just wanted to check up on you two."

"We're doing fine. We're going out tonight in fact. Dinner and a movie."

"I know," laughed Erika.

Daniel pulled over and Zachery recognized him. "Hey, Danny, my friend."

Daniel reached over and opened the door. "Hop in, man, it's too cold."

Zachery got in the truck. "I appreciate it."

Daniel accelerated back onto the road. "So where ya headed?"

Zachery clicked his seatbelt and smiled. "I was headed to see you."

Daniel shook his head. "Funny how that whole thing works."

"They want to meet with you again."

"And by 'they' you mean the Council?"

"Is there any other 'they' I would be talking about?"

Daniel nodded thoughtfully. "Do you know what they want?"

"Man, they don't tell me that kind of stuff. I know who you are and I know who they are. I'm a human ally. They don't owe me an explanation."

Daniel switched gears. "When do they want to meet with me?"

"Tonight. Same place, same time."

Daniel focused his eyes on the road and thought about meeting with the Council again. He hadn't had a bad dream lately and enjoyed feeling like a somewhat normal college student. Zachery and the meeting only reminded him that he was different: that the isolation his mother forced on him as a child made some sense, and was maybe even necessary. Images of himself as a child, often alone and sheltered, along with other memories trapped in time resurfaced as he considered the preceding couple of months.

Zachery tugged at his seatbelt and as it finally released, the metal buckle flew into the passenger window snapping Daniel from his thoughts. He spun toward Zachery and took in a couple of deep breaths.

Zachery laughed and pointed toward the café they were passing. "Well hey, now that I have your attention, how about I buy you another cup of coffee? I know how you half-angel, half-human college students are always broke."

The two walked into the café and Zachery smiled in anticipation of aromas of coffee beans grinding. "Gonna try something different this time? You had Pine Needle last time, right?"

Daniel nodded. "Yeah, I'll try something else this time."

Zachery smirked. "Yeah, you really need some variety in your life."

Daniel locked eyes with Zachery. He wasn't sure if he liked his attempts at humor, but as far as he knew, Zachery was his friend, so Daniel produced a smile.

"How's the Cold Blood blend?"

Zachery cut his eyes up to the blend list as though he had to see the name of the blend before he could comment. "Oh yeah. That's a good one. It's got some fig powder in it and the purple of the fig with the brown of the coffee bean makes a reddish color. Like blood."

"Is it cold?"

"No. But it's a great antidote for cold blood. Of course, they all are 'cause they're hot."

"Got it."

"Think I'll have one, too."

The two sat down with their coffee and sipped it.

"How do you like it?"

Daniel smacked his lips. "It's really good. Just a little sweetness from the figs, but not too much."

"Yeah, that's about it." Zachery leaned in like he was going to whisper something to Daniel. But he spoke normally. "Do you trust the Council?"

Daniel raised his head from his coffee and looked around the café. They were alone. "What do you mean?"

"I mean that you don't know if these guys are who they say they are. So how do you know they're not really the bad guys?"

Daniel lowered his eyes from Zachery to his cup. "At this point, I don't trust anyone completely. How could I? I mean, this is… crazy."

Zachery took a deep gulp of his coffee.

Daniel once more checked the room for other people. "How did you get involved in all this?"

"Well now, that's something I've never talked about." Zachery looked up at the ceiling, tracing the boards with his eyes as he recalled. "I was a teenager. Seventeen. Driving my dad's car on a date with a girl who I loved, named Tabitha. It was a cold winter and since you're from Spring Hill, you know what black ice is. On a back road curve I lost control and slid off the road into a tree."

Zachery took a sip of coffee. "I was fine, other than a bump on my head. She… well it was obvious to both of us she wasn't going to make it. Her back was broken and she was bleeding everywhere. She'd have frozen to death before I could have gotten her anywhere anyway, because the car was totaled, and we didn't have cell phones then.

"She forced out a 'good bye' as she suffered. We had both given up. Then a dark hybrid, or 'vampire' as most humans call them today, walked out of the trees. He told me he could save her."

Zachery again sipped his coffee, staring into the table. "He bit her. I still hear her scream in my sleep sometimes. It was the last innocent sound she ever made. From that point on, she was a monster, unable to fight off the darkness that he put inside her. Her thirst for blood made her like a drug addict. It's not like she could tell anyone. And no one knew but me."

The woman working the counter approached the table. "Ya'll need anything?"

Daniel smiled, "No, we're fine."

As she walked away she called behind her. "Well, let me know if I can get ya anything."

Zachery picked up where he left off. "She used to follow killers so she could drink the blood from their victims. Eventually though, she couldn't keep herself from me. She wanted my blood. I cut myself shaving one morning and she lunged for me. I tried to fight her off, but she was remarkably strong. I was helpless.

"When I stopped fighting, because it was pointless, she felt my body go limp. Her fangs scraped my neck as she was about to bite me. It was then she realized what was happening. She pulled back from me and looked stunned at herself. She left and I watched out the window as that dark hybrid waited for her. He knew it would happen. He had just recruited another to the fallen ones. And I never saw her again."

Daniel cleared his throat. "I don't know what to say. I'm sorry Zachery. When did the Council get involved?"

Zachery finished off his coffee and held the cup up to where the cashier across the room could see. She walked over to the table. "What were you drinkin' hun?"

"Cold Blood."

She turned to Daniel. "Would you like a refill too?"

"Yes please. The same."

"Okay, I'll be right back with fresh cups."

She walked away and Zachery continued. "The Council approached me. I didn't know who they were and when they told me, I didn't want any part of it. I lumped them in with the dark angels and hybrids who had taken Tabitha from me. But it's not like I could talk about any of this with anyone. And they were the only ones with answers. They said I'd received a 'baptism by fire' in my education on the fallen ones and asked me to join them as a human ally. So I did. I didn't have anything better to do and I guess I thought that maybe they could help get Tabitha back. That was a long time ago."

Daniel pressed his lips together. "So you still don't trust them after all this time?"

"I didn't say I didn't trust them. I asked you how you could."

Daniel ran his fingers through his hair, his eyes dull. "It feels like I'm in the same boat as you. They're the only ones with any answers."

Zachery chuckled darkly. "Yes they are, my boy. They are."

The cashier returned with two cups of coffee. "Here we go. Sorry about taking so long."

Daniel took the cup off the tray. "I'm sure it was worth the wait."

Zachery took his cup and she held the tray to her side. "Let me know if you need anything else."

Zachery again waited until she was a distance away. "Ya know, I often lay up at night dreaming I have your powers. You know what I'd do if I had 'em?"

Daniel shook his head.

"I'd march over to those fallen bastards and I'd get Tabitha back. But I talked to Uriel about that and he said it's impossible. She's too far gone. Too much monster, not enough person left."

Daniel glanced thoughtfully at the bottom of his cup. "I wish I knew what to say. I wish I could fight them for you."

Zachery shot his eyes up at Daniel. "You'll fight 'em soon enough, Danny. Too soon." He took another sip of his coffee as Daniel looked on.

Daniel called Hannah from his truck. She saw the phone screen and answered. "Hey there, I was just needing a big strong man to help me rearrange my room. But you got out of it because Natalie helped. She's pretty dang strong."

Concern flashed across Daniel's face. "Well, that's good. Sorry I wasn't there to help. Listen, I need to cancel tonight. I've got to do something... help someone out.

Hannah listened to the acceleration of Daniel's truck

for a few pensive seconds, realizing he wasn't going to say anything further. She'd learned not to push him. It's not that he was totally secretive, but there were times he just didn't want to go into detail. "Okay. Do I get a rain check?"

"Yeah. We'll go out real soon. And the dance is in a few days anyway, so…"

"Yeah. Be careful."

"I will. Bye."

Hannah hung up the phone. She glanced at Natalie, who smirked in self-satisfaction.

Daniel drove the dark road to the state park. He parked and walked to the wood bridge as before. Once he reached the middle of the bridge he yelled into the cold. "I'm here!"

He calmly waited as minutes passed without anything happening so he began pacing the bridge. "Hey fellas, let's get this show on the road. Your freak is here!"

Daniel searched the lake and the shore, wondering if he should just dive in. He watched the water just beside the bridge for any movement and finally saw something swirl in the water. He prepared to speak, expecting Jonathan to climb up. Instead, Lucas approached from the opposite side of the bridge. Daniel didn't recognize him.

"Good evening, Daniel. I don't think we've been properly introduced." They shook hands. "I'm Lucas. I work closely with Uriel."

"I think I remember your face. No lake diving tonight?"

"No, that's not necessary tonight. Uriel has always been one for dramatics. The ones we were trying to screen you from aren't nearby at the moment."

"So what can I do for you?"

Lucas looked away from Daniel's eyes and smiled slightly. "Well, Daniel, that's a question you're going to answer for me."

Daniel shrugged in confusion. "How will I do that?"

Lucas curtailed his smile. "In time Daniel, we'll both learn a thing or two about you, but for now, I want to tell you a little about me."

"Okay."

"As I said before, Uriel can tend to overdo things and I'm afraid that he gave you a somewhat narrow picture of our reality."

"In what way?"

Lucas motioned toward the far side of the bridge. "Walk with me?"

Daniel hesitated, but after seconds of consideration walked toward the woods as Lucas asked.

"Daniel, as an immortal, I've learned to be what I consider an open-minded individual. In fact, I'd say I consider Uriel to be something of an absolutist."

Daniel considered his words. "In what way?"

"I'm not one to get into the specifics or to point fingers, but let's just say I'm not as fast to dismiss all the concerns held by some of those in the angelic underground."

Daniel blinked. "Angelic underground?"

"Well now, just because one happens to disagree with who's in charge or what angels pull the strings, doesn't necessarily mean that one is 'dark' or 'fallen' as Uriel might say. I say that there are some angels who are pushed into a subculture. They're alienated for merely having different ideals."

The two walked in silence as Daniel contemplated Lucas' words.

"So you're saying that Uriel has—"

"All I'm saying, Daniel, is that you should keep an open mind. I've seen hybrids in your shoes before and I can't say that I've approved of their decisions. I've seen them throw away power and influence, because Uriel disagreed with, or expelled, certain angels who could have put them in commanding positions. And I'm telling you that eternity is a long time to be under the thumb of someone who only sees things in black and white."

Daniel took a deep breath and let it out. "So, I'm immortal even though I'm just half angel?"

"Daniel, you can't cut forever in half. You're as immortal as any angel, and I am in a position to tell you that there are plenty of angels who envy your particular arrangement. You see, Uriel has kept information from you."

"I've only just met him once really, so I don't know if I'd say he's kept it from me."

"Daniel, Uriel and the Council have been keeping up with you since the day you were born and they've never bothered to tell you who you are. They just let you rely on bits and pieces of information from your mother, and what you learned for yourself. You know only a fraction of your abilities. But, if you will, allow me to be the first one to give you a demonstration of your unique skills."

Lucas stepped to the side of the path and with one

arm pushed a tree off its roots toward Daniel. Daniel instinctively fell backwards but caught the tree. Just as he pushed it aside, Lucas drew a dagger from his coat and threw it at Daniel who knocked it away as it neared his throat. Lucas lunged at Daniel to punch him, but Daniel stepped aside and kicked Lucas' feet out from under him.

Lucas spun away from Daniel's downward punch and hurled the fallen tree at him. When Daniel threw his arm up, he shattered its trunk.

Daniel stared at his arm and then at the fragments of wood on the ground, speechless.

Lucas paced half a circle around Daniel, grinning. "Well now, I'd say that was rather spectacular for a guy who still lives with his mother."

Daniel positioned himself to continue fighting Lucas but Lucas let his arms relax. "They used to call your kind 'the Nephilim,' but that name became derogatory, so it was changed, over time, to hybrids. I've seen several hybrid manifestations, even giants. You, however, intrigue me the most."

Daniel only now began to lower his guard. "And why is that?"

"Versatility, Daniel. Along with who your father is."

Daniel's eyes glinted. "You know who my father is?"

"I do."

"Tell me."

"Come now, Daniel, I'm not going to dump all this on you in one night."

Daniel stepped closer to Lucas. "I've waited long enough! Why does everyone want to keep this from me?

You said Uriel kept things from me; well you're doing the same thing."

Lucas grinned at Daniel, fascinated. "Daniel, I love the aggression. Just between you and me, I think your rage will serve you very well. It can get you exactly what you want."

"Will it get me the answer I want right now?"

Lucas walked past Daniel, picking his words. "You can do something for me. And if you do it well, you'll get your answer."

Daniel walked away from Lucas and picked up a piece of the broken wood, examining it as he considered Lucas' words. "I'm listening."

Lucas beamed with delight.

Chapter 7

EXHAUSTED AWAKENING

Six days later, Hannah listened as the local weather-man predicted more cold and snow. Tennessee winters were often unpredictable with ice storms, wind, snow or even mild days when jackets weren't needed. The varying altitudes of the mountainous areas caused temperatures to fall lower than forecasters predicted. Hannah missed the sunlight, the warmth of summer, and not having to wear layers with two pairs of socks everywhere she went.

The most snow, as of yet, was supposed to come the next day during the Valentine's dance.

"At least it'll make pretty pictures," Hannah reassured a complaining Erika. The two sat on Hannah's bed attempting to study for an upcoming test.

"Well I guess so. The dance is tomorrow and Anthony still hasn't asked me."

"Guys can glaze over details like that sometimes. Why don't you mention it to him? He can't read your mind you know."

"Like Daniel can read yours?"

Hannah blinked. "What do you mean?"

"Oh come on, Hannah. It's like neither of you has to say a word and there's mile-high fireworks."

Hannah messed with a fingernail, trying to look casual until she knew what to say. "Well, to be honest with you, this isn't at all what I had in mind. I planned to focus on classes and not let guys or drinking distract me again. But it's like he's both. He's the bad boy I've been hiding from since I flunked out the first time. But he isn't like the others who've left me passed out at parties, or said they'd kick me in the stomach if I got pregnant. As pathetic as it sounds, my world basically revolves around him right now. No one's ever had this kind of power over me."

Erika looked up from her notes. "It sounds like you've been through hell with the wrong guys. I'm sorry. Daniel's not that way, I promise. I love Anthony and all, but I've never felt what you described before, for anyone. I envy you." She sighed as she thought back to her frustration. "Well at this point he can still bail himself out if he asks me. He said he had plans for tonight and wanted to run them by me when we donate plasma. I guess he wants to get some money first. I'll be so glad when one of us has a job so we don't have to keep getting blood sucked out of us."

Hannah wondered how the plasma clinic could stay in business without college student donors. There were probably one hundred students who went almost every week to make money. She changed the TV channel to music videos and looked through her closet to find ideas for the dance the next day. She turned to Erika. "Do you know if Natalie has a date to the dance?"

Erika looked out the corner of her eye. "I don't know. But I never see her hanging around any other guys or people in general other than our group."

"Has she ever had another love interest besides Daniel? He says they're like brother and sister."

"I don't know. Nothing like Daniel though. It's always been him since she was a little girl. I know what he says about their relationship, and I do think that's how he feels… at least now. By the way, I'm sure she's going to want to dance with him tomorrow night, you know. Like maybe just one dance. They went together last year and during high school. The only reason she's at this school is because he's here. She was fine without college until Daniel decided he might need it."

"Well, I guess I'd be an obsessed child if I didn't let her have one dance with him. I mean, since they've been friends for so long. As far as he's concerned, that's all it is. Right?"

"I'm impressed. I wouldn't let her near Anthony if she had a thing for him. She's relentless when she wants something. It's crazy."

"Is she going to donate plasma with you today?"

"No, she said she was done with that after what happened last time. So it's just me and Anthony. Unless you'd like to earn some money too. You've already got the paperwork taken care of."

Hannah thought for a moment. With her savings disappearing faster than she had anticipated, selling plasma would be a quick way to earn some cash. "Yeah, I'll go with you two today, if that's cool."

"That's great! I'll take all the support I can get."

During the ride to the clinic with Erika and Anthony, Hannah went back and forth in her thoughts on whether or not she could handle the needle. She'd never been good with them or anything having to do with blood and remembered getting dizzy and weak when she gave blood a few years ago.

Daniel called, rousing Hannah with the distraction. He had firewood to chop until the afternoon, but asked if she would like to help him pick a shirt to wear to the dance. "I need a new dress shirt anyway," he said.

Hannah smiled. "Yeah that sounds like fun."

"And we can grab a bite to eat, too. There's a great Thai food place near there."

"You had me at 'help you pick out a shirt', but okay. Can't wait."

"Okay, I'll pick you up around five."

"Great. See you then."

Erika had overheard Hannah's side of the conversation. "So you're going to help Daniel pick out a shirt for the dance?"

"Yeah."

"So he *asked you to the dance*?"

Hannah smirked, realizing that Erika asked these questions to try to get Anthony's attention. "Yes."

"So he didn't just assume you two were going to the dance together because you've made out a few times?"

Hannah was mildly annoyed. "What does that even mean?"

"I'm just saying that it's nice he didn't just take for

granted that you'd go with him just because you two are together, that's all."

Erika looked back at Hannah and saw her displeased expression. She tilted her head toward Anthony and widened her eyes as if to ask Hannah to just go along with it.

Hannah rolled her eyes. "Yeah, it's nice that he asked instead of just assuming we'd go together since we've seen each other naked."

Anthony tapped the brakes and shot his eyes up to the rearview mirror. "You two have seen each other naked already?"

Erika backhanded Anthony's arm. "That's none of your business! Why don't you worry about your own relationship?"

Anthony sat quietly for a moment, looking puzzled. "I didn't know there was anything to worry about."

Moments of awkward silence passed before Hannah spoke. "Anthony, to answer your question, it's not any of your business, but no, we haven't seen each other naked yet. I was just making a point."

Anthony nodded his head while watching the road. "What point?" Erika laid her head back and sighed as they pulled into the clinic parking lot.

Erika got out of the car quickly and cut her eyes to Hannah. The two walked ahead as Anthony turned the car off and locked up. Erika whispered to Hannah, "Why did you say that thing about you two seeing each other naked, if you haven't?"

Hannah smirked. "I thought if I used 'naked' in a sentence it'd get his attention."

"Oh! Right."

The two laughed as they got to the door of the clinic. Erika held the door for Hannah and waited on Anthony. He walked inside and smiled to Erika. "Thanks, babe."

"Well, that's me. I don't take the one I love for granted."

Anthony's eyes narrowed. "If you're trying to hint at something you're doing a piss-poor job of it!"

Erika didn't acknowledge what he said and walked to the front desk. "Appointment for three."

The woman behind the desk tapped keys on the computer. "What're the names?"

"Anthony Jackson, Erika Hunter, and Hannah Sawyer."

"Okay, we're ready for you. If you'll all come back together, we'll get you going."

Daniel heaved his axe into a log that sat on the chopping stump. The wood split perfectly and he stood another log in place to meet the same fate. A stick snapped in the nearby woods just before the axe cut through the log. Daniel raised his head and traced the area with his eyes. He sensed someone there and walked toward the edge of the woods, leaving the axe stuck in the stump.

He didn't try to mask the noise of crunching leaves and patches of snow under his feet as he neared a cluster of trees. He stopped as he heard more movement and then a voice. "I should've known I couldn't hide from you." Natalie stepped out from behind the trees and grinned mischievously, her blond hair caught back from her face with clips.

Daniel smiled slightly. "Did you walk here? I didn't hear a car."

Natalie approached Daniel. "Ran, mostly."

"You *ran?*" His suspicions of her grew tenfold.

She nodded. "Sure. I like to run."

"I've been thinking lately, about what you said about us being different from other people. And wondering just how different you are. You're strong; I know that. And fast. You're right, maybe we've always been the same." He knew, or at least he thought he knew, what she was. One thing had left him puzzled. "Natalie, why is your blood red?"

She raised her eyebrows and smirked. "Now there's a question you don't hear every day. Why wouldn't it be?"

"Because if we're the same, it shouldn't be."

She approached him, hazel eyes narrowed, wearing that same small smirk. "Well what makes you think my blood's red?"

"You donate plasma at the clinic. You wouldn't do that if it was white like mine." He hesitated, unsure of how much he should say. "I've met some others like us, and they've filled in some of the blanks."

She raised her manicured eyebrows. "And who is it you've met?"

No going back. "They're angels. They call us hybrids."

Natalie crossed in front of Daniel. "Is that so?"

"Yeah. You don't sound surprised."

"I had wondered…"

Daniel stared at her, dawning coming on him. He continued. "It doesn't make sense to me that my blood is white, and yours is red unless…" But he didn't want to say it. He'd known Natalie all of her life.

Natalie stepped closer. "Unless, what?"

Daniel's mind raced. "Unless… you're a vampire."

Natalie raised her head, and chuckled softly, "That's an unusual accusation."

"Are you?"

Natalie walked past Daniel, toward the stump and the axe. She pulled the axe loose and placed a piece of wood on the stump. "Have I ever been a normal girl, Daniel?" She drove the axe down through the log effortlessly, splitting it clean through.

Daniel stared expressionless at her eyes. "So are you going to tell me?"

Natalie raised her head slowly from looking at the stump. Her breath escaped in pants as her face dropped and she started to cry, mascara running. She reached out to Daniel, but he stood motionless. "Daniel, please," she sobbed.

Daniel walked to her. She wrapped her arms around him and laid her head on his shoulder. "Daniel, you used to know me so well."

Daniel narrowed his eyes in confusion. "What happened?"

Natalie continued without raising her head off his shoulder. "I met someone. He was like us. I pretended he was you when we…" Natalie exhaled. "I didn't know him very long. He told me there were others and that I could join them, and that you'd be joining them soon. He said that real angels didn't accept hybrids. He told me about the Council and that they rejected those who didn't walk in step with them. He said they could keep me safe from the Council angels."

Daniel stroked her hair before lifting her head from his shoulder. "Then what happened."

"He told me that in order for me to be under their protection I had to become one of them. He went to feed one night and I went with him. He bit someone and I drank from the bite because he said that's the fastest way for a hybrid to turn. He left me after that. It was like he recruited me and once I signed up he was done. And now all I think about is blood. Mine used to be white like yours, but it's red now, because I drink it."

Daniel stepped back from Natalie and her arms fell to her sides. He set his eyes on hers. "You kill people?"

Natalie stepped forward, but Daniel held up his hand. "Stay there. Answer me."

"It doesn't take as many as you might think. One or two a week."

"One or two a week? You're a murderer!"

Natalie looked down slightly and bit her bottom lip. "That's not very nice Daniel. You think I want to be this way? You think I want to be a living nightmare?"

"No, I didn't say that."

Natalie raised her eyebrows and smirked. "Well, maybe I do a little."

Daniel squinted slightly. "So when you passed out at the clinic it was—"

"I was weak. I hadn't fed in ten days because I was trying to quit. Regular food does almost nothing for me. It only makes me hungrier."

Daniel's astonishment showed in his eyes. He knew

this meant a constant worry for him over his mother, Hannah, and his friends. Why hadn't he seen it coming? Would Natalie attack them? Would the Council go after her?

"Oh Danny, does this destroy my dreams of a white picket fence and a house in the suburbs with you?"

Daniel didn't speak as she approached and put her arms around him again.

"Don't worry your pretty little head about me, Daniel. Being immortal has a way of healing broken hearts. All I have to do is outlive her. And, well, I can't die unless there's no blood for me to drink. So I like my chances." Natalie hovered her open mouth next to Daniel's neck as her fangs slowly expanded from her gums. She pressed her lips against his skin and kissed him. "Yummy."

Daniel placed his hand in the middle of her chest and gently pushed her away. "You need to be careful. You should go."

"Well, okay then. I wasn't going to bite you. They told me not to drink hybrid blood for some reason."

Daniel's expression remained solemn. "That's not the reason. I just have work to do and I don't have time to deal with this new version of you right now. But I'll talk to you later."

"It's a date then." Natalie held eye contact with Daniel for a few seconds before she turned and walked into the woods. He watched her walk away, searching his mind for solutions and answers to the mixture of troubles that continued to mount. His thoughts took him nowhere, except back to the commotion of threats that his mother and friends faced for being part of his life.

Daniel dropped the axe in the bed of his truck and sat behind the wheel. The engine shook as it started and Daniel put it into gear. Fifteen minutes of driving ended at the state park and he found himself walking to the wood bridge. He stood in the middle of the bridge and tried to determine whose name he should call. Before he could decide, he felt steps on the bridge and spun in their direction. Lucas stopped walking once Daniel faced him.

"Hello again, Daniel. What a pleasant surprise."

"I came to talk."

"Of course, my friend. I'm here for you."

"My first question is about you asking me to—"

"We can't talk about that here. Not right now. We don't have the privacy. What was the other matter?"

Daniel swallowed and looked around the lake. "My friend, Natalie, is a vampire. I saw her fangs and her blood is red. A dark hybrid changed her."

Lucas clasped his hands together behind his back and walked a few steps away from Daniel. "And how does that affect you?"

"How does that affect me? Are you kidding?"

"Uriel told you they existed."

"Yeah, but he didn't say one of my childhood friends was one, or would become one. She's like a sister to me and now she's killing people to drink the blood out of their bodies. Is that not supposed to mess with me just a tad?"

Lucas grinned slowly and stepped closer. "And there's that temper again that I love so much about you, Daniel. That's why I convinced Uriel to let me be your contact with the Council. I'm the only one who truly sees your full potential."

Daniel rubbed his forehead in frustration. "Lucas, you're not answering me."

"Who are you to question me boy?" Lucas snapped. The words had barely left his mouth when he back-handed Daniel to the ground and the bridge quaked from the force. "Go back one hundred thousand years before you were even born, and I was there! Before your great grandfather sucked his mother's tit, galaxies were at my command!" His voice echoed across the lake and through the woods.

Daniel's eyes were wide with shock as he pushed his sleeve against the white blood streaming from his lip. He looked at Lucas, whose pupils had turned a sharp yellow above his smile. Lucas stooped and put his hand under Daniel's chin. "Now Daniel you see what you made me do? I hurt a friend." His smile dropped. "My advice to you concerning Natalie is that you don't worry about it. You live your life. You go to the dance and you have a good time. Then the next day, you keep your end of our deal. After that, I'll tell you who your father is and you can walk away in educated bliss. How does that sound?"

Daniel's instincts told him to fight. He imagined himself smashing his fist into the side of Lucas' head. But he spoke differently. "That sounds fine."

Lucas reached his hand out and helped Daniel to his feet. "Daniel, I can be your most powerful friend, or your worst enemy for all eternity. Surely you recognize the logical choice." He turned and walked away from Daniel, disappearing into the woods.

Chapter 8

ANGEL ASSASSIN

DANIEL OPENED THE door to the dorm and Hannah
stood from the lobby couch. He didn't speak. She walked
over to him with a smile. "Hey."

Daniel pushed Lucas to the back of his mind. "Hey.
So are you ready to help me pick out a shirt?"

"I'll do my best, but I have to work with what I've got,"
Hannah said mischievously. She had flirted with Daniel
before, but not in a teasing kind of way. Some guys didn't
react well to that and she held her breath in anticipation
of his answer.

He grinned. "I'm in your hands."

"Are you?" she asked, smiling.

During the ride to the mall they joked about how
Anthony still hadn't asked Erika to the dance. Hannah
was optimistic. "Maybe he'll ask her tonight. He's taking
her to a nice restaurant."

Daniel tapped the steering wheel. "Did *he* say that?"

"No. Erika just said that he wanted to take her somewhere tonight and since he got paid for donating plasma
today she thought it might be somewhere nice."

Daniel chuckled. "I think that's wishful thinking on her part. Anthony's a tight wad. Burgers and milkshakes are a nice night out to him."

Hannah laughed. The conversation dissipated for a few minutes. Daniel seemed completely comfortable with the silence and smiled to Hannah. Hannah decided that now was as good as any time to ask the awkward question she'd been avoiding. "So you and Natalie used to date, or something?"

Daniel lowered his eyes from the road for a few seconds, but not before Hannah saw them flick to a dull silver color. "Yeah. We've known each other forever. She even lived with us for a while when I was a kid. Some of my mom's friends adopted her after her mom died and she never knew her dad. Like me. So we kind of had an instant connection. Still do."

Hannah didn't know how to respond. She didn't like that Daniel still felt he had a connection with Natalie, but thought to herself that jealousy could only make her seem immature and unattractive.

"Hannah?"

She turned back to Daniel. She hadn't heard him talking to her. "I'm sorry, I was just thinking. Did you say something?"

Daniel smiled at her lost in her thoughts. "I said I think of her as a sister now, and that's all. Then I asked if you'd been to this mall yet since you've been back in college."

"This time?" Hannah chuckled. "Not yet."

Daniel turned the wheel into the mall parking lot. "It's

got a few new stores, but not much has changed. Seems to be quite the goth hangout though."

The two walked into the mall entrance and instantly stood out in a flowing river of black jeans, wallet chains and spiked hair. Hannah grabbed Daniel's hand and pulled herself close to him. "Keep me safe." She smiled up at Daniel who lowered his head and kissed her. It wasn't near the intensity of some of their kisses, but it had been two days since they'd really kissed and she'd take this one, even if it was simple and quick.

The teenagers walking by eyed them as though they were strangers crashing a party. Daniel noticed. "If I pierced my eyebrow and dyed my hair black, I think everyone would stop looking at me."

"Would that mean I'd have to get some torn fishnets?"

Daniel smiled. "Oh please, yes."

Hannah smiled flirtatiously. "Does that do it for you?"

"Oh, like you wouldn't believe."

Hannah jokingly cleared her throat. "Well that's good to know. I'll be sure to remember that for summer." She turned toward a storefront. "Oh hey, I need to go in here for a minute."

Daniel looked up at the sign for the ladies clothing store and raised an eyebrow. "Why don't we meet back here in fifteen minutes? I'm going to see about getting one of those wallet chains."

Hannah grinned. "You know, I could see that looking good on you. I mean, sometimes."

"Well I'm really just looking, but you never know." Daniel pulled Hannah in for a peck kiss. "Fifteen minutes."

"Got it."

Daniel walked further through the mall and into a store playing music so loudly that it pounded through its walls. He walked past tie-dyed shirts, shot glasses, black lights and incense accessories before stopping in front of a small selection of wallet chains. He lifted a chain and held it next to his pants. A clatter of items hitting the floor pulled his attention to the back of the store where three high school boys in football jerseys surrounded a pudgy kid with black hair and goth clothes.

One of them snarled, "So you wanna bleed, Cain? 'Cause if you wanna look like you're dying, I can help!" He punched Cain in the face, grabbed his collar and forced his head back up for another.

Daniel dropped the chain and walked toward them. The attacker had "Rod" printed on the back of his jersey. He pulled his fist back to hit Cain again, but Daniel's words caught his attention. "Are you Rod, the quarterback I keep hearing about?"

Rod let go of Cain, turning to face Daniel. "Yeah I am. Now why don't you go mind your own business?"

"Well I would, it's just I heard you have a really unique throwing motion."

Rod chuckled, looking at his friends, and flattered. "Look I can't get into this right now. I'm busy."

"Well I'd just really like to see it is all. I've never seen a quarterback throw underhanded like an anorexic, pre-pubescent girl with a nerve disorder."

"What?"

Daniel smirked. "I mean, that's what I heard. But I guess for you it's really just a natural throwing motion."

Rod's face shook with fury as he glared back at Daniel.

He sprinted and threw his body to tackle him, but Daniel moved aside and struck down on Rod's back, slamming him to the ground. Some of Rod's teeth split and broke from the force of his jaw hitting the tile and driving his mouth together. He moaned and coughed face down in a bloody mess.

Daniel looked up at the others. "You two are the worst cheerleaders I've ever seen. And your uniforms suck."

One of them took two quick steps and chambered his arm to hit. Daniel didn't move and the punch struck his face. He barely turned from the hit and then slowly shook his head. "So disappointing." He punched the athlete in the face, spinning him around and into the back wall where he slid to the ground.

The final of the three walked ahead with his hands up. "Hey man, I don't want no trouble."

Daniel noticed him slowly clinching a fist, expecting Daniel to relax. "Oh come on dude. I'm on a roll." Daniel punched him in the stomach and then raised his knee into his dropping head. The knee strike blasted the bully backwards and onto his back.

Daniel eyed his three fallen victims and then looked up at Cain. "You okay?"

Cain went from a dropped jaw to a wide grin. "Dude! That was bad ass!"

Daniel looked around at the mess. "Who's watching the store?"

Cain dropped his smile. "Well, I was. But the last shift should be here any—"

"Cain! What happened?" A petite girl in all black,

fishnets, and a nametag that said, "Janel" stood with her arms held out, stunned by seeing the wrecked store.

Cain surveyed the knocked out jocks and damaged products. "Call security and tell them these guys were fighting and did this."

Daniel walked out of the store. Cain ran to catch up, calling behind him, "Janel, tell security I have injuries and I'll talk to them tomorrow."

He ran up next to Daniel. "Dude, that was sick! Those guys have been giving me crap for months."

"Glad I could help. So, no offense, but why did your parents name you Cain?"

"My parents didn't name me Cain. That's what I choose to call myself."

"Did you do that for the same reason you got the nose ring?"

Cain thought for a second. "Yeah, pretty much."

"And what reason was that? To piss off your parents?"

Cain again went back to that place in his head that gave him the answers. "Yeah, pretty much. So what's your name?"

"Daniel."

The two walked in silence as Daniel began to feel pestered by his new fan.

"Dude, your timing was perfect. It was like you knew right when to walk in."

Daniel stopped and looked at Cain. He was right, his timing *was* perfect. Much too perfect. Daniel spun in the opposite direction and observed the nearby faces. After several dismisses he landed on a set of eyes too focused on him to be a shopper. The man's black leather jacket hugged his muscular torso and his dark brown hair fell more than half way down his back. Daniel scanned the mall for others.

Cain was clueless. "What's up?"

Daniel turned to him, considering his safety and usefulness in the situation. "I need you to do me a favor."

"Dude, you name it. I owe you."

Daniel studied the crowd. He noticed mall security finally walking into the store he and Cain had left. He turned back to Cain, keeping the stranger in the corner of his eye. "I need you to distract the guy who's standing by the kiosk staring at me. Don't look." Daniel's command caught Cain just before he turned his head.

"How am I going to know which one if I don't look?"

"You can look when I walk away. And that's when I need you to go over to him. He'll still be looking because he hasn't taken his eyes off me yet."

"So what do I do?"

"Talk to him. Just try to keep him from watching me for as long as you can."

"Got it."

Cain turned and walked toward the staring man. Daniel watched until the man's eyes shifted to Cain and then he ran to the store where he'd left Hannah. Once inside, he saw her examining a top and sprinted to her.

"We need to go *now*."

Hannah put the top back on the hanger. "What's wrong? What about your shirt?"

"That doesn't matter right now."

He took her hand and they ran out of the store into the main part of the mall. Daniel looked over his shoulder and the man in the black leather jacket was marching toward him. The glare in his eyes removed all doubt of his intentions. Cain hurried behind the man, raising his voice to get his attention again, but the man ignored him.

"This way!" Daniel pulled Hannah toward the exit.

"Daniel this is crazy! Tell me what's going on!"

Daniel didn't look at her, only back at the man following them and then toward the door. "Just trust me! You're in danger. Come on!"

Hannah struggled to keep up as Daniel sprinted, pulling her along. After running through the automatic doors with Hannah, he jumped and smashed the door's motion detector into useless pieces.

Halfway through the parking lot he turned to see the man examining the shattered detector and looking for a way out. Daniel watched as the chaser punched and kicked his way through the glass doors.

Daniel let go of Hannah's hand beside his truck. "Get in!" He sat down and started the engine. The tires screeched as Daniel reversed through the parking lot. The truck faced the mall entrance as it raced backwards.

"Daniel, tell me what's going on! Who's this psycho and why is he chasing us?"

Daniel turned the wheel and slammed the brakes to a skidding stop on a road that connected to the parking lot. He rammed the gear stick into first and floored the pedal.

The man caught up to the truck and ran at its side.

Hannah screamed. "Holy crap! Daniel please, what's going on?!"

The man struck the truck with his arm, denting it

from the force. The truck swerved slightly, but Daniel turned onto another road and the man stopped running.

Daniel watched in the rearview as the attacker disappeared from sight. Hannah now sat directly beside Daniel clutching his arm with her head lowered against his shoulder, hair cascading over her face.

"How was that possible?! Who was that?"

Daniel sighed. "It's a long story."

"Well how about we start with why that guy was chasing us?"

"I got in a fight at the mall. I think it was a set up. He was probably trying to take me to the ones he works for. Or maybe he was going to try to kidnap you and force me to do something for them to get you back. I'd rather run, than risk your safety."

"You've got to be kidding me. *Why*? Who *are* you?"

Daniel shifted his eyes to the steering wheel, working out where to begin. "Hannah, this is pretty complex."

"I was honor roll every year in high school. Try me."

"Alright, fine, but don't say I didn't warn you."

Daniel pulled off the road and into the empty parking lot of an old church. He parked the truck and turned to Hannah.

"My mom said all my life that I was different. For the most part I believed her, but she used to say some stuff that I thought was just what a mom would tell her kid, because his dad left – to be reassuring – you know, just made up stuff about how magical I was. But recently, I've had my doubts completely removed about what she told me. She actually wasn't making stuff up. She was right.

And it's out there." He glanced nervously away from her. "*Way* out there."

Hannah took Daniel's hand in hers. "Just tell me."

Daniel took a deep breath. "I'm half angel."

She turned her face, biting a grin, keeping her eyes on him.

"You're half angel?"

Daniel nodded.

Hannah snickered. "If you don't want to go out anymore, you can just say so. I'm a big girl. You don't have to tell me some—"

Daniel pressed the truck key against his arm and slashed it away. White blood oozed out of the wound and trickled down his arm. Hannah pushed herself against the door, fear and horror painting her face. Her breaths tuned heavy and her heart began pounding.

"Daniel, what the hell is going on? Are you okay?"

Daniel opened the glove compartment in front of her. She watched fearfully as he moved some items around. He uncovered a bandage and wrapped his arm.

"It's okay, I'm a fast healer."

Hannah stared straight ahead, trying to make sense of what just happened. "Angel blood is white?"

"Hybrid blood is, at least. I don't know if pure angels even have blood. They can take on human form, but I don't know all the details."

"You're half angel?"

Daniel nodded.

"Like, angels in the Bible or something?"

"I think so. I'm still learning."

"So your mom is—"

"No, it was my dad. I never knew him."

"You're an angel hybrid? Are you kidding me? What does that even mean? Can you… fly or something?"

Daniel chuckled. "I haven't tried."

Hannah looked down at the seat with an expression that suggested his claim was starting to add up in her mind. The white blood, the strength, his instincts to detect the immediate future. "Is that why you're so strong?"

"Yes. It's also why we were being chased. I think he was an angel."

"Then why would he be chasing you? Aren't angels supposed to be good?"

"It depends which ones you're talking about and how you define 'good.' There are rebel angels or some call them dark angels. A lot of this is new to me, too, but basically the dark angels want me to join them and they're not really concerned with whether I want to talk about it or not."

"So I guess calling the police wouldn't do any good."

Daniel laughed again. "Nope."

Hannah glanced out the window and thought about what he'd said. Now that the initial doubt and fascination had dissipated, her stomach fluttered with anxiousness as she considered his words. The fact that she even believed his story scared her, but when combined with the implications of Daniel actually being half an angel and facing dark angels, Hannah struggled to catch her breath.

She cleared her throat. "I need to process this; it's a lot to take in. But I trust you, and it doesn't affect the way I feel about you." She leaned in to Daniel's chest and he put his arm around her.

"I think you're taking it really well."

"We didn't get your shirt," Hannah said.

"I noticed. There's a clothing store on the way. I figured we'd stop by, if you're still up for playing wardrobe consultant."

"Yeah, but only since you're going to the dance with me. I can't have you looking anything other than handsome."

Daniel smirked, but didn't comment.

At the store, Daniel and Hannah went through several different shirts before narrowing it down to three that they both liked. Hannah held up two and looked back and forth between them. Then she hung them on a hook and put both hands on Daniel's face. She leaned in and kissed him. "Any chance I could influence your vote?"

Daniel picked up one of the shirts, and looked at the other two. He liked them all equally, but wasn't going to tell her that.

"Maybe," he grinned.

Hannah smiled briefly, but then her face quickly fell and her eyes drifted away from Daniel.

"What's wrong?"

"I'm just still processing it all. It's a lot to take in… and then to just go shopping."

Hannah's phone vibrated and she pulled it from her pocket. She opened the message and looked up at Daniel in disbelief.

She held the phone up where he could see Erika's text.

Anthony dumped me!

Chapter 9

SLOW POISON

DANIEL PAID FOR the shirt Hannah liked most and they walked to his truck.

"Are you going to call Erika?" Daniel asked.

"Yeah, I was just thinking of how to calm her down. But I guess I might as well stop delaying." Hannah pushed *talk* on her phone.

"Hello?"

"Hey. How're you doing?"

"Not good."

Hannah waited several seconds expecting Erika to go off but there was only silence. "Did he give you a reason?"

"He said something about the world spinning out of control and that he wasn't ready for this. Some crap like that."

"Erika, I'm so sorry. We're just a few minutes away. Want me to stop by so we can talk?"

"That'd be good. I'm just sitting here alone in my room."

"Alright, we'll be there in five."

Erika released a quivering sigh. "Okay, bye."

Hannah ended the call and turned to Daniel. "She sounds bad."

"I wonder what's going on with Anthony. I better talk to him."

"We're going to try to get them back together, right?"

"Well that's up to them, but right now I just want to know what's in Anthony's head."

"But you've got to try, okay?"

"I'm not going to discourage him from it, but something is going on and I need to talk to him."

Hannah watched the trees zip past the window. She laughed to herself over the irony that only minutes ago Daniel had told her he was half angel, yet now they were going to attempt to be the voice of reason and sanity to a couple of their friends. "I'll be lucky to make a 'D' this semester," she mumbled to herself.

Daniel dropped Hannah off at the dorm and dialed Anthony's number.

"Yeah, you heard right," Anthony blurted without even saying hello.

His greeting caught Daniel off guard. "Okay, well you wanna grab a drink or something?"

"Did Erika put you up to this?"

"I don't have to be 'put up' to get together with a friend."

"Alright, I'll be in the lobby."

Daniel drove down one hill from Hannah's dorm and up the other to the men's dorms. He turned into Beck Hall and Anthony got in the truck.

Daniel put on his most pleasant smile. "Where would you like to go? Totally your call."

"Well if it's my call, then I want a beer."

"Sure."

Daniel turned into an old Irish pub that was popular with students and townies. "Is this good or—"

"This is fine."

Daniel and Anthony walked in and sat at the bar. After ordering beers, Daniel got to the point.

"What happened?"

"So you didn't just want to hang with me. Fine. It just felt like I couldn't breathe. Like the world was crashing down. You ever been under that kind of pressure?"

Daniel cut his eyes to Anthony and took a slow breath. "The pressure of what?"

"She's been pushing me for a ring. I mean, she wants me to propose, dude."

"You're only twenty-one. What's the hurry?"

"Yeah, I'm not ready yet. I mean, I just didn't think she'd want to do that before we finished college."

"Did you tell her you weren't ready?"

"No. She just kept mentioning it and I'd try to change the subject. Then I just decided I couldn't take it anymore and I told her we needed to back off a bit. She freaked out."

"You just want it to stay how it was for now?"

"Yes."

"Then just tell her that. It's a simple solution. Either she takes that, or you two go your separate ways. And for the love of Moses, please just ask her to the dance!"

Anthony slowly moved his eyes from Daniel to the whiskey bottles on a shelf behind the bar.

Daniel recognized something in Anthony's expression. "That's not why you broke up with her."

Anthony snarled back in disgust. "What did I just say?"

"You were just making something up."

Anthony fumed, "So now I'm a liar? Is that what you're saying, muscle man?" Anthony knocked over his beer bottle and stood up as though he was threatening Daniel.

Daniel looked around at the other people in the bar. The volume of chattering had dropped and most of the customers nearby were watching them.

Daniel slowly looked back at Anthony. "Calm down. Have a seat."

Anthony glared into Daniel's eyes for a few seconds, but Daniel didn't look away. Finally, Anthony sat back down. "Sorry."

Daniel spoke softly. "You want to tell me what's really going on?"

"Don't worry about it."

Daniel looked closer as Anthony stared at the wooden bar, hazel eyes wide and angry.

"Just tell me."

Anthony bit the inside of his cheek. "Why don't you just mind your own business?" He stood and stormed out of the bar, leaving Daniel to be stared at.

Daniel squinted as he watched Anthony speed down the steps, confused at his extreme change in behavior. He laid some cash by their beers and as he walked through the door, his phone rang. *Hannah*.

"Good timing. Anthony's pissed at me. We went to a

bar to talk and he freaked out. I think something's really wrong with him."

"Where is he?"

"I don't know. I guess he just walked back to campus. How's Erika?"

"She's doing better. Pretty hopeful that your talk would do some good."

"I think I made it worse. But he's hiding something. Something's going on."

The next day the campus buzzed about the dance. Professors announced it in classes, social clubs wore cupid tee shirts showing the time, and uninvited girls wept in the cafeteria in hope of last minute sympathy offers.

Erika had become a muted version of herself as she gazed into space during lunch with Hannah. Minutes passed and Erika did nothing but chew and stare at the corner of the wall.

Hannah had to say something. "Have you heard from him?"

Erika shot a half-second glance at Hannah. Her eyes were red-rimmed. "No."

Hannah noticed Natalie coming toward them, carrying a tray of food and a newspaper under her arm. She paused by the table and took note of Erika's expressionless face before asking Hannah to slide over in the booth.

Natalie put her tray down. It held a bowl of tomato soup and she began sipping at spoonfuls.

Hannah was determined to be friendly. "Happy Valentine's Day, Natalie."

Natalie turned to Hannah with what initially appeared to be anger, but then she smiled as though it took her a moment to realize Hannah wasn't taunting her. "Ah yes, Valentine's Day. The day to remind me just how single I am. Thank you, Hannah."

Natalie laid her head back and closed her eyes, apparently searching for something in the taste of the soup: something that wasn't there. She leveled her head and settled her eyes on Erika, who continued to stare blankly past both girls. Natalie titled her head into Erika's line of sight. "What's up with you?"

Erika shifted her eyes to Natalie's. "If you bothered to go online you'd know my status changed from 'in a relationship' to 'single.'"

Natalie took another sip of soup. "I'm too busy to go on the Internet."

Erika's eyes finally showed energy. "Too busy doing what? You haven't been in Art History in weeks."

Natalie took a final sip of soup and patted her mouth with a napkin. "Well, girls, thanks for the company. I guess I won't see you until the dance tonight." She stood with her tray.

Erika returned to her blank stare. "I won't be at the dance."

Natalie cocked a well-plucked eyebrow. "Is that going online, too? Because your fans need to know."

Erika narrowed her eyes at Natalie, but didn't speak. Natalie smiled. "Bye, Hannah." She walked away, turning the heads of guys who stared at her unseasonably short black skirt.

Hannah had no idea what to say to Erika, or whether she should say anything at all.

Erika snapped out of it long enough to dig in her backpack. "Don't feel guilty that you're going to the dance with Daniel. I'm happy for you."

"I wish you'd come anyway. We'd still have a good time."

"I'm really not in the mood, but thanks. You're a good friend." Erika checked the time on her phone. It also gave her an excuse to see that she hadn't missed a text or call from Anthony. "I've got to get to class. Have fun tonight."

Hannah stood and gave Erika a hug. "I think if you just give him some time, it'll be okay."

"Thanks. See you later." Erika walked her tray to the disposal belt and turned to leave the cafeteria. Daniel entered and she stopped in front of him.

"Hey girl, how're you doing?"

"Not good. So he seemed pretty sure last night?"

"Yeah, I'm sorry. I wasn't ignoring you if you tried to call; my phone died after I talked to Hannah."

Erika's face fell into her hands as she burst into a sob. Daniel opened his arms and she buried her forehead into his shoulder. She fought the tears enough to speak, "Daniel, I didn't see this coming. It hurts so much. Was I really that bad of a girlfriend?"

"Of course not. He's just going through something."

"Well why wouldn't he want me to help him through it? It doesn't make any sense."

"I know. After he's been alone and had some time to

work this out, I bet he'll come back. He loves you, I know it."

"You're going to keep talking to him, right?"

"Yeah, I'll be working on him and trying to help him see he's made a mistake. Okay?"

Erika put her head back on Daniel's shoulder for a few moments to compose herself. "Thanks, Daniel." She pulled away from him and left.

Daniel walked over to Hannah who had been watching. "Hey, I can't stay. I'm heading over to campus mail. Walk with me?"

Hannah dumped her tray and went into the cold with Daniel. They held hands as they walked the cobble stone path toward the Student-Life building. Daniel pulled her close to him. "I haven't checked my mail in about two weeks."

"So that's why you didn't say anything about my letter."

"Uh oh."

Hannah grinned. "I guess you'll just have to find out."

Daniel smiled and nodded his head, but after a few steps his expression turned somber. "Erika's having a hard time."

Hannah nodded. "So Anthony was pretty messed up last night?"

"To be honest, he was being weird. I've never see him that way. It was bizarre. But let's not talk about it anymore. It's Valentine's Day."

"Okay. So what do you want to talk about?"

Daniel stopped walking and reached his arms around her, pulling her tightly to his strong chest. "Who said anything about talking?" He pressed his lips to hers and they kissed for several minutes, passionately.

She pulled back, breathless, heat rushing through her body. "Dang, you're good at that."

"Well you know I practice using my tongue to tie knots in cherry stems," he said, twirling a curl of her hair around his finger.

"Is that what it is?" she said, laughing, and pulled his face in for another round.

Daniel pulled away. "Okay, this is getting boring, let's get to campus mail."

Hannah playfully pushed Daniel. "Oh *whatever!*"

He laughed as he opened the door for her. She gripped his hand again. "Hey, do you have anything else planned for tonight? Do I need to be ready for the dance early or something?"

They arrived at Daniel's mailbox and he opened it with his key.

"Let's see. You didn't buy any fishnets at the mall because I had to rescue you from a dark angel. So…" Daniel's playful expression dropped as he removed two letters from his mailbox; one from Hannah and the other had no return address.

Hannah poked his arm. "So… ?"

"Hang on." He opened the envelope with no return address to find a thin piece of wood with tree bark on the side. The next day's date was written in lead pencil.

Daniel had almost forgotten about the deal he'd made with Lucas.

"What's that?" Hannah asked.

"It's a reminder."

"Is that somebody's fancy way of reminding you that you've got to chop their firewood?"

Daniel looked at Hannah, but his thoughts were elsewhere. "Something like that."

Hannah squinted, knowing there was something more, but decided to leave it alone. "Well there's another one," she commented, handing him a small, square envelope.

Daniel tore the top off and removed a card in the shape of baby Cupid that hinged at the wings. The message read, "Don't make me bring in the big gun! Be my Valentine!"

Daniel smiled. "Okay, I surrender."

Hannah chuckled and kissed Daniel's cheek.

"You know," Daniel smirked, "if I were the easily offended type, I guess I could claim Cupid was offensive. You know, a half-naked angel baby who shoots arrows at people. Kind of derogatory to my kind if you think about it."

"There must be something I can do to make it up to you."

"I'll start compiling a list of my demands." She chuckled and Daniel put an arm around her as they slowly walked toward the door. He reached to push the door open, but a woman's voice stopped him. "Hannah Sawyer?"

Hannah turned to a woman with curly, black hair holding her arms out as though she expected Hannah to recognize her. Nothing came to mind, so Hannah smiled and took a guess. "Hey... don't we have a class together?"

"We did, about seven years ago. It's Tiffany Barker."

Hannah remembered the name and could now connect the face. "Yes! Tiffany, how are you?" Hannah released Daniel's hand and the girls hugged.

Hannah noticed a wedding band. "You're married?"

"Yes, I married Rob Stallings about two years go."

"That's great. Congratulations! So what are you doing here?"

"I could ask you the same thing. I work here as a student advisor."

"Well, I'm a student again. So I guess now I know someone on the inside."

"Yeah, here's my info if you ever need to contact me." She handed Hannah a business card.

"Thanks. I'll take you up on that. If anything just to go out for coffee or something. By the way, this is Daniel."

Daniel raised his eyes from examining the wood note again and Tiffany reached to shake his hand. She could get a closer look now that he wasn't staring down. She made an expression as though she recognized him, but responded neutrally. "Nice to meet you."

"Same here."

Tiffany turned to Hannah with a strange look. "Are you two going to the Valentine's dance tonight?"

Hannah squeezed Daniel's hand. "Sure are."

Tiffany blinked as though she had received bad news. She made herself say something. "Well I hope you have fun. If you'll excuse me, I need to get back to work. I'm sure I'll see you around." She walked down a nearby hallway and went through a door.

Daniel watched, quizzically, until she disappeared. "Something wasn't exactly right about that."

"Do you know her?"

"Nope. Never met her before in my life." Daniel put his hand on the small of Hannah's back and guided her toward the door. "Never mind, we need to go."

"Oh yeah, where are we going?"

"I've got to run some errands. So between now and five you're gonna put on something cute and then I'm taking you out to eat before the dance."

"Is that so?"

"It is. And I'll be the one in that blue shirt you picked out."

Chapter 10

DARK DANCE

Daniel drove Hannah back to her dorm. She leaned over and kissed him before jumping down from the truck. She waved as she walked away. "See you tonight," she called behind her.

"Hey," Daniel yelled, "I won't be in the truck tonight. So don't be looking for it."

Hannah hurried back to the truck window, curious. "Should I expect a limo?"

"Don't expect. How 'bout that?"

Hannah grinned and leaned in for another kiss, butterflies fluttering in her stomach. "Sounds good. See you at five." She walked off, smiling with excitement about the coming evening.

Daniel drove the truck through the back roads where the snow had almost completely melted. A lot more snow was apparently on the way for the night and radio stations couldn't stop talking about it. His truck fishtailed going up the gravel road to his house and slid to a stop in the front driveway.

He dropped the piece of wood with the message

written on it, along with the truck keys, into the passenger seat. Lowering the visor, Daniel held out his hand, catching a small key to the lock on the door of an old wooden shed behind the house. Once inside, Daniel turned the light on and walked a circle around a scratch-free, black 1968 Mustang GT. He opened the driver's door and took a small white box along with some tools from the seat. Next, he lifted the hood and propped it up before cutting open the box with the end of a screwdriver. He turned the box over and an engine part fell into his hand. Installing the part took him only minutes after removing the old one.

He measured the oil level, double checked his work and then sat in the driver's seat. The engine started with a thunderous roar and Daniel grinned.

He drove the car out of the shed and down the gravel drive. The new tires and the power of the rebuilt car made quick work of the Tennessee back roads. After ten minutes of test driving Daniel parked the car behind the truck in the driveway and went inside to clean up.

After showering, he stood wrapped in a towel and looked himself over in the bathroom mirror. He needed a haircut. A knock came from his bedroom door and Marie called from the other side, "Daniel?"

"Just a minute, Mom." Daniel put on his pants and the shirt Hannah had picked out for him before opening the door. Marie walked in and sat on the bed, taking note that he was dressed to go out. "You and Hannah ready for the dance tonight?"

"Yeah, I'm taking her to supper first."

"She seems like a sweet girl."

Daniel smiled. "You've only met her once."

"I can tell, Danny. Just be careful. There are people out there who might try to hurt you by hurting her."

"I know that already, but why are you just now telling me this, Mom?"

Marie stood and walked toward the door, but turned before going out. "Because I knew they'd talk to you when it was time."

Daniel shrugged. "They?"

"You know who I'm talking about, Daniel. Don't keep things from me. Be careful tonight." Marie walked out of the room and pulled the door closed.

Daniel stood in disbelief until the ringing from his phone snapped him back to the moment. *Natalie.*

"Hello?"

"Hey, what time are you picking me up?"

"Funny. What's up?"

"I just wanted to ask you to save a dance for me."

"Okay, I'll do that."

"Are you giving her the first ride in the Mustang?"

Daniel walked to the window and scanned the outside. "Are you here? How'd you know I had it ready?"

"I was walking in the woods near where we built that tree house when we were kids. I headed to the road after that and saw you drive by."

Daniel turned from the window. "Hannah gets the first ride."

"I see. Well then I guess I'll see you tonight."

"Yeah, see you there." He hung up and concern clouded his eyes. He shook his head to free it from the worrisome thoughts.

Daniel finished getting ready and walked through the house to the kitchen. He grabbed scissors from a drawer and walked out the front door. The blades sliced through a rose stem from the small garden in front of the house. Daniel sat in the car and laid the rose gently in the back seat before turning the key. He admired the growl of the engine for a few seconds, but looked back at the rose bush thoughtfully before going over and cutting another one. He sat it next to the other in the back seat.

Hannah met Daniel in the lobby and wondered what he was grinning about as he sauntered through the front door.

"Maybe he thinks he's getting some tonight," she thought to herself. Her heart pounded. He looked so fine. His blond hair was a little long in front, hanging towards his eyes, which creased at the corners with his wide smile.

Hannah wore a sage green chiffon dress. Strapless, with a shirred bodice and cinched at the waist, it fell into loose handkerchief drapes to her knees. A pair of burgundy stilettos showed off her shapely calves. Wearing a shade of lipstick to match her shoes, she had piled her curls loosely on top of her head, letting some individual ringlets tumble freely down the sides of her face and nape of her neck.

Daniel drew a shaky breath when he saw her. He pressed an intense kiss against her lips, stopping only when he felt all of the tension leave her body. "Happy Valentine's Day. You look *beautiful.*"

Hannah smiled, pulling herself back from the lightheadedness. "Happy Valentine's Day to you, too. And thank you." She put her hand to his face, trailing her fingers down his jawline, and kissed him again, softly, playing with his lips.

When they broke apart, she grabbed her black woolen dress coat from a nearby chair, and Daniel helped her into it. He put his arm around her and they walked outside where Hannah scanned the parking lot for a likely vehicle. He stood watching her spin around in search.

"What's up?" Daniel joked. "I told you I wouldn't have my truck tonight."

"I halfway thought you were joking or trying to keep me on my toes," she smiled.

"Nope, I was serious. I have a different set of wheels tonight." Daniel led her by the hand to the far side of the parking lot to an old station wagon and pretended to be proud of it. "I polished the fake wood just for tonight." He crossed his arms and smiled.

Hannah tried to act impressed while walking toward the passenger door where Daniel waited to let her in, but then he frowned. "You know what, I'd rather drive something else—something a little more intense." He walked away from the station wagon and neared the shining black Mustang, motioning toward the passenger door. Hannah hesitated and then rolled her eyes. "What? Is this a joke, too?"

Daniel patted the roof of the car. "Come on."

He opened the door and she looked at him. "Seriously? Daniel, this is *awesome!*"

"You haven't ridden in it yet."

As Hannah sat down Daniel ran around to the

driver's side, climbed in, and turned the key. He revved the engine and Hannah smiled at his excitement.

Daniel showed off the capabilities of the engine on the way to the restaurant, earning a squeal or two from Hannah.

After driving past the Nashville city limits, he pulled into the parking lot of a restaurant with gray bricks and several men in white button-up shirts standing near a sign that read "valet parking." He stopped the car by the front door and a teenager with black hair emerged from the group and ran over to greet them. "I'll park that for you sir."

Daniel examined his eager face and red tie. "No thanks, I'm just going to park it myself. But it looks like *they* need some help." Daniel looked in the rear view mirror and motioned to the minivan that had just pulled up behind him. The teen's face fell as he drudged toward the middle-aged man holding out the van keys.

Once inside, the two were seated and the server went to get their drinks.

Hannah looked up from her menu at Daniel who was scanning his. "So do you eat anything special or do you always eat normal human food even though… you know."

Daniel lowered his menu, revealing a smirk. "Yeah, I'm fine as long as no one brings the Kryptonite around."

Hannah laughed loudly, but caught herself after seeing stares from diners around them. "Does that make me Lois Lane?"

Daniel's mouth leveled slightly. "That brings back memories. Superman was one of the few shows Mom let me watch as a boy. Maybe she was trying to get me familiar with the idea of being more than human in a world of humans. Apparently she wanted me to learn something from cartoons."

The two returned to their menus as the server came back with their drinks. The waiter opened his notepad. "Have you had a chance to look over the menu?"

Daniel and Hannah ordered and each had a glass of red wine. After they had finished eating, Hannah held the glass up and looked into what was left of the dark red liquid. "My parents would freak if they knew I was drinking again."

Daniel raised his glass toward her before swigging down the last bit. "And don't forget dancing. Drinking and dancing."

"Well, I don't think they'd object to this kind of dancing."

Daniel glanced down at his phone. "Speaking of dancing, we need to get going." He paid the bill and they headed to the dance in the Mustang.

Hannah put her hand on top of Daniel's as they rode. "Do you think Anthony will show up?"

"I seriously doubt it."

"Erika told me Natalie will be expecting a dance with you and I wanted you to know that I'm okay with that. I know you two are close."

"Well that's good, 'cause I already promised her one."

Hannah felt a twinge of jealousy. Not because Natalie liked Daniel or because they were going to have a dance, but because he and Natalie made plans to dance without first talking to her. But after a few minutes the feeling evaporated and optimism for the evening resumed.

The campus swarmed with nonstudent boyfriends and girlfriends who were there to dance with their significant others. Dorm parking lots were completely full, but Daniel found a spot behind the gym and he and Hannah walked halfway across campus. Snow flurried as they neared the entrance to the hall and Hannah could hear music.

"I love this song!" She playfully wiggled in front of Daniel with her back to him. The line moved quickly and within a few minutes they were inside the banquet hall, and Hannah found a hook to hang her coat on.

Slow music played and students danced, socialized, and ate finger foods. As they walked beside the dance floor, friends from various classes greeted them, and Daniel leaned over to whisper to Hannah, "I'm so bad with names."

"Me too!"

An extremely skinny man with brown hair and glasses approached Daniel. "Hey Dan, introduce me to your date, buddy."

Daniel motioned to Hannah, "Hey… man, this is Hannah."

He shook Hannah's hand. "Your boyfriend's a great guy." He gave Daniel a half hug like they were great friends and walked away leaving Daniel with wide blue eyes shining in the low light. He looked over at Hannah, whose eyebrows were raised. "Not a clue."

Hannah laughed and a slow song started playing as the lights dimmed further.

Daniel took Hannah's hand. "Would you like to dance?"

Hannah smiled flirtatiously. "Would you?"

They walked onto the floor and started slow dancing. Daniel pushed a loose strand of Hannah's hair behind her ear. "You really do look beautiful tonight," he said in a low, hungry voice.

"Thank you. And you make that blue shirt look very, very good." She playfully leaned in close to him, running her fingers over his upper contours. "I noticed how your shirt reflected the color of your eyes earlier."

Daniel returned the smile. "So have you thought any more about a major, now that we're halfway through the semester?"

"Great dance conversation. Yeah, definitely psychology."

Daniel smirked. "Oh yeah? So are you going to hypnotize people?"

"If I have to, I guess. I'm sure I'll learn how if that's something I need to do some day."

"The guys on TV swing a watch back and forth and get you to look in their eyes."

Hannah chuckled. "I think you've watched too much TV."

Daniel shook his head. "I think there's something to looking into another person's eyes. I still remember the first time I looked into your eyes when you finally opened them. I had no idea who you were, but I remember thinking that I'd never forget those beautiful green eyes."

Daniel gathered her in his arms and crushed his

mouth to hers, far from caring if everyone noticed. They lost themselves in the kiss, and the moment.

Jeff from the cafeteria danced with his date a few feet from Daniel and Hannah. "Get a room, you two." He playfully slapped Daniel on the shoulder, interrupting their kiss.

Daniel squinted, doing little to hide his annoyance. "Having a good time, Jeff?"

"Sure am."

"Awesome." Daniel turned with Hannah and danced her away from Jeff and his date. She rested her head on his shoulder as they continued to sway with their bodies pressed close to each other.

The slow song ended and the beat of the next one vibrated the floor. Freshmen guys who thought they were being funny did goofy dances that caused most of those watching to feel embarrassed for them.

Hannah stood beside Daniel and looked around to see if she recognized anyone. She spotted the faces of a few girls from one of her classes and waved to one who smiled and waved back. The girl walked away and Hannah flinched at the sight of Natalie who had been standing on the other side. Natalie stared at Hannah for a few seconds and then walked toward her. She looked ravishing in a tight red dress with black stockings, and incurred the lusty stares of guys as she moved. Hannah's stomach stabbed with jealously with every step Natalie took.

"Hi, you two. Having a good time?"

Hannah didn't smile. "Yes, we are thanks."

"Well you ought to be. Because you look beautiful." She turned and ran her hand down the sleeve of Daniel's shirt. "And you look handsome." Without taking her eyes off Daniel she asked, "Hannah, could I have my dance on the next slow song?"

Hannah wanted to say *no* and tell her where to shove it, but she feared any demonstration of jealously or insecurity would only empower Natalie, and could push Daniel away. She put on a pleasant smile as though Natalie was her dear friend. "Sure, you two have a good time."

Daniel looked down at Hannah, trying to gauge her thoughts.

Natalie waved to the DJ who nodded his head and started a slow song. She reached for Daniel's hand and pulled him to the far side of the room where Hannah could hardly see them.

Natalie put her head on Daniel's shoulder as they danced. "I needed this Daniel. It brings back memories."

Daniel gave her a small smile.

She lifted her head and made eye contact with him. "Listen, about the whole vampire thing."

Daniel chuckled. "You say that like it's a sorority you've pledged to or something."

"Yes, I know Daniel. It's bad. I get that."

She placed her head again on Daniel's shoulder and a tear fell from her eye onto his shirt. "I'll stop for you, Daniel." She looked up again and continued. "I don't need blood. Humans make blood from their food, so why can't I figure out a way?"

Daniel lowered his eyes. "You think that'll work?"

"It's got to Daniel. I've just got to find the right food. Then you'll believe how much I truly love you."

Daniel shook his head. "Who says I don't believe it now?"

Natalie moved her face close to Daniel's. "Well I'm going to show you that I'd do anything for you."

Her fangs grew from her mouth, but Daniel didn't flinch. "Why are your fangs out then?"

Natalie covered her mouth as though she were hiding a cold sore. "It happens when I'm hungry. But I'm stopping Daniel, I swear."

She returned her head to his shoulder and Daniel spun the two of them toward the front door, jostling her enough for a fang to scrape his neck. Daniel took a quick breath and Natalie met his eyes as she covered the wound with her hand. "I'm sorry, that was completely an accident."

She uncovered the cut. "Dan, you're bleeding."

His eyes sparked with panic. "Someone could see."

"Don't worry; I'll take care of it." Natalie licked the white blood from below the scrape and up to where it leaked out, pulling a few awkward stares from those around them. But all that anyone could see was Natalie licking Daniel's neck and she passed it off as making out.

Daniel led them to an empty area on the floor. "I thought you weren't supposed to drink hybrid blood."

Natalie tilted her head and squinted back at Daniel. "Oh come on, Daniel, this could be crazy hot if you'd just give it a chance. Besides, I don't think a little bit will hurt me as long as I don't drink a lot of it." She took one final lick and closed her eyes, inhaling in jagged breaths as they continued to dance. "There, I think it's stopped and we both know it'll heal itself in five minutes anyway."

Daniel looked where he'd left Hannah, but the collage of couples blocked her figure out.

Hannah had given up trying to watch them and instead talked to Jennifer from one of her classes. "So do you like the psychology program?"

"Yeah, over all I do. The professors are nice and most of the work is pretty interesting, I guess. I'm just glad to be done with the basic stuff."

Hannah looked again through the crowd for Daniel and Natalie. "Is it just me, or is this a really long song?"

Jennifer glanced toward the DJ. "This *has* been a long song. Has it repeated or something?"

Hannah walked a few steps, alternating directions, but still couldn't see them.

Natalie pulled her body closer to Daniel. "Thanks for the dance." She pressed her lips to his and he allowed the kiss for a split second before quickly pulling away. But the dancing couples had parted at just the moment for Hannah to see them kissing. And for all she knew, it had lasted an eternity.

Chapter 11

FUGITIVE ANGEL

DANIEL LOCKED EYES with Hannah, but dancing couples blocked his way. He pulled away from Natalie's arms and zig zagged through the labyrinth of bodies.

He yelled for Hannah across the room, but the music drowned out his voice and she was gone by the time he found a clearing. He ran through the front doors. The snow fell like a thick fog, and when combined with the night, made seeing beyond a few feet impossible.

Daniel raced in the direction of Hannah's dorm, and his vision adjusted. His nighttime eyesight had dramatically improved in recent weeks – some hybrid thing, he suspected – and he saw Hannah in the distance and again yelled for her. She turned around, shocked to see him. She held up her pointer finger. "Okay, first of all, how could you possibly see me? I only knew you were there when you yelled, and I couldn't see you until you were right in front of me."

"That doesn't matter right now. What you saw—"

"What I saw was reality. Are you really going to try to explain it away? Like it was up for interpretation?"

"*She* kissed me! Alright? You saw everything because the whole thing didn't even last two seconds before I stopped it."

Hannah crossed her arms. "Has it happened before?"

"You mean like—"

"I mean since we've been together!"

Daniel pocketed his hands and looked at the ground.

Hannah assumed his answer. "Are you kidding me?" Tears stung in her eyes as she shivered.

"Look it's really complicated. I've known her all my life and she's loved me ever since we were old enough to talk. I… have strong feelings for you and I don't have to tell you that my situation is—"

"So because you're half angel, I'm supposed to put up with this crap?"

"That's not what I'm saying. I'm saying that she's my friend and she's messed up. We're connected, and if you're going to be with me, you have to understand that she's going to be my friend. We can deal with her together, but you're going to have to—"

"Who in their right mind would let a girl act that way and tell his girlfriend that she's got to deal with it? It doesn't make sense if you're really committed to me! What do you mean you've got a 'connection' to her? Just because you've known her for a long—"

"She's a hybrid!"

Hannah's eyes fell from Daniel's as his words sunk in. "She's half angel too?" she almost whispered.

Daniel nodded.

Hannah shook her head in disbelief. "How many are there? I mean, is Erika one too? Who else—"

"No. I don't know any others. It's an extremely rare thing."

Hannah tilted her head back and closed her eyes as the snow brushed her face. "You know, I keep thinking maybe I'll wake up from this. I mean, just when I think things can't get any more insane you add something else. What else are you not telling me?"

"I'm not keeping anything from you. Ask me anything and I'll tell you."

"Daniel, I don't even know what to ask." Hannah sighed and folded her arms, hugging herself from the cold. "Okay, look I'm going to do my best to understand that it's not what it looked like with Natalie, and that she's obsessed with you, but that you're not going to end your friendship with her over it. And I'm hoping that the hybrid thing makes her more like a sister or something. At least I'm going to tell myself that. I'll try to think of her as a crazy relative or someone that you can't really disown, but—"

"Perfect! That's exactly how you should feel because that's pretty much how it is."

Hannah smirked at Daniel. "You know, you've got to be the luckiest guy on earth! I mean you kiss another girl and can smooth it over with your girlfriend because the two of you are half angels and the regular rules don't apply. I can't believe I'm okay with this! It's like you've got a get-out-of-jail-free card or something."

Daniel smiled and put his arms around Hannah's waist. "And here I was looking forward to the handcuffs."

Hannah laughed. "It's cold. Walk me to my dorm?"

They walked toward her dorm lobby and after a few

seconds of their feet crunching in the snow, Hannah cleared her throat. "Look, just promise me you'll do your best not to end up alone with her anywhere. Okay? But if you have to, you've got to keep up your end of treating her like the crazy relative and calling her on her crap. I expect you to do that for me from now on."

Daniel pushed the lobby door open for her. "Sounds like a plan."

Hannah walked in and turned back to Daniel. "I must be crazy myself for not throwing a fit over this."

Erika stood from a lobby chair in front of the TV. "You two are back early. Did you have a good time?"

Hannah forced a smile. "I guess. Some of it was good."

Daniel put his hand on the small of Hannah's back. "I better get going before the roads get worse. I have a long day tomorrow. Unless you want to go back to the dance." Daniel looked at Hannah and motioned toward Erika with his eyes. Hannah concealed her nod back to him.

"I'm over the dance. Will I see you tomorrow?"

"I'm not sure. I've got a favor to do for someone."

"Okay, well call me then." She kissed Daniel goodbye and they hugged.

Daniel pulled away slightly, stroked her cheek, and met her eyes. "I'm sorry."

"It is what it is."

"I'll call you."

"Goodnight."

Daniel walked through the heavy snow toward the car. As he approached where he had parked, he noticed someone leaning against the car. He stopped twenty feet away. "Lucas?"

"Hi, Daniel. Did you enjoy the dance?"

Daniel nodded, annoyed. "Sure."

"Now tell me again why you socialize with the mortals. They're such pathetic little sheep who take themselves too seriously. You're so much better than that."

Daniel scanned the parking lot for anyone who might overhear. "Am I?"

"How can you stand to be around such temporary creatures anyway?"

Daniel released an uncomfortable snicker. "I'm dating one."

"I know. And there are so many problems and conundrums with that that you don't even know. But I won't insult your intelligence by pointing out those."

"So what can I do for you, Lucas?"

"I just wanted to make sure you were clear on our little deal. That there weren't any last minute questions or requests for my assistance."

"No, I've pretty much got it. And after it's done, you'll tell me what I want to know, right?"

"Absolutely, my young friend. Cross my heart and hope to die."

Daniel smirked and got into the car. He watched Lucas shrink in his mirror as he drove away and exhaled in relief to be leaving him for the moment. Suddenly, Daniel remembered the roses and turned to see them in the back seat. He'd had plans for them, but it had skipped his mind.

Hannah and Erika went to the third floor and into Hannah's room. Erika walked in and sat on the bed. "Well, I'm glad somebody had a good time tonight."

Hannah sighed. "It wasn't as good as it could have been. I was actually ready to dump him."

Erika scooted to the edge of the bed. "You're kidding! What'd he do?"

"It was more about what he allowed. Natalie kissed him and he didn't put up much of a fight. Well, I guess he put up a little bit of one, but—"

"And you saw it?"

"Yeah. He pulled away and turned toward me. I just ran out. He caught up to me and sweet talked me. But, now that I think about it, it wasn't really that sweet."

Erika stood and paced. "We're going to have to do something about her. I mean, she's got to respect boundaries."

"Daniel convinced me that she should get a pass because she's crazy. And that I shouldn't make it a condition that he kicks her out of his life in order for us to stay together."

Erika locked her eyes on the wall across the room. "Do you think Anthony has somebody else?"

"What? No. I think he just needs a breather. I'm sure we'd know if there was someone else."

Erika walked toward the door. "I'm sure you're right. I feel sick. I'm going on to bed." She walked out the door before Hannah could say anything.

Hannah lifted a heart-shaped box of chocolates with Daniel's name on it from her dresser. She shook her head, flustered, and walked to the bathroom to get ready for bed.

Sleep stayed a step ahead of Hannah. She couldn't fight off thoughts about the evening and how Daniel hadn't given her a gift for Valentine's Day. The one moment she felt herself slipping away her heart jumped at the sound of Natalie slamming the door to the connecting suite. *Where had she been?*

Hannah couldn't remember when she fell asleep but at eight o'clock the ringtone blared from her phone sitting on the windowsill. She barely caught it before it went to voicemail.

"Hello?" Her voice cracked sleepily.

"Hannah, it's Dad."

"Is Mom okay?"

"What? Yes, why would you ask that?"

"Well, I haven't heard from you all semester and barely heard from her, so I figured somebody had to be hurt or dying."

"Okay, that's not funny. We gave you a little space and you certainly could've called us if you wanted."

"Okay. So how are things?"

"They're fine. I actually called about something going on with you. I got a call from the college dean, whom I've known since I was a student there. We'd both like to meet with you this morning. He checked your schedule, so I know your first class isn't until ten-thirty. Would you please meet with us in his office around eight-thirty?"

"Uh, sure. Yeah, just let me go so I can get ready."

"Alright princess, see you soon."

"Okay, bye Daddy."

Hannah's feet hit the floor and she staggered toward

the bathroom. *He hasn't called me princess since I was a little girl. What's going on?* She wondered.

Hannah showered and got ready, grabbing a quick cup of coffee to take with her. She walked across the snow-covered campus to the administration building. Once inside, she followed the arrow that said, "Dean's Office."

The hall was silent and mostly dark, with only occasional sections of lights on. The building wasn't used for classes and Hannah figured they left the lights off until the start of office hours. She heard nothing but her own footsteps for the first few seconds as she turned the corner to go deeper into the building. Finally, she heard male voices behind a door on her right. She held her phone up to the door and from its light read, "Dr. Kenneth Burcham."

Hannah felt a jolt of nervousness in her stomach as she raised her hand. She paused and took a breath before hitting the door with her knuckles.

The talking stopped and Hannah waited seconds before the door opened. She recognized the slightly over-weight, white-headed man as Dr. Burcham from one day in the cafeteria when he had walked around introducing himself to students.

"Hello, Hannah, nice to see you," he spoke as though he hoped he was right about her name.

"Hi Dr. Burcham. Nice to see you too."

Hannah's dad, Marty, stood and walked over to hug her. "Princess! Aren't you the trendy student?"

Hannah looked down at her clothes, not thinking they looked especially trendy or like a student.

"Won't you sit down, Hannah?" Dr. Burcham motioned to two chairs outside Hannah's line of sight and she turned to see a short, brown-headed, middle-aged policeman seated in one of them.

The dean allowed the uncomfortable moment of silence and then clarified. "This is Officer Starks."

Hannah's mind raced; searching for anything she might have done wrong, but she stepped forward before her hesitation seemed more than simply reacting to a stranger.

She smiled and reached out her hand. "Nice to meet you."

Officer Starks stood and stopped smacking his gum long enough to force a small smile. "Hi."

He retook his seat and Hannah plopped down in the empty chair beside him across from her dad and Dr. Burcham. Dr. Burcham rubbed his chin. "Well, Hannah do you have any idea what this is about?"

Hannah glanced back and forth between her dad and Dr. Burcham before turning for a quick glance at Officer Starks. "No. Not a clue. Should I?" She looked at Marty for a comforting expression, but he seemed completely fascinated with the wooden floor between his feet.

Dr. Burcham continued, "One of our staff members who knew you when you were a student before contacted me a few days ago. She was concerned about some company you're keeping, with a certain young man. Does the name Daniel Keith ring any bells with you?"

Hannah tried to disguise her bewilderment. "Yeah… yes I know Daniel."

Marty finally spoke. "How well do you know Daniel, Hannah?"

Hannah looked into his eyes and realized that this was the most interest he'd shown in her since she attended college last time. But she also detected care in his eyes, despite his usual discomfort with anything that required him to feel. "I'm dating him, Dad."

Marty didn't hide his disappointment. "Hannah." He propped his face up in his hands and resumed his staring contest with the floor.

Dr. Burcham fidgeted in his chair. "After Tiffany told me her concerns, I contacted Officer Starks and he informed me of some recent issues that I felt your dad should know about, and he drove over here to—"

"I'm sorry, what's the problem with Daniel?" Hannah's mind joked with her as it pointed out that he was half angel, that she'd seen him break a man's arm while standing fearlessly at gunpoint, and that he had gotten in a fight at the mall before rushing her to safety from an attacking dark angel.

Dr. Burcham wasn't lacking material. "Hannah, about five years ago Daniel was arrested for assault. The man almost died, but for some reason he dropped the charges and changed his story. The state couldn't prosecute because they had no witnesses, but that's just the start." He raised an open hand to Officer Starks who stood and walked to a laptop on Dr. Burcham's desk. One click of the mouse and Hannah watched a video of Daniel from their recent trip to the mall.

The room looked on as Daniel pounded the teenagers to the ground. He appeared to have a slight smile on his mouth throughout most of the beating. The video froze frame and Officer Starks turned to Hannah and crossed his arms.

Dr. Burcham and Marty raised their eyebrows to Hannah, giving her a chance to present an explanation, if she had one.

Hannah shook her head. "I know that looks bad, but do you even know why he was fighting?"

Officer Starks snapped back. "Do you?"

Hannah absorbed the situation. She realized that when Daniel explained why the man at the mall was chasing him, he hadn't mentioned why he got in a fight. And she might have asked him more about it if he hadn't shocked her with the half angel confession. "No, I don't know. But couldn't it have been in self-defense?"

Officer Starks ran the video backward and stopped at the spot where the third person walked up with his hands raised. "He wasn't defending himself there." He continued the video and the room watched Daniel beat the teen bloody.

Hannah didn't have a response, but Officer Starks had more to say. "We haven't yet spoken with the person watching the store when that event occurred; this is just what the mall brought to us yesterday."

"So you're here to question Daniel?"

"After we arrest him, yes."

Hannah held her stomach and leaned forward.

Marty lifted his face from his hands. "Hannah, are you alright?"

"I just need to go to the bathroom."

Officer Starks stepped toward Hannah. "I'll walk you

there." He took Hannah's arm and walked her out the door into the hall. He looked both ways, unfamiliar with the layout of the building.

Hannah pointed in the direction of where she thought the bathrooms were, but didn't speak. He walked her to the bathroom door and looked as though he was considering going in with her. Instead, he opened the door and looked around the bathroom noticing that no one could fit through the small window inside. He let go of her arm. "Let me know if you need me."

Hannah nodded and walked in. She entered a stall and spun the lock on its door. *I can't believe he didn't take my phone.*

She scrolled to Daniel's name and wrote a text: *Don't come to campus. Police are here looking for you over the mall fight! Don't reply. Delete this.* She deleted the record of the sent message and flushed the toilet so that Officer Starks could hear.

She went to the sink and turned on the water so he'd think she was washing her hands. Finally, she opened the door and found him waiting on the other side, leaning against the wall.

He stood up straight. "Did you throw up?"

"Yes and I'm lightheaded."

"Here, I'll help you." He put his arm around her, uncomfortably close to her hip, and grabbed her arm with the other hand. Hannah pretended to be dizzy all the way back to Dr. Burcham's office.

When she walked in, Marty immediately replaced Officer Starks at her side. "Are you okay?" he asked.

"I just need to sit down."

Dr. Burcham looked over at Starks. "Wait a minute. Where's your phone, Hannah?"

Officer Starks looked at Hannah, the phone bulging from her side pocket. "What phone?"

Dr. Burcham threw his hands in the air and let them fall. "Dad-gummit, Woodrow!"

Officer Starks seemed surprised to be called by his first name, but it quickly transitioned to a stern look at Hannah for deceiving him.

"Hand me your phone."

Marty objected. "On what basis?"

"On the basis that she could be aiding a fugitive from the law." Marty lacked a response and turned to Hannah.

"Hand him your phone."

Woodrow took it from her hand and held it out where he and Dr. Burcham could look it over. "How do I get to your texts?" He walked the phone over to Hannah and positioned himself where he could see what she was doing. She made a couple of swipes with her finger and her outgoing texts displayed on the screen.

Woodrow walked back over by Dr. Burcham. "Well, it doesn't show a recent text."

Dr. Burcham frowned at Hannah. "She could have just deleted it." He took a deep breath. "Did you text or contact him in any way to warn him?"

Hannah didn't blink. "No."

Woodrow put his arms on his gun belt and stared at Hannah. "Well, you're not to have any contact with him until further notice. If he's innocent, the system will release him."

"He had a reason for what he did. I know it. He didn't just fight over nothing!" Hannah protested.

Marty slammed his hand on the desk. "He's dangerous!"

Hannah smiled, slowly nodding her head. "I know."

Daniel walked into his room after showering. His phone showed a new text and he read Hannah's warning, deleting it afterwards as forewarned.

He dressed and walked out of the house to the Mustang, figuring he needed to leave in case the police came to his house. The roses were still in the back seat and Daniel sighed at the sight of them. He pulled some sunglasses from the glove compartment and put them on before speeding down the driveway.

After maneuvering the back roads, he turned onto Main Street near campus and slowed down to watch the people walking the sidewalks. After several minutes of scanning both sides he finally found what he was looking for. He pulled over by a parking meter, rolled down the window and hollered, "Zachery!"

Zachery walked to the passenger door and got in the car. "Nice wheels, Dan!"

"Thanks."

"By the way, please don't say my name where everyone can hear it. I'd rather not advertise to my enemies."

Daniel merged back into the small-town traffic. "I'm glad I found you."

Zachery snickered. "No, I found you. Or do you not know how that works yet?"

"Apparently there's still some things I don't know."

"Okay, it's like this; the part of you that's a guardian angel is drawn to me when I'm in a dangerous situation. But with the help of Uriel and some other interesting characters, I've learned to draw you in without having to put myself in actual danger."

"So you just go out and wait for me to drive by?"

"That's what happened the last couple of times."

"Okay. Well as interesting as that is, I had some other questions that I thought you might be able to answer."

"Why not ask Uriel or Lucas?"

Daniel glanced down from the road. "I don't like being around the Council. I just don't trust them and with all the stuff going on in my life, I don't want to deal with that too."

"I see. But you've had a lot of conversations with Lucas recently, right?"

"Yes, but he initiated those most of the time."

Zachery pushed his hair out of his eyes. "But you trust me?"

"Yes."

"Okay, cool. Well, let the questioning begin."

"Well, I need to tell you some things first. I was in a fight at the mall. I think some dark angels set me up, like Uriel warned could happen. They used a kid to lure me in and tried to get me, or maybe Hannah. And I got a text a while ago from Hannah saying that the police were on campus looking for me so—"

"So you're on the run then. Gotten into the thick of things now, Danny boy."

"There's more. My best childhood friend is a vampire

who's in love with me, another close friend just dumped his girlfriend who is also a close friend, and he seems to have changed in just the last few weeks. I haven't talked to him in a few days. And to top it all off, I'm supposed to do something for Lucas today, so that he'll tell me who my father is."

Zachery spun on Daniel. "The Council hasn't approved you being told about your father. But you're saying that Lucas said he'd tell you if you did him a favor?"

"Right and—"

"What'd he ask you to do?"

Daniel suddenly locked his eyes on the rearview mirror. "Cops are behind me."

"Just calm down, it's probably nothing."

The police car trailed as Daniel turned right onto a highway. Daniel kept the car under the speed limit and after a few minutes the police car passed him and turned down another street.

Daniel hung his head in relief. "I've got to find Cain."

Zachery blinked. "Who's Cain?"

"He was getting beat up at the mall and I got the guys off of him—and then some. I need him to talk to the police. Cain should have already, if the mall was doing any kind of investigation into this."

"Okay, does whatever Lucas asked you to do have anything to do with that?"

"I don't think so. He gave me directions and a time and told me I'd be meeting someone who needs my help doing something. If I help him, he'll tell me what I want to hear."

Zachery looked concerned, but then noticed the roses from the night before still in the back seat. "Two roses?"

"One was for Hannah, and I figured I had to give one to a girl named Natalie. The vampire. We've been friends all my life. But it was a pretty wild night and I ended up forgetting about them."

"The roses or the girls?"

"The roses."

Zachery chuckled. "You really know how to get in messes, my friend. But that one is your mess. Do you need help finding Cain?"

"Yeah, why, do you know him?"

"No, but based on your story, you found him with your guardian abilities. So you can find him again."

"But I didn't mean to find him. It was because he was in danger, right?"

"Right. But I've been observing angels for about twenty years now. I guess you could say I'm an ange-lologist. I can reverse engineer your guardian senses. It's easier for me to do with hybrids because the human side softens some of their defenses."

"Reverse engineer?"

"In other words, he doesn't have to be in real danger for you to find him. We can access your ability to get to him."

Daniel pulled the car to the side of the road. "Okay, what do I have to do?"

Zachery grinned. "This might sound a little out there, but just trust me and we'll find him."

"I don't have much of a choice."

Zachery situated himself in the seat. "Okay, I want

you to just breathe and try to resist analyzing anything. Just get to the point where you're following and feeling your instincts."

Daniel leaned against the door, took a deep breath and closed his eyes.

Zachery waited a few moments before continuing. "I want you to see Cain's face in your mind's eye. I want you to picture him being attacked by those guys, but you're watching the fight from a distance. You run to help him, but it's as though the ground under his feet is moving him further away from you. Next, the sun dims and night falls. Your eyes adjust in that hybrid way that makes you the only person around, other than his attackers, who can see him. You run toward him as a punch lands against his face. You hear the bones crack and see the blood fall from his nose."

Daniel flinched and Zachery's voice grew louder. "You run toward him, as fast as you can, but no matter how hard you try, you can't get to him." Zachery took a knife from his pocket and turned up Daniel's right hand. Then he quickly stuck the sharp tip of the knife into Daniel's hand, drawing the white blood. Zachery looked up at Daniel's closed eyes. He seemed unfazed by the stab. "You sprint toward Cain as fast as you can, but he falls to the ground and—"

"Stop!" Daniel's eyes opened and he stared straight ahead, the picture of focus. "I know where he is. I just saw it."

Zachery laughed in celebration. "Easiest one so far!" Daniel put the car in gear and accelerated onto the road.

The two were silent for the first several minutes of the trip, but Zachery had a reason to speak again.

"When's the last time you spoke to Uriel?"

Daniel kept his eyes straight ahead on the road, as though he hadn't heard the question. "I only met him that one time."

Zachery shot his eyes at Daniel. "How is that possible?"

"What do you mean?"

"How could you have only met with Uriel once? There's so many things you need to know, and there's a plan that involves you that I thought was progressing."

"Lucas told me that he was my contact with the Council."

Zachery looked out his window. "Is that so?" Moments passed without Zachery speaking. "And you tell me that one of your close friends is a vampire?"

"Yeah. She dated this dark hybrid who dumped her after he turned her. She said it was like he recruited her and was on to the next recruit."

Zachery stared expressionless at Daniel. "Yes, that's exactly what he did! How do you not know that? You should be informed enough to know how they work at this point. They've been recruiting hybrids for centuries; it's part of their strategy. They'll come after you, too, until you're either fighting against them or you join them. They make you choose."

"So what should I do about Natalie?"

"Well she's your friend. You could try to save her if their hooks aren't too deep into her already. Do you have much influence on her?"

Daniel snickered. "I think it'd be easier to list what she *wouldn't* do for me. So yeah, I have a lot of influence on her."

Zachery smirked. "I'll overlook the arrogance in that, and just say that if you care anything about her you need to get her away from them before it's too late. And I need to talk to Uriel because either the plans have changed or something's not right. Lucas shouldn't be your contact with the Council and you should know a lot more than you do. I don't think Uriel is aware of some of this."

Shortly after crossing into Nashville, Daniel turned into a subdivision.

Zachery looked around. "You know this area?"

"Some. My mom drove through here on her way to nursing classes when I was a kid. She took me with her sometimes when I couldn't stay with kids who had parents she trusted. And some of my friends donate plasma there." He pointed to the plasma clinic.

After they passed a couple more blocks, Daniel slammed on the brakes. "That's the house!"

Zachery turned to see a house with light blue siding and dark navy shutters. "So is this where he lives? What did you see in your head?"

"I saw him open the door from the inside of this house. An exterminator came to the door and he answered it."

Zachery pointed to a pest control van parked a few houses down.

Daniel put the car in park and the two walked to the door. The doorbell sounded and several seconds later Cain answered. He didn't say anything as he examined

Zachery first and then his eyes flashed familiarity when he looked at Daniel. "Hey! It's you!"

"My name's Daniel. You remember me?"

"How could I forget? You're the badass who beat up those three anal wads. How'd you find me?"

Daniel smiled. "Just lucky I guess. Listen, what happened at the mall? Did you tell them that I was just defending you?"

"Nah, man, I got sick that night. Puked all night. Been sick ever since."

"They didn't call you or anything?"

"Yeah, I saw it on the caller ID, but I didn't answer. I don't want that job anymore."

"Well you've got to tell them what happened because I've got cops after me. All they saw on the tape was me fighting those guys. They didn't see what happened before that."

"Yeah, man, I'll totally call 'em. I owe you."

"Why don't you call them right now?" Daniel stepped into the house and Zachery followed.

"Yeah, sure." Cain walked down the hall and into his room. The walls were plastered with posters of gothic bands and one of a gothic woman wearing skimpy clothes. A Nirvana poster hung from an opposite wall.

"This brings back memories," Daniel said.

Cain picked up his phone from the night stand and walked over beside Daniel. "Curt Cobain. Yeah, he's a legend, man. Started it all back in the day."

Daniel smiled. "I remember when he was new."

Cain dialed a number and held the phone to his ear. "Hunter? Hey it's Cain." He listened for several seconds as Hunter gave him an earful for not calling in. Then he told him he was fired. "Yeah, okay, but that's not why I'm calling. I'm calling to talk about that fight that happened." Cain listened to Hunter and then covered the phone before turning to Daniel. "He says the police were out there the other day when they called here. I'm supposed to call a number they left." He surveyed his cluttered floor and finally found a pen. "Okay, go ahead Hunter." He wrote down the number. "Okay and yeah I get that I don't have a job there anymore and you can kiss my—"

He looked at the phone screen and then at Daniel. "He hung up!"

Daniel grew impatient. "Okay, go ahead and call that number he gave you."

"Right." Cain dialed and waited. "Hi, my name is Seth Jackson and Detective Kemp told me to call about a fight I witnessed at the mall a few days ago. Yeah, I'll hold."

Daniel smirked at him. "So your real name is Seth?"

Cain nodded and then turned away to focus on the call. "Yes sir. I was working at the mall and three guys who go to my school came in and pulled me over to the wall and started punching me and saying they were gonna kill me. Then this blond guy walked in and sees what's going on and fought them off of me. That's pretty much it." Cain listened to another question and turned back to Daniel. "He had blue eyes, blond hair. Kind of built. Not ugly or anything."

Zachery rolled his eyes.

Cain responded again. "I'm sixteen. No, I didn't know him. Never seen him before until then and I don't know where he is." He turned to Daniel with wide eyes as he listened. "Yeah, I can do that. Okay, thanks, bye."

He turned back to Daniel and Zachery. "They want me to come in sometime today or tomorrow to sign a statement or something like that. They want to talk to you, too, if they can find you."

Daniel turned to Zachery. "I think I should just go talk to them today now that he told them what happened."

Zachery laid down an incense holder he'd been looking at and turned to Daniel. "Might as well face the music. They probably just want you to sign a statement too and they'll want you to stay in town while they're investigating. It's best to appear cooperative. At least until they try to arrest you."

Chapter 12

PIECE OF WORK

DANIEL PULLED THE car keys from his pocket. "Want to go with me, Cain?"

Cain's mouth gaped as he mulled it over. "You want *me* to go with you?"

"I just figure they're less likely to arrest me if they have your statement on file first."

"Alright then."

The three walked to the front door and started toward Daniel's car. Cain realized they were walking to the black Mustang. "Is this your car?"

"Sure is."

"You've got to be kidding me!"

Daniel smirked. "Nope."

Cain circled the car and stopped in front of Daniel. "Dude, you have the perfect life." With that he opened the door and sat in the back seat.

Daniel turned to Zachery who repressed a laugh before speaking. "Well, Mr. Perfect Life, let's ride down to the police station so you can confess to beating the snot out of a couple of teenagers."

Daniel grimaced and sat in the driver's seat, starting the car and revving the engine for Cain's benefit.

Dr. Burcham poured himself a second cup of coffee and held it behind his desk while he reached into a drawer and pulled out a bottle of scotch. He then stared disappointedly at Hannah.

"No one blames you for being won over by him, Hannah. Young ladies often come to college and get enamored by some punk with biceps who gives off that bad-boy vibe. And we're not saying he's an evil person. He's just misguided. With never knowing his father, and his mom away from him so much trying to make ends meet."

Hannah crossed her arms and dropped her eyes from his only to cut them back. "You don't know him."

Marty stood from his chair. "And neither do you, Hannah! Do you think a couple of months with him means you know him?"

Hannah glanced at her cell phone as Woodrow groped it. "Maybe you're right." Just then the phone rang, startling Woodrow and bringing Marty and Dr. Burcham over to look at the caller ID, which clearly displayed *Daniel*. Hannah was stunned by the invasion of her privacy.

Dr. Burcham took the ringing phone from Woodrow and handed it to Hannah. "Put it on speaker." Hannah knew she didn't have much of a choice and hoped Daniel knew what he was doing.

"Hello?"

"Hey, sexy."

Hannah noticed her dad's eyes squint in anger as he listened. She tried to answer with something that would keep Daniel calm and not cause him to give away his location. "Hey there."

"I thought I'd call and let your friends know that I'm an innocent man. And I have the proof in the car with me now. They'll know soon enough. I just wanted you to know really."

Dr. Burcham mouthed words to Woodrow. "Can this be traced?"

Woodrow shrugged and answered out loud. "I guess if we would have planned a little better."

Dr. Burcham smacked himself in the forehead. "And whose job would it have been to plan, Woodrow?"

Woodrow pointed to Hannah and put a finger in front of his lips.

Hannah cleared her throat. "I'm glad you called. I assume you're going to the right people with the proof and that I'll hear from you or someone about it."

"Yeah. You'll hear soon."

Hannah's phone beeped once signaling that Daniel had ended the call.

Woodrow stomped closer to Hannah. "Call him back and ask him where he's going!"

Dr. Burcham wasn't amused. "Woodrow, the man's no fool. He's not going to tell us where he's going or what he's doing. He was taunting us. It's probably a police station somewhere or he agreed to meet a cop somewhere private."

Woodrow lowered his eyes in disgrace at Dr. Burcham's failure to take him seriously. He spoke softly this time. "Should we keep her here or does it even matter anymore?"

Marty pressed his lips together. "You *can't* keep her here. She hasn't done anything wrong, so unless you can name some law she's breaking or show me a court order, I'm going to take my daughter and go."

Dr. Burcham didn't look up, but fidgeted with some papers on his desk. Woodrow stammered, "If you hear from him, you contact me."

Hannah nodded and stood beside Marty, who put his hand on her back as they walked out of the office.

After the first few silent steps, Hannah had to ask, "What changed your mind?"

"What do you mean?"

"You seemed to be on their side, thinking I was terrible for dating him, and that he was some kind of criminal fugitive."

"Well I don't know what I think about him – I don't know him – but I didn't realize when I came into this that they were going to keep you in that office and do whatever it was they were doing. I thought they'd just ask you some questions and see if you'd been in contact with him. But I do think we need to see what kind of proof he's got."

Hannah inhaled slowly, puzzled. "That doesn't make much sense, seeing as how you seemed to be going along with them and even yelled at me."

Marty grunted as though he was covering up a laugh. "When you have children of your own, you'll understand that sometimes you have to be firm. Try to put yourself in my shoes. I hear my daughter is dating someone danger-ous. What would you have done?"

Marty opened the door for them to go outside, but Hannah stopped walking and waited for him to return her gaze. When he did, Hannah gauged his sincerity as best she could, determining that he seemed to have her best interests in mind.

Marty glanced down at his watch. "Can I take you to lunch?"

Hannah turned her head and looked around campus. "I've already missed my morning class, even though I was told I wouldn't, so why not?"

Marty smiled. "The car's this way." As they walked, he continued the conversation. "You think he's innocent?"

Hannah looked straight ahead, but internally, her thoughts were a windstorm. "I'm not saying he's a boy scout, but he's got a good heart. If he beat up those guys, they deserved it."

Daniel parked the Mustang and he, Zachery, and Cain walked through the entrance, pulling the stares of multiple officers.

Cain, knowing he needed to go first, walked to a counter and waited until the woman behind it looked up at him.

"Hi, I'm here to see Detective Kemp."

The secretary, an older woman with short, curly hair and a name tag that read, "Tullis," glanced back to her computer. "What is this regarding?"

"He wanted to talk to me about something I saw… or witnessed."

She raised her head to get a better look at Cain through her thick glasses, and then examined Daniel and Zachery. "And your name is?"

"I go by 'Cain', but my real name is Seth."

She sighed. "And what is your *real* last name, Seth?"

"Jackson," he whispered.

"One moment, please." She picked up the phone, pressed an extension button and waited several seconds before saying, "Sir, I've got a 'Seth Jackson' here to see you." She listened to the response and then returned the receiver to the cradle. "Please have a seat." She pointed to some chairs against the wall, but before they could take more than a couple of steps, the deep voice of Detective Kemp called out. "Seth, come with me please."

Daniel and Zachery sat and waited for half an hour, until Detective Kemp and Cain rounded the corner again. Detective Kemp stood in front of Daniel and crossed his arms. "Well, Mr. Keith, I didn't recognize you, since you aren't throwing punches this time."

Daniel turned to Cain. "You told him who I was?"

Cain shrugged. "They already knew."

Detective Kemp turned and began to walk down a white-tiled hallway. "This way, Mr. Keith."

Daniel followed Detective Kemp to a room without pictures or furniture, other than a table with two chairs. Kemp pushed a chair out from the table. "Have a seat." Daniel sat and looked around the room, noticing the blandness and the scuffmarks on the floor. Detective Kemp remained standing and crossed his arms.

"This is a temporary discussion room. The other one is being remodeled." He walked to the other side of the table and leaned on it with his hands. He smirked at Daniel. "Well, you're quite a piece of work, Mr. Keith."

Daniel remained expressionless. "In what way?"

"You seem to have some impressive fighting skills."

Daniel weighed Detective Kemp's words and concluded that Kemp was probably trying to bait him into bragging about some of the fights he'd been in. "I guess it was just adrenaline. You know, seeing those thugs hurting an innocent kid."

"Alright, Mr. Keith, tell me what happened."

"I walked into the store and saw a guy holding Seth's arms behind his back while another one punched him in the stomach."

"How many were there?"

"Three."

"Go on."

"I said some things to distract them. I wasn't nice about it. And they attacked me. I think you saw the rest on tape."

"What about the last one Mr. Keith? He raised his hands, trying to surrender."

Daniel tilted his head. "I didn't trust him. I thought he had a weapon. Can't take any chances with people who would gang up on an innocent kid like that."

Detective Kemp leaned back in the chair and locked eyes with Daniel, trying to pull some sort of reaction that might show he was in cahoots with Cain to tell a made-up story. Daniel didn't blink.

"Okay, Mr. Keith. Thank you for your time. We will

continue to investigate and will be in touch with you if we need you. Don't go any further than a couple of hours away from the area until you hear from me."

Detective Kemp had Daniel sign a few papers then walked him out of the room and motioned toward the waiting area. Daniel walked past Cain and Zachery, who followed him outside to the car.

Cain closed the car door. "So they didn't lock you up. I guess it went like you planned."

"Pretty much. We obviously had the same story and apparently they don't have the entire video anyway. I wish they did, but either way, they pretty much have to come down on my side. Or at least, I'm thinking they just don't have evidence to charge me with anything."

Cain released a cleansing breath, glad to be out of the police station and relieved that it appeared his hero wouldn't be locked up. As long as Daniel walked the streets, Cain wouldn't have to worry about being the victim of any bully, even if he didn't really know that for sure. The story of Cain's mysterious friend hospitalizing three star football players had spread around the local schools, and people who typically gave Cain a hard time for the way he dressed or his weight hadn't spoken to him derogatorily since.

"Are you going to take me home or am I hanging with you guys all day?"

Zachery sat up and found Cain in the rearview. "I think it'd be best if we dropped you off today. We have some errands to run. They're not fun."

"It's probably better than what I have to do."

Daniel chuckled. "And what's that?"

"Some homework I *may* consider doing. And I'll probably microwave something that used to have cheese in the middle of it. Then I'll probably burn some incense and take a nap, face down in the carpet."

Daniel blinked. "Ever thought about taking a girl to see a movie or something?"

"I think I need to lose about fifty pounds before that could happen. I'm not you, ya know."

"It's eighty percent in your head, bro."

"What a crock of crap. I'd say it's eighty percent in your face and biceps. Plus, only goth girls are even in the universe of possibilities. Regular girls just think I'm weird and smell funny."

Daniel, considering Cain's words, sniffed the air, but could detect nothing. "Well, *do* you smell funny?"

Cain laid his head back on the head rest. "Yeah... I reckon so."

Daniel turned into Cain's driveway. "Take care, man."

"Okay, but what if I need you again?"

Zachery got out of the car and opened Cain's door. "He'll be around."

Cain got out and stood, awkwardly holding the door open while he struggled for words. "Uh, yeah. Later, dudes."

Daniel dialed Hannah's number and she answered, "Are you okay?"

"Just wanted to let you know that the issue has been cleared up. They might have to make a phone call, but I talked to a detective in Nashville and he didn't arrest me. Before that, he talked to the kid I helped so he's got the full story now."

"Great. I'm having lunch with my dad, so I'll tell him."

Hannah ended the call and explained to Marty what Daniel had said. Marty sipped his drink and seemed to only catch the highpoints. "Okay, Hannah, but talk is cheap. Maybe he's telling you the truth; maybe he's lying. Either way, he's got a past record to explain as well. I'm worried that if you stick with him, that it will be just a matter of time before you're at the end of his fists."

"He wouldn't hit me! You've got the wrong idea, Dad!"

Marty looked at Hannah as though she were a little girl who didn't understand how the world works. "Of *course* you want to think that. But it doesn't matter how much *he* thinks he cares about you. All it could take to set off that rage of his is for you to upset him. You saw what he did to those guys in the video! I don't care if he didn't start it; he enjoyed himself. You think I'm going to trust someone like that with my little girl?"

Hannah grimaced as she replied, carefully taking the time to calm herself, brushing some lose hair from her eyes. "Daddy, first of all, I'm not a little girl. Secondly, it matters more what *I* think about him, than what *you* think about him. And in this case, I—"

Hannah stopped herself before she said it. She had used the word "love" only once in her life and that ended miserably. He was the guy who had introduced her to alcohol. When he left, she tried to hang onto him by hanging onto the drinking and partying.

"Hannah?"

"Look, all I'm saying is that I appreciate your concern and that I'll be careful, but you don't know him at all. Please don't judge him on this. He's a good person, Dad.

I do know what I'm doing… *this* time, at least. Okay? Could we please change the subject?"

The day passed and the sun eased behind the mountains. Daniel and Zachery had spent the day practicing reverse engineering Daniel's guardian skills. Daniel had gotten pretty good at doing it himself, even without Zachery's assistance or cutting. Once Daniel managed to see the location of one individual in his head, they moved on to a new person. Marie, Hannah, and Natalie were the easiest for him to see. He had difficulty finding Anthony at first, but eventually saw him walking into a bar and ordering a beer. Daniel found it tricky to keep focused on him.

They rode in silence as Daniel headed to the location Lucas had described. Lucas had specified 'sundown' as the time for Daniel to show up. Zachery was increasingly concerned.

"Look Dan, to clarify what we talked about earlier, I'm concerned that Lucas has been your only contact with the Council, and that he hasn't educated you like they would any hybrid they wanted aligned with them. I don't mean to put doubts in your head, but something isn't right. Be cautious."

"I thought you trusted the Council?"

Zachery's countenance fell as he carefully selected his words. "It's not that I don't trust the Council. It's just that, as you know, not all angels are trustworthy. There are power struggles, mutiny—"

"Mutiny with *angels*?"

"Why not? Some of them are angels of light, some of them are dark. You've got to be careful about who you're dealing with." Zachery noticed concern on Daniel's face. "What are you thinking?"

"I'm thinking Lucas isn't a Council loyalist."

Zachery didn't look surprised. "Why?"

"It's just adding up to me after being around him and what you said. I've trusted him, dismissing things that should've concerned me, because I thought he represented the Council. All this time he's just been isolating me and making sure he's the only voice I heard."

"I'm glad you see that. It's what I think too. We need to talk to Uriel. What was it Lucas wanted you to do for him today?"

"I'm supposed to deliver a message to a dark angel."

Zachery's eyes widened. "What message?"

"He said it was a message of peace. That I was to tell them my name, that I'm under his protection, and that I'm there to help them with something. He wasn't specific about that part. He just said that I could be the one they'd been waiting on to reunite the rebel angels with the Council."

Zachery slugged the door with his fist. "That lying bastard! I know exactly what he's doing. He didn't send you to unite anybody. He sent *you*, because he didn't want Uriel or another Council angel to know he was anywhere near the rebels or that he was taking you to them. Telling them who you are, and that you're under his protection, will be some kind of sign to them from him and probably trigger some sort of planned response. They'll likely capture you and torture you until you join them."

Daniel clenched his jaw, his entire world now uncertain. He drew a deep shaky breath. "You're right, we need to talk to Uriel."

"I'll take care of that. You just be there like you told Lucas, so no one suspects anything. I'll bring Uriel and some others, but we've got to hurry."

Chapter 13

CONDITIONAL IMMORTAL

DANIEL STOPPED THE car on the side of the road and let Zachery out. Daniel leaned over the passenger's seat. "Don't you need me to take you to the lake or something?"

Zachery smiled with confidence. "I'll be fine. Besides, we don't want Lucas to wonder where you are. I'll find Uriel. You just do what Lucas expects you to do, without worrying about us. Understand?"

"Got it." Daniel drove away as Zachery watched.

The car lights flashed across the entrance sign to Daniel's old high school and he parked behind the gym. He got out of the car and started walking. Memories filled his mind as he looked around the track, the football field, and some of the buildings. He remembered Natalie. Holding her hand during P.E. Kissing her behind the gym and going to dances with her. As he neared the edge of the woods, he resumed his focus on the matter at hand. He looked back and forth down the tree line and into the darkness of the woods.

Stories about those woods were like legends when Daniel was a teenager. It seemed that most of the forests in this part of the state had some sort of attached horror story. Missing kids, old ladies who lived as witches in caves, monsters of different sorts, rabid animals; Daniel had probably heard them all. But this time, the story was real and he was part of it.

Crunching leaves turned Daniel's head, but he couldn't find the source. He took a couple of steps back and became still, bracing for what approached.

Suddenly, a tall, thick figure stepped from behind a cluster of trees. As the massive silhouette advanced into the moonlight, Daniel recognized him from the mall as the dark angel who had chased him.

"I see you're not running away this time, Daniel."

Daniel felt the hair stand on the back of his neck. "I wasn't running away. I was protecting someone."

"Ah yes. I enjoyed watching her flee. Please tell me you were able to take that pink thong off her that night."

Daniel swallowed his anger, refusing to show offense. "And who are you?"

"My name is Kore. You know enough of the rest."

"I'm here with a message for you. I came to tell you who I am, which you already know, and that I'm under the protection of Lucas."

Kore stepped closer, slowly circling Daniel. "And?"

"And that I'm here to help you with something. Lucas said you needed me for a mission."

"*Need* is too big a word, but I do have something for you to do." He walked closer to Daniel, stopping inches from his face. "We would like the services of a certain young man. He's thick boned and his name is Anthony. I understand you know him."

"What do you want me to do?"

"Bring him to us. We'll take care of the rest."

"And if I don't?"

Lucas stepped from behind the trees, leering at Daniel, eyes black and manic. "Then all you'll find of Hannah will be that pink thong," He snickered loudly.

Daniel charged after Lucas and lunged with a massive punch that Lucas dodged and countered with a fist to Daniel's stomach. Daniel doubled over and Lucas elbowed him in the back of his head. He fell to the ground and rolled a few feet away. Kore took a large stride with his oversized legs and threw a kick into Daniel's ribs and head. White blood streamed from Daniel's nose and mouth as he struggled to push himself off the ground. He collapsed on his back, face up, blinking at the attacking angels.

Lucas leaned over Daniel's face. "Join us now... or die."

Daniel breathed in gulps, getting just enough air to speak. "I'm immortal, I can't die..."

Lucas squealed with laughter before kicking Daniel in the side. Daniel groaned as he felt a rib snap. Lucas put his foot on Daniel's chest, pressing his weight down on him.

"Do you feel that Daniel? That's what it feels like to be dying. That's why you're called a *conditional* immortal. Because you're immortal only until I break you in two!" Lucas laughed hysterically just before Kore delivered a final kick to Daniel's side. Daniel groaned in agony.

Lucas mockingly put his hand to his ear to hear Daniel's muffled response strangled in his throat. "Did you say something?"

"What about the Council?" Daniel managed.

Lucas exhaled and smirked. "Screw the Council." He turned to Kore and the two of them smiled darkly. "Daniel, do you remember all those times when you were a kid all by yourself and you felt so lonely? Or that time when that bully, Thad, beat you up in front of everyone on the playground because your mom had told you never to hit back, since it wouldn't be a fair fight?" Lucas again leaned over Daniel's face. "You've lived the life of a freak! It's time for you to know your place. With us."

Daniel wiped the blood trickling from his forehead and saw Natalie approaching.

Lucas laughed again. "Don't look now Daniel, but as you know, your ex-girlfriend got herself turned into a vampire, which means she's on our side now. And she doesn't like being second place."

Daniel's eyes widened in confusion as he watched Natalie's fangs extend from her open mouth. She circled him and stopped as Lucas and Kore continued to laugh and mock him.

Natalie stooped to one knee and straddled Daniel before leaning over face to face with him. She licked the blood rolling down his face and the edges of his bleeding lips. "Yummy. Now I'll know what it's like to drink all of you." She teasingly slapped him across the face and stood, while all he could do was watch her, shocked, unable to move. She pulled her leg back to kick him, but just before impact, the leaves crunched behind her, under the sound of running footsteps.

Natalie ducked to the ground and covered Daniel as Uriel leaped over them and kicked Lucas in the head. Sparks flew from Lucas' head like flint against stone. He was thrown through the air and smashed into a tree, folding it over with a loud splintering pop. The top of the tree pinning him beneath

Kore ran toward Uriel and punched furiously, but the older angel dropped below his reach and kicked Kore in the side of his knee, snapping it. Kore shrieked in pain and fell sideways, grasping his broken limb.

Uriel lifted Daniel onto his shoulders and he and Natalie ran to the Mustang. She sat in the back and Uriel laid Daniel down with his head in her lap. He took Daniel's keys from his pocket, started the car, and sped out of the school parking lot.

Natalie pushed Daniel's hair away from his eyes. "Daniel, I'm so sorry. I'd never mean to hurt you, I'm so sorry." Ripping a piece from the bottom half of her shirt, she gently wiped blood from his nose and lips. "Danny? Can you hear me?"

Daniel slowly turned and opened his eyes, trying to find Natalie through his fogged vision and vertigo. His blurry eyes met hers, while she slowly caressed his cheek. "It's okay, I'm right here."

Daniel felt something in his arm and raised it slightly. Natalie noticed. "What is it?" She groped under him and uncovered the thorn-stemmed roses from the night before.

She looked curiously at them and back at Daniel.

He cleared his throat, mustering the strength to speak. "One of those is for you. Happy Valentine's Day."

Natalie smelled the wilted petals and smiled back at him. She leaned over and kissed his cheek. "Thank you so much, Dan. That means the world."

Natalie brushed her bobbed blond hair away from her face, inhaled, and looked meaningfully at the other rose.

Daniel closed his eyes. "For Hannah, of course."

Natalie nodded her head and after inspecting the flower for a moment, carefully laid it aside.

Daniel turned his head toward Uriel and pushed himself to speak loudly, "Am I going to die?"

Uriel kept his eyes straight ahead. "You'll live. The key was getting to you before they killed you. Since we did that, you'll heal up."

"And what about Lucas and Kore? They're immortal?"

"Conditionally, like you. But their strength is far more developed at this point."

"Angels are only conditional immortals?"

"Before humans fell, angels were all immortal with no conditions. But some angels were part of the fall and sided with their leader. That's when they became conditional immortals. Even today, some good angels fall. Like Lucas."

Daniel lifted his head. "Why would he fall?"

"Power. Most who fall, figure they can defy the odds long enough to build a following to protect themselves. But eventually we find them."

Daniel slowly wrapped his hand around Natalie's, gripping it firmly. "Then what?"

"Then we either kill them, or lock them up."

"Lock them up? Where?"

Uriel watched a car cross at a four-way stop before he answered. "Hell."

Daniel and Natalie stared at each other, wide-eyed.

"A bit overwhelming, isn't it?" Uriel muttered. "I owe you an apology, Daniel. I thought I could trust Lucas in spite of his hunger for control. He assured me that he would educate and train you properly if I delegated that responsibility to him. Obviously, he betrayed us all."

Daniel closed his eyes for a few moments, gathering his thoughts. "What's next?"

"You won't heal from this as quickly as you have other injuries. You were struck by angels and they didn't just break skin and bones. There's more to it than that. It will take a few days for you to recover. Then we'll begin your training."

Daniel looked at Natalie as she pushed his hair back behind his ear. "We've got to find Anthony before they do. They'll come after him and as messed up as he is right now, he might—"

Natalie put a finger to Daniels lips. "Don't worry about anything right now. You just need to focus on getting yourself well."

Hannah walked into her dorm room, reflecting on the day's events. Following lunch with her dad they had walked around campus looking at landmarks that he remembered from his college days. It was the most they'd talked in years. At one point, Dr. Burcham called him and said the police were no longer seeking to arrest Daniel.

"I still think he's trouble," Marty had told her, but she

shook away his words. He didn't know Daniel. They didn't talk much about him after that as father and daughter chipped away at several years of distance.

Hannah hung her coat in the closet and kicked off her shoes. Her phone rang from the coat pocket. *Daniel.* She answered, "Hey."

A female voice responded, "Uh, hi."

"Who's this?"

"It's Natalie."

Hannah felt light headed at hearing Natalie's voice on Daniel's phone. Her developing fury conjured images of Natalie making out with him. "Why are you calling me from Daniel's phone?"

"Hannah, Daniel's not well."

"What do you mean? What's wrong?"

"He got in a fight with two..." Natalie hesitated momentarily... "dark angels. It didn't go well. He asked for you, but his ribs are swollen. It's hard for him to talk. We're at his house."

"I'll be right there."

Hannah flew down the roads until she arrived at his house. She knocked on the door and Marie answered. "Hi Hannah. He's in his room."

Daniel was asleep. Uriel and Natalie stood at his side.

"Is he okay?" Hannah rushed to the bed.

"He's asleep." Uriel extended his hand to her. "You must be Daniel's beloved Hannah. I'm Uriel."

Hannah recognized his name from past conversations. She examined Daniel's bruised and scraped face. She lifted the blanket and saw bandages wrapped around his ribs. She turned to Marie. "Why is he in such a deep sleep? Did he take pain killers or something?"

"I put him in a type of hybrid sleep that calibrates his body in a mode of hyper healing," Uriel explained.

"Faster than usual?"

"No, but faster than he would have if I hadn't. He'll wake in the morning feeling a bit stronger, but still sore. In about three days, his bones will be healed completely and he'll be himself."

Hannah looked at Marie's resigned, emotionless expression. Uriel walked over to her. "It's going to be alright, Marie; I'll make it right."

Marie nodded and Uriel turned toward Natalie. "How long has it been since you've had blood to drink?"

"A while. There was just what I got from Daniel. It seems to pack more of a punch than human blood."

"Yes and that was unwise, Natalie," Uriel replied.

Hannah stood and leaned away from Natalie, shocked. "What are you talking about? You drank some of Daniel's blood? Are you one, too?"

Uriel held a hand up. "I was with her the entire time. She didn't hurt Daniel; she helped us rescue him. It was a stunt to keep their attention and make them think she was on their side." Uriel returned his gaze to Natalie. "I don't know if you *can* stop drinking like you're wanting. It's only ended poorly before."

Hannah looked back and forth between the two of them in dismay. "Wait a minute. Stop drinking what? Blood?"

Uriel calmly turned to Hannah. "Natalie is what some humans call a 'vampire.'"

Hannah's eyes widened as she backed to the door where she could see all of them.

"Stay away from me. All of you." She set her eyes on Natalie and then Uriel. "How do I know she won't try to bite Daniel while he's asleep?"

Natalie frowned. "I wouldn't do—"

"I didn't ask you!" Hannah didn't take her eyes off of Uriel.

Uriel looked down at Daniel and placed a hand on his head. "I know this is all a lot to take in."

"I'm dating a guy who's half an angel and bleeds white. I've learned how to take it in, but that doesn't mean I have to like her."

Uriel continued. "She loves Daniel far too much to hurt him. I'm afraid you'll have to trust her for now. She needs to stay with him."

Hannah gestured to nowhere and let her hand fall. "And why can't I stay with him?"

Uriel smiled warmly, "You're welcome to stay, I'm sure, but he needs a hybrid with him at least until tomorrow, even a hybrid who's a vampire. In the rare event that Daniel has complications from this type of sleep or the attack, he'll need her eyes."

To Hannah, that sounded ridiculous. "Her eyes? What does that even mean?"

Marie pressed her lips together. "He could need her to put her face against his so that their eyes are very close and locked together. It can keep him from having a type of seizure following a beating like that. The seizure could kill him."

The room fell silent. "I'm staying too, then," Hannah

said. "I just need to get some things from my dorm." Hannah ran through the house, out to her car, and drove away.

Uriel turned to Natalie. "We're going to set aside the dark hybrid issue for now so we can take care of Daniel. But in the near future you'll have to make some major decisions."

"You say that like I'm deciding what to major in or something. Like there's anything I can do about my situation."

"I'm not saying it's easy, but there is a way to make you a clean hybrid again so that you don't need blood."

"I heard that's a fairy tale."

"It's not. You don't have to decide yet. Just while you're still transitioning. It takes about a year before you lose the ability to turn back. Just take care of Daniel right now. He may wake up soon and he'll need to drink water. Then he'll need to go back to sleep until tomorrow."

Natalie pushed her hands into her pockets. "Okay."

Following a glance toward Marie, Uriel left the room. The sound of him closing the front door resonated through the old house.

"I'll make some coffee." Marie walked out, leaving Natalie alone with Daniel.

She walked around to the other side of the bed and knelt down, bringing herself close to Daniel's face. She touched his arm lightly, running her fingers over his skin, looking for a response. Receiving none she stood again, but fell back to her knees when she heard Daniel whisper her name.

"I'm here."

Daniel looked around the room, recognizing it after a few seconds. "I'm thirsty."

"I'll get some water." She disappeared into the bathroom and returned with a cup. She lifted Daniel's head as he drank. "Daniel, you're only going to be awake for a few minutes so I want to tell you something while we're alone. I know you love Hannah, but I know you also love me. But I can be with you forever. She can't. I love you."

Daniel nodded and after a few minutes of silence his eyes closed and his head fell back into the pillow.

Marie returned carrying a tray holding three cups of coffee. She looked at Natalie for a few seconds, preparing to speak. "Natalie, for Daniel's sake, I'm asking that you try to be civil with Hannah."

"We're civil. Up until she found out I was a dark hybrid, we were doing okay. Well other than the thing at the dance."

"What thing?"

Just as Natalie opened her mouth to answer, the sound of the front door opening and closing signaled Hannah's return.

Hannah hurried to the bedroom and Natalie forced a smile. "That was amazingly fast."

"I called ahead and had Erika waiting at the door with my stuff. And I didn't use the brake all that much." Hannah saw the three coffees and motioned toward them. "One of those for me?"

Marie turned to leave the room. "I'm going to get the cream and sugar now."

Hannah called after her. "None for me thanks. Black and strong."

Natalie echoed. "Me too." She looked at Hannah who stared back for a few seconds before the two turned their eyes to Daniel.

Marie went to bed around midnight and Natalie sat in a chair on one side of the bed while Hannah sat on the other. Neither had spoken in hours. Hannah had entertained herself by messing with her phone and occasionally kissing Daniel's cheek, almost taunting Natalie.

Natalie finally met Hannah's eyes. "I'll go make us some more coffee."

Hannah didn't answer, somewhat taken back that Natalie would offer to do anything for her. Hannah examined Daniel's face, noticing that the bruising had healed significantly. She couldn't help but share her joy with Natalie when she returned with two cups of coffee. "Look at his face, the bruising is a lot better."

Natalie sat the cup for Hannah on the nightstand and leaned over to see Daniel's face. She turned back to Hannah with a smile. "You're right. He's a tough one."

Hannah looked at his wounds. "But he healed quicker before. I've seen him heal from cuts in minutes."

"I've seen that too. But like Uriel said, he was attacked by angels. It's different. It's not just about how hard they hit him. He could've taken that. It's who hit him. They've got spiritual power that adds another kind of force. That's the best way I know how to explain it. I'm still learning about some of this, too."

"You learned from the dark angels?"

Natalie didn't respond. Hannah watched her closely,

awareness flooding her again of Natalie's supernatural state. "Can I ask you some questions about…" Hannah searched for the right words.

Natalie helped. "About being a vampire?"

"Yes."

Natalie flashed an amused smile. "Go ahead."

"How do you go out in the sunlight?"

Natalie laughed. "Pop culture is so cute. There's only one kind of vampire that can't go out in sunlight."

Hannah's eyes narrowed. "There are different kinds of vampires?"

"Yes, there are several different types of us out there. There are angels who turn dark. There are hybrids who are bitten or who drink blood from a vampire bite. And then there are the runts on the totem pole, humans who've been bitten by any kind of vampire, but not fully drained of blood. To answer your question, only humans who've been turned into vampires can't go into the sun, at least not much. That's why there's not nearly as many of those. They're not worth as much to the dark angels since they can't run errands during the day."

Hannah soaked up Natalie's words, wanting to prevent as many future surprises as possible. "Do all dark angels turn into vampires?"

"They're more versatile than the other types of vampires since they don't have to feed to live. They just drink human blood to become more powerful. It's temporary though. Each time they drink someone's life away, they get some sort of a power high. It's addictive."

"So you kill people by biting them, right?"

"Well it's not like it's my job, but I have to live. I've

mostly stuck with biting bad people like child molesters and murderers. But I try to go as long as I can without drinking."

"How long has it been since you fed?"

Natalie looked toward the ceiling as she remembered. "A week."

"Who was it?"

"I've paid close attention to the newspapers and also have a source who gets me to the lowlifes. It was a man who robbed a gas station. During the robbery he shot the owner in the leg. They had to amputate. The thief only got three years in jail and I got him the day after he was released. When I walked up to him, I could tell he thought he was about to get some of this. You should've seen the look on his face when he saw my fangs." Natalie smirked.

Hannah looked to the ground, scared to ask Natalie what she was thinking. "So are you hungry now?"

Natalie smirked darkly. "Yes... very."

"And do you want to bite me?" Hannah tried to smile as though she was joking.

Natalie sipped her coffee, letting the question linger in the air. She sat down the cup and met Hannah's eyes before answering, "Yep."

After recovering from the sudden pit in her stomach, Hannah thought, *I can't let her intimidate me.* She tried to think of how to change the subject, but Natalie beat her to it.

"I'll be right back." Going to Daniel's dresser, she picked up his car keys. Hannah watched her leave the room and heard the front door open and shut. A few seconds later the same sounds interrupted the house's silence and Natalie returned holding a rose.

"This is for you."

Hannah's eyes fell to the wilted rose Natalie pushed into her hand. She glanced away from the flower as she tried to make sense of it.

Natalie waited until Hannah looked back up. "That's from Daniel. He meant to give it to you on Valentine's Day, but you know how that went."

Hannah, stunned Natalie would even bother to make sure she got the rose, searched for the words to reply.

Natalie left the room again and came back with a vase. "You'd better get that in some water. The cool weather preserved it some while it was in the car, but it'll get worse."

Hannah took the vase and walked toward the bathroom. "Thanks," she said before turning the corner. She filled the vase with water and went back into the bedroom, where she placed it on Daniel's nightstand.

"It'll make Daniel happy that you got the rose. Which makes me happy."

"So does this mean I can have him to myself?"

Natalie's face went blank. "Over my undead body." Hannah chuckled uncomfortably and two minutes of awkward silence passed before Natalie walked to the window and looked out suspiciously. "Anthony's in trouble."

"What do you mean? For skipping classes?"

"Not that kind of trouble. The dark angels want him to join them."

Hannah's eyes widened. "What if he doesn't?"

"They'll probably threaten someone he cares about. Or they'll vampire him and just use him at night, I guess."

"Vampire him?"

"Or they might keep him human so that he can screw up as many lives as possible for them during the day, without giving it away by being a freak. Don't worry, Uriel knows and will do what he can."

"Why do dark angels want to hurt humans?"

"For one thing, to distract the Council and keep them running around trying to protect people, since most of the Council members are guardian angels. That helps the dark angels pull in more allies and launch more attacks against the Council. But Uriel will do all he can to get Anthony back, I think."

"How do angels attack each other? I mean, do they fight or shoot at each other or what?"

"They wouldn't use guns or anything. It's pretty complex, but sometimes they can transfer power into things like a knife or when knocking down a tree. But a punch or kick from an angel is a much more powerful weapon because it's not just physical; it's spiritual too. They can use both sides here in the physical world even though they're limited by it some."

"What about hybrids?"

"We're more affected by the physical than angels, but can access spiritual power in much stronger ways than humans. What they did to Daniel would have killed a normal man. Maybe the whole point of it was to let him know they were going after Anthony. Just trying to get into his head. Things were much simpler when Daniel and I were kids. I can see him now. His hair was so blond, almost white. And he had those dark blue eyes and a big smile. I'd love to go back to those days."

The night gave way to the morning sun and Daniel opened his eyes to see the two girls asleep in their chairs. He smiled to himself that they both had spent the night in the same room to stay with him, in spite of their cold relationship with each other. Natalie woke and turned to see Daniel's smiling face. She stood and leaned down to kiss him first on a cheek and then his lips. But Daniel turned his face and looked back at her with a cocked eyebrow.

Natalie smiled and touched his face. "Your bruises are gone."

He rolled out of bed carefully, so as not to wake Hannah. Opening a chest of drawers, he took a tee shirt and winced while dressing. Soreness riveted through his body. Then he walked to Hannah, gently picking her up and laying her in his bed. He pulled the blankets over her and quietly took Natalie, by the arm, to the kitchen.

Marie stood at the stove making pancakes. "Those smell really good, Mom," Daniel said, putting his arm around her.

"I knew they were your favorite and hoped you'd feel like eating some."

"I definitely do."

Marie turned to Natalie. "And how about you Miss Natalie? Still watching the carbs?"

"No ma'am, not anymore. Taste is the only way food affects me now."

Marie looked down at batter frying in the pan. "That must be nice. Where's Hannah?"

"She's still asleep," Daniel replied.

Marie took the plate of hot pancakes to the table for Daniel and Natalie. "I'll make some fresh when she gets up."

Daniel and Natalie dug in. After a few bites, he turned to Marie. "Aren't you going to eat, Mom?"

"I already have. You two enjoy. I'm just going to make some more coffee and—"

"Would you make some eggs too?" Daniel smiled.

Marie smiled warmly. "Sure."

Daniel looked at Natalie across the table and felt his pulse quicken at the sight of her fallen bra strap sticking out of her shirt sleeve. He pushed his thoughts elsewhere, and knowing Hannah wouldn't want them having breakfast alone, said, "I'll be right back."

He walked down the hall and into his room. Hannah still slept and Daniel walked over to watch her for a few seconds. He leaned over and held himself up on the mattress to watch her more closely. Her red hair covered her eyes and Daniel brushed it aside. He lowered his head and kissed her. Her lips reacted, kissing back before her eyes opened. She smiled up at him. Confusion shaped her face as she realized Daniel was supposed to be lying where she was.

"Daniel. You're up! How do you feel?" She sat up and Daniel sat beside her with his feet on the floor.

"I feel good, considering. I'm a little sore, but that's all. And I love seeing you in my bed."

Hannah smiled, blushing, before reaching out and gently touching his ribs where the bandages were still wrapped. "That doesn't hurt?"

"No."

She slowly unraveled the bandages, revealing unblemished skin without a bruise or cut. "That's incredible!"

Daniel smiled and kissed her. "You know what else is incredible?" Hannah grinned and shook her head. "My mom's pancakes. Come on."

The two went into the kitchen and joined Natalie at the table.

"Well good morning Hannah," said Marie. "How are you this morning?"

"I'm great. Daniel looks like he's completely healed. I can't believe it!"

"He's close at least. Thank God Uriel and Natalie did what they did."

Hannah glanced at Natalie, who winked an eye back at her.

Chapter 14

MESSENGER

THE NEXT WEEK of classes brought with them feelings of anxiousness and dread for Hannah. Uriel had warned them that Daniel's refusal to join the dark angels put a target on her. And Natalie's betrayal endangered her as well. Because of Erika's connection to Anthony, Uriel suggested the four stay close together until further notice.

Daniel escorted Hannah and Natalie to their classes and back to the dorm. Because Erika didn't know about hybrids and dark angels, Daniel didn't let her catch sight of him as he watched over her along the way.

At the end of the week, Zachery sent word from Uriel that Daniel, Hannah, and Natalie should explain everything to Erika. He also informed them that he had not been able to find Anthony. So Friday night, the group of friends ordered pizza to Erika's room and after eating, as planned, Daniel began the revelation.

"Erika, we need to talk to you about Anthony."

Erika squinted in suspicion, wondering if this was some sort of insensitive intervention to tell her to get over Anthony and move on. "What about him?"

"We've know each other since we were kids. You trust me to tell you the truth, right?"

Erika looked around at Hannah and Natalie, trying to guess what this could possibly be about. "Yes, you know I trust you."

"We'll see. I've been keeping something from you for as long as I've known you." Daniel cupped his fist with the other hand and looked down as he tried to think of the best way to explain.

"Daniel," she said, "you picked me up from elementary when you were sixteen. Just tell me, okay?"

Daniel raised his eyes back to Erika's and held her gaze as he took a breath. "You know there's something different about me, right? You've always known that."

Erika looked puzzled. "Yeah, well I've always suspected. I mean, I know you're unique."

"I'm half angel," he blurted.

Erika paused, then grinned and looked to Natalie and Hannah for confirmation that he was joking, but neither smiled. "You've got to be kidding me. Do you really expect me to believe that?" She shook her head, disgusted that he would kid her at such a vulnerable moment in her life. "I mean how is that even possible?"

"My father was an angel. I'm what's called a Nephilim. They're talked about in the Bible, some."

She examined each face in front of her, unable to fathom that they could be serious. "Daniel, what are you talking about?"

"I'm telling you the truth, because it's important that you know."

"Prove it, then. Do something angelic."

Natalie stood. "Oh good grief." She moved over to Daniel and held his arm where Erika could see it. She faced Erika and rolled up the sleeve exposing his skin. She smiled so that Erika could see her teeth extending into fangs. Erika recoiled in shock.

Natalie batted her eyes sarcastically. "It can be a little shocking, can't it? Well it gets better." She raised Daniel's arm to her mouth and punctured his skin with her fangs. When she let go, white blood leaked from his arm. Erika screamed, jumping from the bed. Natalie sprang beside her and cupped a hand over her mouth. Natalie faced Daniel but spoke beside Erika's ear, "Nothing quite like it, is there?"

Daniel pressed his hand against the wound. "Erika, I know this is a shock, but I'm still the same guy I've always been, I just had some secrets."

Erika moved her head, trying to speak behind Natalie's hand. Natalie faced Erika. "I'll let you talk, but you're not going to scream are you?" Natalie flashed a smile ensuring that her fangs could be seen. Erika, with eyes wide, shook her head in compliance.

Natalie released Erika and crossed her arms as she waited for her response.

Erika pointed to Natalie but lowered her hand as she tried to catch her breath. "What does a vampire have to do with you being half angel?" she gasped.

Daniel cut his eyes to Natalie and back to Erika. "There's only a slight separation between the two. It's complicated."

"You?" Erika looked at Hannah, eyebrows raised.

"No, no," said Hannah, "I'm just—"

"Mortal," snickered Natalie.

Erika shot a leery eye back at Natalie, her head spinning. "What does this have to do with Anthony?"

Daniel sat down in a chair behind her and uncovered his arm. The fang wound had completely healed.

Erika rubbed the same spot on her own arm and stared perplexed at the man she thought she knew only ten minutes ago. He cleared his throat. "It's just that we haven't heard from Anthony in several days and—"

"Neither have I," Erika interrupted.

"Some bad people, who know about us, are looking for him. I've tried to call him, went to his dorm room and an angel friend of mine has tried to get in touch with him. We're not sure where he is, but the fact that you two dated means you could be a target."

Erika pushed back tears. "Is Anthony okay?"

Daniel nodded. "I hope so. But it's possible they want to use him to get to me."

"But Anthony's your friend. He wouldn't hurt you."

"If they turn him into one of them, they might be able to change him from the person we knew."

Erika cut her eyes to Natalie who shook her head. "Oh don't worry, I'm not evil really. I just have fangs."

Erika crossed her arms. "So what's next? How do we find him?"

"We're waiting on the Angelic Council to tell us." Daniel replied.

"That's it? We're just supposed to wait around while Anthony could be a prisoner of a bunch of monsters?"

"We couldn't possibly take them on by ourselves.

It's not even close." He motioned to Natalie and back to himself. "Only the two of us are even—"

"If Anthony's in danger, I'm going! You're not going to just leave me here."

Daniel nodded, understanding Erika's feelings. "It's not my decision."

Little was said the rest of the night. Natalie finished off the pizza, jokingly showing Erika tomato sauce on her mouth that looked like blood. Erika didn't appreciate the humor. Though Daniel expected a list of additional questions, Erika didn't speak or eat. She watched Daniel and Natalie like they were coiled snakes who might strike at any second.

Natalie left first, realizing that her attempts to joke about the situation had only made it more difficult for Erika to accept. She smiled as she walked down the hall, forgiving herself, since it had been Erika who encouraged Hannah and Daniel to get together in the first place.

Daniel watched Natalie leave and felt that Erika might brighten up with her gone. He sat next to her and gently rubbed her back. She flinched at his touch as if it burned.

"Erika, it's just me."

Erika stood and spun to Daniel. "That doesn't help me, Daniel! I don't really know who or what you are. Everything I thought I knew about you and freak girl was built on the fact that you two were human. That's the first thing you assume about someone. But that was a lie you let me believe my whole life! And now some other freaks that you've upset have come after Anthony. So how could it 'just being you' possibly bring me any comfort?"

Erika stomped to the door and held it open. Daniel

and Hannah took the hint and walked into the hall as Erika slammed it behind them.

Daniel and Hannah went to the dorm lobby in silence and dropped into the chairs in front of the TV. Daniel's eyes glazed off to somewhere past the dorm wall. Hannah rubbed his arm and kissed his cheek trying to cheer him up. He responded with a slight smile, but his face showed his frustration, and his jaw was clenched.

Hannah nudged his arm. "It's just a major shock when you first hear it. I can tell you from experience."

Daniel nodded. "I know. It's just that she acted like I betrayed her by not telling her all this stuff years ago."

"I guess she has a right to feel that way."

"I didn't say she didn't. But I have a right to keep certain things to myself. It's not like she's told me everything there is to know about her. And I don't want to know all her private stuff."

Hannah continued to try to explain Erika's reaction, while being supportive of Daniel. After a few minutes of thinking out loud, she decided she wasn't getting anywhere and rested her head on his shoulder. Several seconds of silence passed and she looked up to see Daniel's eyes wide and locked on the TV. Hannah sat up.

"What is it?" Hannah asked.

Daniel leaned forward in the chair. "I know that face."

Hannah looked at the screen to see a picture of a girl in her twenties and text beneath it saying, "Abduction victim." The report ended and Hannah turned back to Daniel. "How do you know her?"

"I had a dream about her. She was running from someone."

"So you're still having the dreams?"

"Nearly every time I sleep. I have dreams about several people each night. Sometimes I don't even see *them*; I just see what's happening through their eyes." He leaned back in the chair, still eyeing the TV. "They're taunting me."

"So do you plan on trying to rescue her or some of the people in your dreams?"

"I've realized I can't. To be able to, I've got to learn more about how to find them consciously, rather than just dreaming. Zachery's been helping me and I think Uriel plans to teach me a lot more once he figures out what the dark angels are working on right now. It's all pretty chaotic at the moment."

Hannah rested her head on his shoulder and laughed softly. "When I knew I was coming back to get my degree, I was kind of excited about possibly having a boyfriend again at some point. I told myself maybe I could have one only after I had focused on my grades for a while. The second rule was 'no drama'. Pretty sure I've broken both of those rules."

Daniel smiled for the first time that evening. "I have a 'no drama' rule, too. Didn't think it'd be my own drama that would break it."

Hannah's phone buzzed on her leg and she held it up to see a text from Erika.

I called a police friend of mine and he told me I should fill out a missing-person's report. I told him a little about the situation and he said you'd both likely be questioned. I didn't tell him the freak stuff.

She showed the text to Daniel. He shook his head.

"They're not going to find him. And that's just going to make her trust us less."

The next few days consisted of awkward moments between Hannah and Erika. In English class, Hannah passed a note to Erika who sat next to her. The note said: *I understand you're upset at Daniel, but that doesn't mean we can't still be friends.*

Erika read the note and pushed the paper back to Hannah without response. After class Erika left ahead of her, but walked back in the hall. "Have the police questioned you or Daniel yet?"

Hannah shook her head and Erika sighed before hurrying away.

A text came through on Hannah's phone from Daniel. *Meet me in the caf.*

Hannah went into the cafeteria and found him sitting alone. She sat down and tried to sound cheerful. "Hey."

"Uriel has an insider at the police station who said they've already dropped Erika's missing person report on Anthony. She said the two of them were broken up, which was flag number one. They called his parents who said they had talked to him last week and he was headed to the beach with some friends."

"So Anthony's at the beach?"

"I doubt it. Uriel said the dark angels probably forced him to call and tell them that. He said they operate best in secret and, if anything, want to make us feel like it's hopeless."

"But what about the Council? I mean don't they know where the dark angels are? Can't they just attack them?"

"I don't know if they know where they are exactly or not, but an attack is not a simple thing. Especially since the dark angels outnumber the Council. Something else I've started thinking about is that Anthony is just one person. He's just a human and the Council has plenty of other things to deal with. I'm not sure what would motivate them to be aggressive about finding him."

"Aren't they supposed to be guardian angels?"

"Yeah, but the number of people needing help is extreme. Maybe that's what they had in mind in the first place. To overwhelm the Council."

"So you don't think the Council will rescue Anthony?"

Daniel's eyes found the window as he realized the implications of his words. "I think they have good intentions, but he's on a long list."

"Why are dark angels doing all this here? Why Spring Hill?"

"I don't know. The mountains? The caves? Maybe it's easier for them to hide. But if the Council can't or won't do anything about it, I can at least try."

Hannah reached for his hand, finding his eyes before she spoke. "But you told Erika that even with you, we couldn't take them on by ourselves. You'll be no good to Anthony dead."

"I'm not sure what I'm going to do. But sitting around waiting while Anthony is turned into a vampire or killed isn't an option. I'm going to see Uriel. I'm tired of waiting."

"What can I do to help?"

"I honestly don't know, but I should do this by myself.

I don't want to put anyone else in danger. Just stick to your classes and go straight back to the dorm." Daniel stood. "I'll call." He drew Hannah in by her waist and kissed her.

Hannah leaned her head against his chest. "Be careful."

Daniel headed across campus to where he had parked his car. Though it was still cold, the sun had enticed many of the leaves of spring from the trees, making it harder to see all of campus. Daniel turned the corner and walked to his Mustang. He opened the door and started to sit down, but noticed someone sitting in the passenger seat. He instinctively raised his hands to fight, but recognized the intruder as Natalie.

A large smile spread across her face. "Did I scare you?"

Daniel's smile was smaller. "Well, I wouldn't say it was relaxing. You need something?"

"We need to talk."

"Can it wait? I've got to go somewhere."

Natalie's smile fell. "You'll want to hear this."

Daniel traced the landscape with his eyes, forecasting the results of his plans if he took time for her. "Quickly." He sat down behind the wheel and turned to Natalie. "I'm listening."

"Drive. Anywhere but here, please."

Daniel sped out of the cobble-stone parking lot and turned right, toward a field where students parked to make out at night. He pulled into the field and drove to its far side where an opening into the trees allowed him to maneuver so that they had complete privacy. "Now what couldn't wait? Are you alright?"

Natalie started to speak, but inhaled as though sucking her words back inside.

Daniel tucked her blond hair behind her ear and smiled, gently turning her face toward his. "Whatever it is, it's okay, I'm right here."

Her face showed consideration of his words, but she didn't return the smile. "Daniel, what if it's not okay?"

Daniel's hand fell to hers. "I can't help unless I know."

"You can't help anyway. It's out of your control now."

Frustration flashed across Daniel's face. "Natalie, just tell me so we can—"

"I'm pregnant."

Daniel pulled back and gripped the top of the steering wheel. The two sat quietly. Images darted through his mind of one of the dark hybrids taking Natalie's clothes off, touching her body. The familiar rush of rage flared through his chest. "Who's the father?"

Natalie seemed to prepare for an explanation rather than provide a name or description. She struggled to find a starting place.

Daniel turned in his seat, furious at her hesitation. "Who? Just tell me his—"

"It's you, Daniel! You're the father."

Chapter 15

THICKER THAN WATER

NATALIE'S WORDS REVERBERATED through Daniel's being.

"What're you talking about? That's impossible. We haven't had sex since—"

"Since we were nineteen. I know. I was there."

"So why are you telling me this crap?"

"Because it's true. Remember when I said they told me not to drink hybrid blood, and when Uriel said it was unwise? There was a reason." She sighed as she recalled what the dark hybrid had told her months ago. "There's life in blood. Turns out hybrid blood is physical and spiritual. Instead of just keeping me alive, it creates a life."

"But you only had a little of my blood. Hardly any."

"I guess it doesn't take much."

Daniel twisted in his seat. "How do you know for sure?"

Natalie gave him a look that said she knew because of reasons she shouldn't have to explain.

"How did you find out hybrid blood could make you pregnant?"

"I put together some of the stuff they told me. And I made a phone call."

Daniel pressed his lips together in aggravation. "Who did you call? Don't tell me it was another hybrid!"

Natalie looked up from biting her fingernail. She suddenly realized the terrible mistake she'd made, and why Daniel was so upset. "Yes. I wasn't thinking."

Daniel slammed his palm into the steering wheel and turned to her with a pointed finger. "Do you realize the hell you've just put us in? If they came after me the way they have, how do you think they'll come after my child? How do you think they'll come after you carrying it?"

"Daniel I didn't think about—"

"You're right, you didn't think! And you've endangered everyone I care about now. You've made an awful situation even worse!"

Tears filled Natalie's eyes. "Daniel, there's got to be something I can do. Something we can do." She buried her face in her hands and turned away sobbing.

Daniel stared out the window for minutes. Natalie calmed herself and tried to wait for him to speak.

"Daniel? Please talk to me."

Daniel turned from the window and met her eyes. "I'll talk to Uriel. Or Zachery. We've just got to make sure everyone's safe. And I've got to tell Hannah. I can't see her taking this well."

"Daniel, other than your blood, I've stopped. And now I have even more reason, since I don't want this baby to be born to a monster. I'm just hoping the father will notice the changes in me, too." She turned to Daniel, wanting to see something in his eyes other than rage.

"Natalie, I don't know the future. Today is enough for

me to worry about. Right now I'm asking you to back off and let me figure this out."

Daniel drove Natalie to her dorm and walked her to the door. "Remember, stay in your room until you hear from me. Don't leave for anything."

"I won't."

They hugged and she stepped back. His eyes moved down her body and stopped midway. He put a hand on her stomach. She covered the top of it with her own and sighed in appreciation for the moment. "I'll be a good mother, Daniel."

Daniel raised his eyes to hers, expressionless, but didn't reply. He turned and walked out of the dorm, heading toward the heart of campus.

Hannah's phone buzzed with a text from Daniel. *What building are you in?*

She hid her phone with the cover of an open book to conceal her texting from the professor. *I'm in the business building, finishing up class. Why?*

I'll be at the front door when it's over.

The professor finished the lecture and asked for questions. Since students typically remained until questions were over, Hannah drew the eyes of most of the room by the grating sound of her chair backing across the floor as she stood to leave.

She opened the front door to find Daniel waiting. She leaned in for a kiss, but stopped when he didn't react. "What's wrong?"

"We need to talk."

Hannah's stomach pulsed with nervousness. It had been years since she'd heard the 'we need to talk' line but all the other times it had been said as a prelude to other lines like, "It's not you, it's me" and, "I need some space."

Daniel led her to a commons area near a cluster of old oak trees. He turned his back for a moment to take the edge off his frustration so he wouldn't take it out on her. She silently waited for him to turn and speak.

"Hannah, I've got something pretty intense to tell you."

She tilted her head sarcastically. "Please Daniel, tell me something intense. Tell me something that blows my freaking mind! That's what I really need instead of this boring world I've gotten used to."

Daniel laughed, since he wasn't sure what else to say.

Hannah wished she could take it back. "I'm sorry. I'm just on edge with all that's been happening. I know it's affected you too. Is it about Anthony?"

"No," Daniel chuckled sardonically.

Hannah smiled, relieved that the issue must be minor. "What's so funny? Come on, tell me."

"It's really not funny. Not at all. But you know how in third grade your teacher told you that if you didn't be quiet, you'd have to go to the principal's office and for some strange reason it seemed funny?"

Hannah stared at him blankly. "No, I never had a teacher threaten to send me to the principal's office."

Daniel laughed sharply. "Really? Okay, well so far this isn't going well."

"Daniel, come on, you're making me nervous. Just say it."

"Natalie's pregnant."

Hannah recoiled slightly. "Sheesh, I didn't know vampires could get pregnant. So does she know who the father is?"

"Really? You're going to insult her now?"

"Oh come on, I didn't mean it that way. So who is the father?"

Daniel lowered his eyes, finding a tree root to look at.

"Daniel?" Her heart began to thud faster.

He forced his eyes up to hers, wishing he could skip this moment in time. "I am."

Hannah's head fell forward slightly as though she was making sure she hadn't misunderstood. "You?" Tears stung the back of her eyes and began to blur her vision.

"But we didn't sleep together!" he added quickly.

Hannah shook her head in disbelief, as the tears spilled over. Then she smirked at him as though he had just denied the existence of gravity. "Do you think I'm a complete idiot? Like I'm totally unaware of how biology works? Oh let me guess, you just brushed up against her and somehow—"

"It was when she drank some of my blood."

"What?"

"We didn't know it could happen, but a hybrid woman can get pregnant by drinking a hybrid man's blood."

Hannah's mouth gaped, her mind racing as though it could no longer find any reality that was certain or safe. She walked away and leaned against an oak tree as she brushed the wetness on her cheeks with the back of her hands.

Daniel followed. "You okay?"

The sound of her heart pounding in her head made

it difficult to hear. "Am I okay? No, I'm not okay. My half-angel boyfriend knocked up a vampire; I think it's my duty as a sane human being to be out of my freaking mind right now!"

Daniel reached for her hand. "I'm sorry."

Hannah snatched it back and walked toward the sidewalk in front of her, her head swimming, wondering if he was even telling her the truth.

Daniel followed. "Where are you going?"

"I'm going away from you. What I should have done the first day I met you."

Daniel stopped dead, as though she'd slapped him. "I don't blame you."

Hannah took a few more steps and turned around. "Look, I didn't mean that. But I need some space. For now, I need to step away from all of this."

Daniel didn't respond, but just regarded her, his eyes glowing icily.

Hannah pushed her hair back and sighed. "I'm sorry, but the last few months have put my world in a blender or something. I don't know which way is up anymore. I just need to get back to a simple life. I should be confused by algebra, not the details of some supernatural soap opera. I can't handle this. I'm sorry Daniel."

She waited for Daniel to speak, but walked away when it became clear he wasn't going to react beyond a brooding stare. Her emotions tortured her, begging her to run back to him.

Chapter 16

DIVIDE

DANIEL WATCHED HANNAH walk away until she turned behind a building, desperately wanting to call her back, or run after her. Of course, she was going to break up with him after finding out about Natalie being pregnant. What had he expected?

I should have ended it myself instead of dragging it out so long, Daniel thought to himself. *It would never have worked out anyway, and I've simply put her in danger when I could've avoided it by breaking up with her ages ago. I should never have involved her.*

Though he tried to tell himself it was for the best, he worked himself into a frenzy of rage, eventually storming away from the commons area toward McGee Hall. He knew Hannah wasn't there because he saw her turn in the opposite direction, but Natalie was.

He pounded on her door and she answered with a look of surprise. "What's wrong?"

Daniel stepped past her into the room and turned back facing her. "What do you think is wrong? I told her and she dumped me." Daniel seemed more angry than hurt.

Silent moments passed before Natalie reached her arms out to Daniel and he accepted her embrace. The sound of the wall clock ticked several seconds away as the two drew comfort from each other.

Holding her was therapeutic. He didn't have to explain anything. If he wanted to kiss her, he could. If he wanted to tear her clothes off, throw her on the bed and take her, she would have welcomed him. There were no games. His anger blinded him to anything but memories of Natalie's passion for him. Something else drew him to her. Something he couldn't define.

He felt outside of himself, as though he could watch his actions but had no say in them. He moved in to kiss her. He stopped with his mouth opened against hers and then quickly lifted his head away as he tried to shake his urges, but Natalie wouldn't hear of it. She closed the gap between them and squeezed his lips with hers. She stepped backward, pulling him with her toward the bed until she fell on the mattress with Daniel on top of her.

She arched her back and sighed as the stubble on his face brushed her cheek. His breath tickled her ear as he slowly moved to where he could taste her neck. Natalie gasped in anticipation as he kissed his way down to the top of her shirt. She sat up quickly and the two pulled off the fabric barrier. Daniel's shirt followed, flung into the pile of his jacket, Natalie's shirt, and seconds later, her bra.

They were sixteen again, wanting nothing else in the world but to remove any space between their bodies.

Each felt the other's breath quicken as they entwined and strained their bodies to experience the sensations they knew were possible.

Daniel's hand found the button to Natalie's jeans and pulled them off, then he reached for her panties. Daniel batted Natalie's hand away from his belt since he could undo it faster. The belt hit the pile on the floor as Natalie tugged his jeans down as far as necessary.

He swiftly maneuvered himself between her legs and their eyes locked together in realization of the moment. Natalie held her hand against Daniel's face and smiled as she reached again for his lips.

The sudden sound of Hannah's door closing sent Daniel's eyes in the direction of her room. He jolted and turned back to Natalie with a look of disbelief, quickly sitting up.

"Natalie, I can't do this. I'm sorry, I don't know what happened."

He stood up from the bed, stepped back into his jeans and reached into the pile of clothes for his shirt.

Natalie followed, gripping his arm. "But I felt it, Daniel, we were—"

"Yes, we're attracted to each other and we always have been."

Natalie raised her eyebrows. "And the bad part of that is?"

Daniel sighed. He walked over to Zeb, who was balled up in his round bed in the corner of the room and patted his head. "How old is Zeb now?"

Natalie pushed her hair out of her eyes and squinted

in frustration. "Well, I've had him since that summer we saw the bear in the woods. So fifteen years?"

Daniel looked up. "That's over one hundred in dog years. So that's why he's lazy all the time."

Natalie frowned, waiting on Daniel to get back to their previous discussion. He put on his shirt and pushed his feet into his shoes.

"Before you told me about the baby, I was on my way to find Anthony. I need you to stay in here until you hear from me. I'm—"

"He's fine."

Daniel cut his eyes from the door to Natalie. "How do you know that?"

Natalie's only response was to grin.

In an instant Daniel was in her face. "Tell me where he is!"

"I don't know where he is. But I know the dark angels want to keep growing their numbers. They told you they wanted him and he's no good to them dead. Just undead."

"That's what I thought." Daniel hurried to the door and turned as he opened it. "Stay here until you hear from me."

"Daniel." Natalie waited until he came to a complete stop before continuing. "Even if you find Anthony, he won't be the same."

"I know."

"No, you just know me. I'm a hybrid and a vampire. Hybrids change a little when we're turned, but we're mostly still who we were before. It's different with humans. They change based on who bit them and Lucas would have made sure Anthony was turned by a very dark angel, since he'd use him to help go after you. He's not your friend anymore, Daniel."

Daniel fastened his belt. "We'll see."

He closed Natalie's door and walked down the hall, stopping in front of Hannah's room with a hand half lifted to knock. But a combination of responsibility and pride prevented him, and his arm fell to his side as he continued toward the elevator.

The Mustang engine fired up and Daniel drove out of the parking lot and toward the park. A mile or two down the wooded road, he saw the familiar frame he expected and pulled over. Zachery plopped down in the passenger seat and pressed in the cigarette lighter without saying a word.

"Hello, to you, too," Daniel smarted off.

Zachery raised his head acknowledging Daniel, but remained focused on the lighter until it popped out. He wrapped his lips around a cigarette and pressed it to the end of the lighter, but it didn't catch fire.

"Doesn't work." He held his finger on what should have been the hot spot to demonstrate.

"Sorry about that," Daniel shrugged, "but we've got more important things to worry about."

Zachery held the cigarette out to Daniel. "You do it."

"What? I can't make the lighter work if you can't."

Zachery frowned. "I'm not asking you to use the lighter. I'm asking *you* to light the cigarette."

Daniel shook his head. "I'm not following you."

"You're an angel; you can light this just by wanting to."

"I'm half an angel for starters, and we haven't gone over the 'hands-of-fire' trick yet."

Zachery put the cigarette in his shirt pocket. "We're really wasting your abilities. It's almost like Uriel is..." Zachery stopped himself as though the idea hadn't been thought through well enough to be given an audience.

Daniel was curious. "Almost like Uriel is what?"

Zachery shook his head.

"Tell me."

Zachery clicked his teeth together as he thought. "I guess it wouldn't hurt. I'm beginning to think the Council doesn't trust you."

Daniel squinted. "Why wouldn't they?"

"I think they see your unique potential but... they figure you could betray them like Lucas. So maybe they've concluded that instead of risking you joining the dark angels, they'd rather eliminate you."

"Eliminate me? So you're saying you don't trust the Council?"

"No, I'm not saying that. I'm saying *you* shouldn't. They have their own agenda and maybe you don't have a place in it since you're not completely an angel. After Lucas betrayed the Council, higher sources have lost faith in Uriel. They don't trust his ability to choose allies and Council members. And it's possible they believe he's chosen poorly in deciding to reach out to you. So what I was going to say earlier was that they were wasting your abilities, unless Uriel was trying to prove a point to the Council. If that's the case, he could let you think you're one of them, and then he'd back off so the dark angels can kill you."

"So, I'm an enemy of the good guys *and* the bad guys?"

"Something like that. Except that, as much as you know about them, I don't think you appreciate just how terrible it is to be on the wrong side of these creatures."

"Okay, so what am I supposed to do now?"

"Well, I guess we've got to convince the Council you're on their side."

"And how am I going to do that?"

"I don't know yet. What'd you want to tell me in the first place?"

Daniel chuckled darkly. "If I've got to win points from the Council then I'm really screwed."

Zachery waited quietly for Daniel to explain himself.

"Natalie's pregnant."

Zachery lowered his head, but kept his eyes on Daniel. "The vampire is pregnant? Well that's not good."

Daniel looked out the window. "It gets worse. I'm the father."

Zachery froze in shock. "Tell me this is a sick attempt at being funny."

Daniel shook his head.

Zachery hit Daniel's shoulder with the back of his hand so that he'd turn away from the window. "You slept with her? Or did she bite you?"

"She bit me. Uriel didn't tell me this could—"

"Geez, Daniel, I think I could've understood it better if you'd just nailed her! How brain dead can you possibly be to let a vampire bite you? You want to be aligned with a Council of angels and you…" He couldn't find the right words, so he punched the dashboard in front of him before turning back to Daniel and getting out of the car. "I don't know why I wasted my time." He slammed the door and walked down the road in disgust.

Daniel rammed the car into first gear and left a layer of rubber on the road as he sped away.

Leaves crunched in the woods, startling Zachery, and he spun to find Uriel. He couldn't tell if Uriel was angry or not. "I guess you heard what I told Daniel."

Uriel nodded his head. "You did well."

"Did you know about the vampire being pregnant?"

"Yes. I'd hoped the help I gave her would win her over, but it looks like she's going to be another tool for them."

Zachery pulled the cigarette from his shirt pocket and put it between his lips. Uriel reached out and squeezed the end with his fingers, causing it to light.

"Thanks. So is that it? Are you finished with him?"

"Hannah won't talk to him. Neither will Erika. Anthony's his enemy now. He thinks we don't trust him and now you've walked out on him. He's completely alone, except for Natalie. And I wouldn't put it past Lucas to use this to his advantage either. We're about to learn a lot about our young friend."

"I don't understand. You're just gonna leave him to chance?"

"No. I'm showing him whose side he's on."

Chapter 17

CONQUER

HANNAH GASPED AND her eyes shot open. She flung the covers off and jumped out of bed. "I can't even take a nap without seeing vampires!" She reached from the bed and pulled a book from her backpack. "Maybe I can catch up enough to pull a 'B.'"

Fifteen minutes passed and knocks sounded on the door. Hannah dropped her face into her hands and sighed. The knocking sounded again, this time faster and louder.

She turned the nob and strained to see through the glaring sunlight coming through the window at the end of the hall.

"Still pretty as a peach I see." He stepped closer, making visible the details of his face and yellow pupils.

Hannah backed away quickly, too perplexed to make a sound, and tried to close the door.

Lucas put one finger to it. Her strength was no match. "This will go much smoother if you just come quietly. I wouldn't want anyone to die a slow, miserable death because you brought us unnecessary attention."

Hannah swallowed the scream rising in her throat, nodded and walked into the hallway.

Once outside the dorm, Lucas pointed to the wooded area behind the parking lot. "Go in there and wait."

Three strides into the woods for Hannah and Lucas stepped from behind a tree. He picked her up as though she were a branch and tucked her under his arm before running further into the forest. Seconds later he stopped and she covered her face, bracing as he dropped her in some leaves. Then he quickly pulled her up and set her on her feet.

He smirked. "You're welcome."

Hannah backed away, scanning the trees.

Lucas stepped closer. "I appreciate your cooperation, Miss Sawyer."

Hannah grimaced and bit her lip. "Like I had a choice."

"Sure you did. Right now you could be a corpse lying on a dorm floor instead of here with me, alive."

Hannah gave a slow nod. "What do you want from me?"

"Just to talk to you about the birds and the bees. And the hybrids." He circled Hannah, looking her over and observing her reactions. "May I tell you what you see in Daniel?"

Hannah squinted sarcastically but on the inside was trying to keep the fear at bay. *"Please."*

Lucas came closer, turning his head to continue eye contact until he walked past her. "He reminds you of someone, but you don't know who. He's the hero you watched in movies growing up, but he's real. He'd annihilate anyone who threatened you, and yet it often feels like you completely and totally bore him."

He paused for emphasis. Hannah sighed. "You know we're broken up, don't you?"

"Yes, only because you've thought about it a time or two so far during our time together. Your brain just won't shut up. But we both know the break up's temporary."

Hannah opened her mouth to speak, but couldn't find the words.

Lucas nodded slowly. "But what of Miss Natalie?"

Hannah returned her eyes to his. "What about her?"

"I'm just wondering if you're happy being the warm up act."

"Excuse me?"

"I mean since the sixty or seventy years at most you'd get with him is just a scratch on infinity's clock. And then she gets him, and you'll be just a passing memory, some random night a thousand years from now, when Natalie scratches her nails down his back."

Hannah's jaw tensed.

"Hannah, Natalie is just waiting you out."

She stared at the ground as his words sunk in.

"I, however, have a counter offer."

Hannah slowly raised her eyes, again finding his yellow pupils, narrowed and shining. "I'm listening."

"Rather than merely being foreplay for someone else's fun, my offer is mutually beneficial and simple. There's a way for you to live forever with him. If you're a vampire, the love story doesn't have to end. Ever. And if *I* turn you, it's a much different conversion than the pathetic infection you'd get from some human vampire. I'm offering you eternal life with the man you love, and all that I ask in return is a mere token of your appreciation."

Hannah crossed her arms. "And what is that?"

"It's quite small, really. I just need for you to provide me with some information."

Hannah turned away, distracting herself by looking at the trees.

Lucas grinned. "Protecting your thoughts from me, Hannah? Then I'll save you the trouble of asking. The information I need would simply require you to keep note of Daniel's dreams. Keep a journal of any ten of those nightmares of his, and I'll transform you in exchange."

Hannah slowly turned back to Lucas, eyes flashing. "So betray him and then just hope he can forgive me at some point in eternity? You can read my thoughts, so I think you know my answer."

Lucas looked toward the sky and seemed to be in deep thought. "Then, I suppose you can at least be of some use."

Hannah tried to determine what he meant, but suddenly felt hands reach from behind and cover her mouth.

Daniel's anger burned as fast as his Mustang around the curves and straight shots. His mind pestered him with Zachery's words, Hannah walking away, and a complex heap of troubles involving Natalie.

As he cleared his head, he remembered Anthony's situation. It had been a couple of weeks since he went missing.

He picked up his phone and dialed Hannah's number.

After a few rings it went to voicemail. "Hey, I didn't expect you'd answer. I just wanted you to know where I'm going so if you don't hear from me in a few days... well, basically I'm an easy target without the Council, so I figured I don't lose anything going after Anthony alone. It wouldn't take long for the dark angels to recognize I have no allies anyway. So, maybe you could tell Mom and Erika if I don't come back. Hannah, I... bye." He hung up, unable to finish.

Daniel turned the key to shut off the engine. He opened the door and stood in the parking lot of his old school, deserted for the weekend. He walked across campus to where he had nearly been killed by Lucas and Kore a few weeks earlier. He crossed the field and entered the woods, passing the new blooms of spring. Once deep enough into the woods, Daniel stopped in a clearing and searched the landscape. After seconds of eerie silence, Daniel turned his face to the sky and yelled, "Anthony!"

He only had to wait a few seconds before he recognized a smug voice. "Hello, Daniel."

Daniel spun to face him. "You!"

Lucas smiled. "Me." He laughed and walked past Daniel, who repositioned himself to retain eye contact. "You're pathetically predictable, you know."

"Where's Anthony?"

"Where he wants to be, Daniel. With us. And you're trespassing... again."

Daniel watched as dozens of figures came out from the trees. Lucas lengthened his grin as he saw the defensive intensity in Daniel's eyes. "So I have one final offer to make you before I show you just how conditional your immortality really is. You can join us. Or you can die. I hear your Council friends aren't making nearly as generous an offer."

Daniel looked over the small army behind Lucas. He turned in the opposite direction and dozens more stepped into view.

Lucas raised his voice. "I need an answer, Daniel! Life or death?"

Daniel walked slowly to his right, beginning to circle Lucas. The two were completely surrounded by a patchwork of dark angels and vampires.

Lucas motioned his hand in the air and a couple of the surrounding group walked toward the center of the clearing. "I thought I'd let you hear a couple of testimonials from some satisfied converts."

As the two neared, Daniel recognized Anthony and Natalie. Lucas gestured toward them. "So, Daniel, tell them if you'd like to hear all the benefits of joining our little group or if you'd rather hear the hell that'll happen to you if you don't."

Daniel glared at Natalie as she walked close to him.

"Oh Daniel, don't act so surprised. I've got leverage now that the little red-headed slut doesn't, and I'm using it. So if you ever want to see our child, you'll join us and be with me forever. Quit wasting time and let's put this little bump in the road behind us."

Daniel could hear his own heart beating as he struggled to catch his breath. He turned his eyes to Anthony who looked every bit the part of a human vampire with dark circles under his eyes and pale skin.

"How are you able to be in daylight?" Daniel asked.

"They've got this down to an art form my friend. I pity the ones who go at it on their own." Anthony walked closer to Daniel. "But I also pity you, Daniel. I've watched you always seeming to get the best chances. You were the best at sports and whatever else you tried. But then I learned why. It's because you're a freak. Well, now I'm one, too. So I don't have to settle for girls who bore me anymore. How do we stack up now, pretty boy?" Anthony took a step toward him and swung a fist. Daniel blocked the punch and landed his own on Anthony's cheek, sending him to the ground where he lost consciousness. Natalie laughed hysterically.

Lucas stepped over Anthony and smirked at Daniel. "You'll have to forgive your friend, Daniel. Enthusiasm for our little cult can sometimes cause members to come across a bit too strong. I didn't say it'd all be flowers and sunshine, but I think you'll soon see that we're quite the happy little family here. You'd have much more support with us than you ever had with the Council. And don't think you can pull off some heroic stand here, Daniel. You have no chance against me. Call it spiritual supremacy if you will." He stepped closer to Daniel and slowly raised his chin as he waited for an answer.

Daniel used his foot to roll Anthony over on his back. His mouth fell open and Daniel saw his fangs. He looked back up at Lucas. "So you think I'll fit in nicely with your little pack of blood suckers?"

"Oh Daniel, don't be such a hypocrite. Humans have their own blood *and* the blood of Jesus and nobody bats an eye. What's wrong with asking them to share the wealth? And just in case you were thinking of doing some sort of rage-inspired kamikaze attack or something, I have my final motivating offer that just sat itself on the table today." Lucas turned to a section of dark angels behind him. "Boys, if you please!"

A cluster of them walked toward Lucas and Daniel. When in range, they fanned out, revealing a redheaded hostage, blindfolded, with her hands tied behind her back. She spoke panicky. "Daniel? Daniel, I'm sorry. I couldn't get away from them."

Daniel stepped toward her, "Hannah!" But Lucas moved between them, face to face with Daniel. "Now, do we understand each other? And this is the part where you dismiss a few of those asinine ideas in your head. You can't run away with hopes of coming back for her. Even if you could escape, I'd make sure that she'd make a thirsty vampire, or ten, very happy. And you can't defeat us to rescue her. So I'm asking for the final time, Daniel. What will it be?"

Daniel again turned his head to analyze the army of dark angels that surrounded him, dropping his eyes before responding. "Lucas, you're right. It seems I've really only got one choice."

Lucas walked toward Daniel with a wicked smile spreading across his face. "I'm always happy when another one comes home." He wrapped his arms around Daniel and pulled his head to his shoulder. "We have a very bright future together, my young friend. I'm going to teach you everything I know."

Daniel raised his head from Lucas' shoulder and smiled. "I'd rather die."

Lucas dropped his smile. "What?"

Daniel chambered his fist and knocked Lucas to the ground. He charged the two holding Hannah and rammed his elbow into one's face. He punched the neck of the other and lifted Hannah over his shoulder, to run.

"That will be quite enough!" Lucas' angry voice echoed through the woods. A vampire seized Hannah, while five others overtook and restrained Daniel. Lucas rolled up his sleeve. "I'm really going to enjoy this, Daniel."

Lucas cocked his arm when a voice projected from the other side of the field. "Lucas!"

The fallen one turned to see Uriel and the Council, with dozens of dead vampires lining the ground at their feet. He examined the faces surrounding Uriel and yelled back, "We'll trade them both alive!"

Uriel didn't move or change expression as he watched Lucas and the others step back toward the woods, a couple of vampires dragging Anthony by his arms.

Daniel removed the ropes from around Hannah's wrists and reached to untie the blindfold, but stopped. "I want to do something first." He leaned his forehead against hers and slowly pressed her lips against his. They kissed for a few seconds before Daniel pulled away and untied the blindfold.

Hannah smirked. "Put it back on."

Daniel heard heavy breathing behind him and turned to see that Natalie had broken away from Lucas and the others. She held her hand on her stomach and glared at Daniel. "I'll hate you as much as I've loved you, Daniel Keith." She saw Uriel and Zachery nearing and backed up slowly before running into the woods with the others.

Zachery put his hand on Daniel's shoulder. "You need to get going."

Daniel smiled back. "So this is the Council eliminating me?"

Uriel stepped close. "This was me knowing that you'd come to see Anthony for yourself, even though you knew he was a vampire. So if Lucas thought we weren't supporting you, then he probably wouldn't bring his entire army when you showed up. And he didn't. That opened the door for us to save you from your own hardheadedness. Second, I wanted to see if there was any way you'd join them. I thought you'd probably join us, but as you know, I can't be sure that would translate into loyalty. You showed you'd rather pay the ultimate price than join evil. That tells me a lot. It's not just about what a man will do; it's about what he *won't* do, even when it means losing everything."

Daniel smiled. He reached for Hannah's hand and the small splinter of the Council walked toward the wood's edge, where the rest waited. Several of the angels gave Daniel pats on his back and said things like, "Welcome" and "Glad to have you." Daniel scanned the faces around him, but couldn't find Zachery. He turned to see him walking slowly to the far side of the field.

Uriel answered the question in Daniel's mind. "No, he's not okay."

Others turned to watch as Zachery neared the edge of the woods on the other side. He stopped and reached out to someone. "Tabitha," he called into the woods.

A woman with dark brown hair walked from the woods and stood just out of his reach. "Zachery, I've missed you so much. But it's over now. We can finally be together."

Zachery smiled and stepped into an embrace with her. Then the two walked into the woods together.

Daniel stepped in front of Uriel. "Aren't you going to do something?"

Uriel reluctantly returned eye contact with Daniel. "We need to leave now." He turned and the angels followed him.

Daniel protested. "So that's it? We're just going to run away and leave him?" He glanced in disbelief at Hannah.

Uriel spoke, but continued to walk. "It's a trap. Lucas wants us to go after Zachery so he can ambush us with his entire army. Zachery is entranced by her. We couldn't stop him without killing him anyway."

"So after all that talk about a man standing up for what's right even if it cost him everything, you're not going to fight to save a friend?"

Uriel spun on Daniel, noticeably irritated. "We're not going to stay to fight because they would wipe us out! We'll find another way to get Zachery back. It's a long war and it can't be won today." He walked away with the Council. Daniel hesitated, but finally put his hand to the small of Hannah's back and the two followed.

Just before Daniel and Hannah got to his car, Uriel walked over to him. "Daniel we need to get started with your training right away. Come to the lake tomorrow morning and we'll begin. And, Hannah, I'd like for you to come too."

Chapter 18

PATIENCE

DANIEL DROVE HANNAH to the dorm and they walked up to her room. She tossed her keys on the windowsill and sat on the bed facing Daniel. "You want something to drink?"

He shook his head before walking through the bathroom and opening the door to Natalie's room. Hannah followed. "What're you looking for?"

"Just thought I'd check on Zeb." The boxer trotted over and Daniel petted his head. "I don't know how she kept him here. How'd she take him out without getting caught with a dog?"

"She told me that the dorm mom didn't really enforce the rules. I guess she's right because I've only seen that woman two or three times the whole semester."

"Let's take the poor guy outside. We can talk to Erika on the way back."

After taking Zeb out they knocked on Erika's door and both were a little surprised when she answered. "We need to talk to you," Daniel said.

Erika slowly opened the door and walked away to

sit in a chair in front of the TV. Hannah grabbed Zeb's collar. "Alright if we bring Zeb in?"

"I don't care."

Zeb followed Daniel in and collapsed on the floor. "He's just going to lie there anyway."

Hannah stared at Daniel, waiting for him to start what would obviously be a difficult conversation. He cleared his throat. "We found Anthony."

Erika's eyes widened and she stood from her chair. "Well, is he alright? Where is he?"

Daniel dropped his head, carefully choosing his words. "He's got a new set of friends now, I guess you could say. Maybe he just thought he needed some new faces to be around or something."

"I don't even know what that means," she snapped. "Do you think I don't notice how vague you're being? Just tell me the truth!"

Hannah cleared her throat. "Erika, we told you the truth before and you kicked us out, and didn't talk to us for ages. Remember?"

Erika rolled her eyes. "Well excuse me for not believing in ghost stories."

Daniel ran his fingers through his hair. "Who said anything about ghosts?"

Erika sighed. "Whatever. So why can you see him, but I can't?"

Hannah responded, "I didn't have a choice. They kidnapped me. I thought they were going to kill me!"

"How? By drinking your blood?" Erika's sarcasm was unmistakable through her tightened jaw. She obviously didn't believe their story.

Daniel walked over to Zeb and gently pulled on his collar to stand him up. "Well we came to tell you that we're not giving up. They've also got Natalie."

Erika looked concerned, but not surprised. "I guess she was easy to lure in. So what, you're going after them with the good angels?"

Daniel replied, "Whatever I have to do."

The three were quiet as Daniel walked Zeb to the door and turned around. "We'll talk soon."

He walked Hannah to her room but didn't go in. "I'm taking Zeb home with me. He'll like all the wide open space on our land."

Hannah kneeled down and scratched Zeb behind his ears. "Well at least you can't scare me out of the shower over there." As she stood she put an arm around Daniel's lower back and kissed him. "Thank you for rescuing me."

"It was more the Council really."

Hannah shook her head. "I know what I know."

"Goodnight." They kissed again and Daniel left with Zeb.

Once home, he walked in the front door of his house with Zeb on a leash. "Mom," he called and walked through the house looking for her. He stopped in the hall in front of her room at the sight of her sitting on her bed sobbing. Daniel ran to her side, "Mom, what's wrong?"

Marie took a deep breath, calming herself. "The house."

Daniel waited as Marie got control of herself enough to speak again. "The city condemned it. It's too old. It has to be demolished."

Daniel shook his head. "How can they do that? This was your grandpa's house. It's private property."

"They say it's no longer a 'fit structure.' We can move into the guest house on top of the hill for now. The movers are coming tomorrow to take everything there. Then they'll bulldoze the house in seven to ten days."

The fog of the next morning burned off a little faster than past weeks as spring grew closer to summer. Daniel and Hannah walked toward the lake from the parking lot and recognized Uriel from a distance.

As they neared, he smiled. "Good morning. You both have a lot to learn, but now that I've gotten to know you each, I think I know where to begin."

Hannah took a step backwards. "Wait, you sound like you're talking about training me too. But I'm not a hybrid."

"No, but we're without an angelologist at the moment. And who better than someone who's been immersed into our world as you have? Plus, Zachery has needed help for a while."

Hannah didn't speak as she processed what he said.

Uriel added, "But we'll talk more about that later." Uriel turned his eyes to Daniel. "A minute please?"

Hannah understood Uriel wanted a private conversation with Daniel so she walked back in the direction of the truck.

Uriel waited until Hannah was out of range and walked across the bridge with Daniel. "Daniel, I want to officially invite you into the Council. That would make you the first hybrid to ever be one of us. But before you accept, I want you to share with me any doubts or questions you have."

Daniel's face burned at the memory of the promise Lucas had made him. "I want to know who my father is. I think I have a right to know."

Uriel dropped his eyes to the ground. "I agree Daniel; you have a right to know. But I don't have the right to tell you." The two walked without speaking as Daniel fumed. Uriel spoke again. "I give you my word that one day you'll know."

"I don't understand how the Council works," Daniel said, frustrated. "It's like you're afraid of the dark angels. What about my child? And my friends? How're we going to get them back if the Council just sits here?"

Uriel didn't hesitate. "I promise you your child will be safe. There's so much you don't know yet about how we work. Many times things can appear to be disasters, but be according to plan and in the long term, we win. It's a war of perseverance and now you're going to learn the inner workings that many angels don't even know."

Daniel cleared his throat. "Why did Lucas run yesterday? Why wouldn't he just fight?"

"He was outnumbered then. And remember, dark angels are conditional immortals. They can be killed."

Daniel squinted in confusion. "I remember you telling me that, but why hasn't the Council destroyed them by now since you're immortal?"

"Well to begin with, we're not all immortal. Some of the Council angels were once fallen, but came back. We call them prodigal angels. Their full immortality

won't return in this age and that's why I said the dark
angels could've wiped us out yesterday. On top of that,
many of the angels who fell were great warriors. They've
given chief angels, like Michael, trouble for thousands of
years. That's why the war continues, especially on earth
where the dark angels outnumber our forces. It's been a
longstanding stalemate."

Daniel glanced over the lake and sighed. "Why me?
Why would a bunch of angels want someone with a
hot head like me who's got a child growing inside of a
vampire?"

"We weren't looking for an altar boy, Daniel. We
needed a warrior. And because you're a hybrid, you play
an incredible role in all of this. You'll learn more about
that in the days ahead." Uriel inhaled and crossed his
arms. "So what do you say?"

"I know I should jump at the chance and this is probably my mom's dream come true for me, but-—"

"This shouldn't be anyone's dream come true. I'm not
offering you membership at a country club. Your life will
become second place to hunting dark angels."

"No wonder you picked me. I've always had a second
place life. But honestly Uriel, I'm still not sure I totally
trust the Council given what's happened in the last few
months. And you still won't tell me who my father is. I
need a few days and I'll get back to you."

Uriel turned toward the woods without speaking.

Daniel walked back toward Hannah, but stopped
at Uriel's voice calling after him, "Think if you must,
Daniel, but we don't have much time. Your training is
key to getting your friends back."

Daniel paused while he considered Uriel's words, but continued, walking onto the parking lot. "I'll be in the truck," he muttered to Hannah.

Hannah felt a rush of embarrassment as she watched Daniel walk away. It wasn't every day that someone stomped away from an angel. She kept her eyes on him and her back to Uriel for as long as she could, to delay awkward eye contact with the angel. When she finally turned around, Uriel stepped close to her, unfazed. "He can be a tad moody at times, can't he?"

Hannah chuckled, "You're telling me."

"That's why I need you to study him. Learn what Zachery knew." From inside his jacket Uriel pulled out a faded book. "This will help. It's years of observations about hybrids by angelologists, including Zachery."

Hannah accepted the book and ran her fingers over the aged, rough cover. "I don't understand. Why would I need to read what humans say, when I could learn from you?"

"For the same reason I can't learn as much about humans by learning from a human. You're too close to the situation to know what I'd need to learn as an angel. Of course, I've had thousands of years to observe humans, so I don't need much insight. But you need to start reading about us immediately."

Hannah shut the car door and Daniel drove out of the parking lot. He tapped on the book in her lap. "What's that?"

"Something I'm supposed to read to learn more about you."

"About me?"

"Well, hybrids and angels anyway. It's Zachery's observations over the years. And some other people too."

Daniel turned the book cover open and fingered through the first few pages between glances at the road. "I want to look over this. I'll get it back to you."

Hannah nodded. "I figured. So you still don't trust Uriel?"

"I don't see why I should."

Neither said a word the remainder of the ride to Hannah's dorm. After parking the car, Daniel walked Hannah to her room. She unlocked the door and stepped in expecting Daniel to be behind her, but turned to see him standing in the hall. "You can come in you know, you're not a stranger."

Daniel cut his eyes to the floor before answering. "I don't think I should come in. If you're going to be studying me and we're working together, I think we shouldn't be involved. Not until this thing is finished."

Hannah sighed loudly. "I thought you weren't sure if you're going to join them or not."

"Yeah, well, I don't want liabilities in case I do. I'll see you later."

Daniel left and Hannah fell back on her bed, wanting to put the day behind her. She lay there, with open eyes and thought how the best decision she could make might be to resign from college again. Her phone buzzed from her back pocket. When she turned it over, Erika's name was on the screen.

"Erika, hey."

"Hey."

Hannah waited for Erika to say something since she was the one who called but nearly laughed into the dead air as the seconds passed. Finally Hannah couldn't take anymore. "Erika, you need something?"

"I want to see Anthony."

"But we've been over this. He's not who—"

"I know he's a vampire. And his parents and everyone else think he's on some road trip because he's going through a college-age crisis or something."

"So you believe us now?"

"I guess. I want you and Daniel to take me to him."

"Erika that's too dangerous. You know what vampires do, don't you?"

"Yes, and that's why I want you to take me to him. I want him to turn me."

"What? You've got to be kidding me."

"If that's what it'll take to be with him, then that's what I want to do."

"You don't know what you're saying."

"Why don't you just let me live my own life, Hannah? And I'll let you live yours."

Hannah paced the room, scouring her brain to find something wise to say. "Will you at least talk to Daniel first?"

"Well, yeah. How else am I going to know where Anthony is? So why don't you call him and set up a meeting for the three of us. Maybe that coffee shop with all the blends."

"Okay, I'll call him."

Hannah scrolled down her phone and pressed Daniel's name. It went straight to voicemail. After the beep

Hannah said, "Hey, call me as soon as you get this. Erika says she wants to see Anthony." She checked the clock to see that she needed to head to class.

She did her best to listen to the professor's lecture, all the time wishing she could go back to being as ignorant about the spiritual realm. Finally, her phone vibrated on the table, drawing the stares of surrounding students and startling the girl beside her. Hannah gathered her things and rushed outside the classroom. "Hey, I was beginning to worry."

"Worry? About me?"

"Well yeah. Did you get my message about Erika?"

"Yep. And I need to talk to her again anyway. And you."

"Okay, well she said we could meet at that coffee shop Zachery liked so much."

"Okay, I'll meet you there at six."

Daniel hung up before she could respond.

Hannah finished class and went to the cafeteria for lunch. She sat alone watching other students eating, laughing, flirting and seeming to enjoy life in general. She remembered when she had an entire table of friends with her at lunch. In getting caught up in Daniel's world she had done exactly what she had promised herself she wouldn't. Now she didn't even know if she'd pass all her classes.

The walk from the cafeteria to the dorm motivated her to focus on studying until it was time to meet Daniel and Erika. After several hours, Hannah had made a dent in areas where she was behind, and in the nagging worry that she was going to fail. The relief and sense of accomplishment fueled her for a couple more hours until she looked at the clock.

"Crap!" Hannah grabbed her phone off the bed and rushed out the door. As she walked the hall, she called Erika.

"Hello?"

"Hey, Daniel said we should meet him for coffee at six. I totally forgot to tell you and lost track of time."

"That's fine, I'll meet you in the lobby."

Erika joined Hannah midstride after she walked through the lobby entrance. Erika pushed the door open. "We'll take my car."

When they arrived at the truck stop, Daniel's car was already there. They walked through the shop and into the café area where Daniel sat with a cup of coffee. He watched them as they quietly approached. A woman walked from the counter to the table. "Ladies, what can I get ya?"

Hannah looked at Daniel's cup. "I'll have whatever he has."

Erika nodded. "Me too."

"Okay, I'll go get those started." She hurried away.

After more than a minute of silence, Hannah started thinking of ways to move things along. "So as I told you, Erika wants you to take her to Anthony."

Daniel sipped his coffee and slowly raised his eyes to Erika. "And do you know what will happen if I take you to him?"

"Well, if things go according to plan, he'll turn my

head and bite my neck. And if he doesn't kill me, he'll turn me into a vampire like him."

Hannah exhaled; still shocked that Erika would ask for such a thing. Daniel didn't seem to react at all. He just lifted his cup and took another sip.

The sound of footsteps meant two more coffees were coming and Erika moved her hands off the table in anticipation.

"Can I get you anything else? A refill for you?" the waitress asked, sitting down the cups.

Daniel shook his head. "No thanks."

"Okay, well I'm here if you need anything." She left again.

"Do you know why Anthony would've wanted to be a vampire, or how he got involved with them in the first place?" Erika asked, leaning forward.

"I don't know exactly how it happened," Daniel said, "but they might've promised him power."

Erika thought over his words and nodded slowly. "His dad is military and apparently always picked on him for not going that way, like his brother. He was always made to feel inferior in the family. So I guess, in some ways, it kind of makes sense that he'd do this."

Hannah picked up her cup and blew at the coffee to cool it down.

Erika's tone changed abruptly. "So will you take me to him?"

Daniel spoke softly. "If that's what you want, I guess you'll just find a way eventually."

Hannah scoffed. "So you'll let your friend be turned into an enemy without even a fight?"

Daniel lowered his eyes. "I was in the woods today

and saw Anthony walking with the big one, Kore. I hid behind a tree and listened to them. They're planning to overthrow Lucas and put Kore in charge. Apparently they have a group of dark angels and vampires on their side."

"So Anthony's still a good guy?" Erika asked.

Daniel took his last swallow of coffee. "Maybe. Or he's just trying to score points with Kore. Either way, it's a big deal and Anthony's in a lot of danger."

Hannah turned to Erika. "You don't still want him to turn you, do you?"

"Of course I do."

Hannah didn't know what to say and Daniel shook his head at the server who pointed again to his empty cup.

Daniel continued. "He had a hood on today and they stayed in the woods under the trees. The sun didn't bother him when I saw him last time, so I'm thinking maybe at some point even vampires who've learned from Lucas can get too much light. Maybe he overdid it." He shifted his eyes to Hannah and back to Erika. "If you want to go, I'll take you tonight."

"Daniel!" Hannah's eyes were wide as she looked back and forth at the two of them. "Do you not know who these freaks are? You're both nuts!"

Daniel's face lost expression. "So are you going with us?"

Hannah sighed. "Yeah, just to try to talk some sense into you two on the way."

✳

Daniel's Mustang rumbled into the school parking lot and he turned the key to kill the engine.

"Now what?" Erika opened the door and looked anxiously at Daniel, who still sat behind the wheel.

"Now we walk." Daniel stepped into the grass off of the pavement and Erika and Hannah followed.

Hannah raised her voice, "I'm going to say it one more time. This is absolutely insane." The three walked in silence and minutes passed as Hannah sifted through ideas to motivate Daniel to reconsider. "Let's at least go to the Council about this. How have we not done that?"

"I've had enough of the Council's big talk with no action."

Hannah stopped walking. "This isn't about you! This is about Erika! And you shouldn't have her here! Or me!"

Daniel turned to Hannah and opened his mouth to respond, but stopped at the sound of a snapping stick. He spun to see Kore, complete with a horde of dark angels and vampires.

Kore stepped closer to Daniel. "Did you not want to die alone, Daniel? Is that why you brought the ladies?" He laughed as he glanced back toward the others.

"I brought someone to see Anthony," Daniel said.

Kore's grin fell. "You think we won't kill you all?"

"I didn't say that."

Kore thought without moving his eyes off of Daniel. "I'll take you to him. Then, if he doesn't like what you have to say, I'll kill you one by one."

Chapter 19

HONOR AMONG THIEVES

KORE WALKED IN front and several dark angels followed behind Daniel, Hannah, and Erika. Minutes passed before they approached a creek with a large tree in front of it. Underneath sat Anthony, wearing the hooded shirt.

Erika took a step to run to Anthony, but Daniel halted her with his arm. "Wait." Erika obeyed, reluctantly.

Anthony stood in recognition. "Erika?"

Before Erika could answer, Daniel smarted off, "The hood keeping you from getting sunburned?"

Anthony cut his eyes at Daniel and then back to Erika. "What are you doing here?"

"I had to see you."

Kore stepped next to Anthony. "Enough with the small talk. I brought you here, now what do you want?"

Erika took Anthony's hand in hers. "I want you to make me like you. So I can be with you."

Anthony looked down at her hand, seeing a ring he'd given her to celebrate their one year anniversary.

A voice interrupted and Daniel smiled in recognition. "I just had to see with my own eyes if it was really true. Daniel, here again? And he brought appetizers with him?"

Daniel turned to face Lucas, smirking as though he was glad to see him.

"Daniel, were you hit too hard in the head last time? I mean don't get me wrong, I appreciate a good suicide as much as the next angel of darkness, but I'm intrigued at how easy you made this for me." He took Erika in his arms and held her out, looking her over as though he were inspecting fruit for dark spots. "But who am I to look a gift horse in the mouth?"

He studied her for several more seconds and then his smile fell. He slowly turned his head to Kore. "You backstabbing son of a bitch!"

Kore's eyes narrowed. "What?"

Lucas released Erika and walked toward Kore. "When I found you, no angel wanted anything to do with you! I made them respect you. I placed you as my second in command and this is how you repay me?"

Kore took a step back, his eyes intense with fear. "Lucas, I've been nothing but loyal to you!"

Lucas pushed a nearby vampire out of his way. "Loyal? You think I'm a fool? You think that if you brag about it, that it's not going to get back to me? Like I can't read their pathetic minds?" He motioned toward Erika and Hannah.

Kore shook his head. "You've got to believe me; I don't know what you're talking about!"

Lucas laughed sarcastically and seized Kore by his shirt collar. He slammed him against a tree, splitting it in two. He turned to the surrounding crowd of dark angels and vampires. "Let this be a lesson to you all, that anyone who plots mutiny against me will get the worst possible of consequences." With his index finger and thumb he grabbed Kore's chin and in one swift motion, turned Kore's head to its back side, projecting a snapping sound that echoed through the woods. Kore's massive body fell lifelessly to the ground.

Lucas turned to his perplexed followers. "I accept nothing but loyalty!"

He scanned the crowd for several seconds and then angrily pushed his way through them. "Where are they?!"

Daniel dodged trees as he ran through the woods carrying Anthony across his shoulders. Hannah and Erika followed.

Erika yelled from behind. "You didn't have to punch him!"

Daniel glanced left and right, selecting the fastest way back to his car. "I had no choice. He wouldn't have come with us if he was conscious."

Hannah could run faster than Erika and moved to within a few feet of Daniel. "What happened back there? How did Lucas all of a sudden know Kore was going to betray him?"

Daniel smirked as he led the group across the parking lot toward the car. "He knew because I told you two about it. Lucas can read your mind and one of you thought about it back there. But it wasn't true anyway. I just made it up as a way to have Lucas and Kore fighting each other so I could get Anthony away from them. I knew you'd think about it once we got there."

Erika opened the car door and Daniel heaved Anthony into the back seat. "Well as impressive as it was to fool a dark angel, what are we going to do now?"

Daniel started the car and turned to Hannah in the passenger seat as he accelerated out of the parking lot. "Now, we go to Uriel."

Erika held Anthony's head in her lap and looked up in realization. "What do I do if he wakes up?"

Daniel looked thoughtfully into the rearview mirror. "If he wakes up, hit him with this." He pulled a crowbar from under Hannah's seat and handed it to Erika.

Daniel turned down a road toward the farm. "But I don't think he'll wake up before we get there. I hit him pretty hard."

Hannah put her head into her hands and exhaled loudly.

Daniel turned toward her. "What's wrong?"

"Are you kidding? We've kidnapped a vampire who used to be our friend and now we're running from a herd of them! It just keeps getting worse."

Daniel grinned, "I can take a vampire."

"Can you?" Anthony asked.

Daniel turned eye to eye with Anthony, his fangs extended and one arm restraining Erika. Hannah screamed. The tires of the Mustang screeched as Daniel slammed the brake peddle into the floor and skidded to a stop on the shoulder of the road. He stepped out of the car, but Anthony was waiting. He kicked Daniel in the head, knocking him back into the car.

"So this is how it's going to be, Daniel? You sucker punch me and haul me off?"

Erika opened the door. "Anthony, please! Why are you doing this?"

Anthony smiled so she could see his fangs. "As if you didn't know." He turned back to Daniel whose white blood streamed from his lip. "It's not like you couldn't have seen this coming. How does it feel to be up against me now that I can be just as threatening?"

Daniel lunged a fist at Anthony who dodged and counter punched again into Daniel's mouth causing his lip to gush more blood.

Anthony grinned as the two circled each other. "You know what happens when a male vampire drinks a hybrid's blood Daniel?"

Daniel blinked, regaining his focus. "I don't know. What load of crap did Lucas tell you?"

"Not a thing. So I can't wait to find out." He swung another punch at Daniel who ducked away. Anthony put his other hand on the side of Daniel's head and pushed until his neck was exposed.

"Daniel!" Hannah yelled from the car.

Daniel flung the back of his fist against Anthony's jaw, propelling him into the side of the car. Both girls screamed and scooted away. Daniel stood and round kicked Anthony's head, knocking him unconscious again.

After opening the driver's door and looking at Anthony lying on the shoulder of the road, Hannah asked, "How do we know he'll stay knocked out long enough this time?"

Daniel put him in the back seat before looking at Hannah. "You drive."

Hannah turned into the farm parking lot and continued onto the grass until she slammed on the brakes and slid to the edge of the lake. Within seconds, two men climbed out of the lake and hurried to Daniel.

Daniel stood from his seat and looked back at Hannah and Erika. "Stay in the car."

Daniel recognized one of the angels as Jonathan. He was the one who first pulled him into the lake the day he met Uriel.

"Jonathan, I need some help with—"

"With a vampire? You brought a vampire here? What were you thinking?"

"I'm thinking Uriel can turn him back."

Jonathan stepped close to Daniel, inches from his face. "Come on Daniel, you had to know better than this!" he barked. "How dare you bring a—"

"That's enough!" Uriel suddenly stood behind Jonathan. "You will not speak to him that way."

Jonathan turned back to Daniel, lowering his head. "I'm sorry."

Daniel turned from him to Uriel. "Can you change Anthony back?"

Uriel walked to the side of the car and looked in at Anthony. "Is that what he wants?"

"I'm not sure. I was hoping you could just do it."

"Daniel, it doesn't work that way." He turned to Jonathan. "Please bring the chains." Jonathan ran to the middle of the bridge and dove into the lake. Uriel continued, "I know you want to save your friend, but you're up against free will. You can't make his decisions for him, even if they're the right ones. That's what being free is all about."

Daniel looked through the car window and saw Anthony's arm moving, dizzily. "So what do we do?"

"For now, we'll restrain him with some special chains so that he can't go hunting at night."

"Does he hunt every night?"

"If he's hungry. And they send him after specific people. Lucas and the others have been building their army by using vampires like Anthony to put people in danger to lure in hybrids with guardian instincts. It works even if the hybrid is evil. I assume Zachery talked to you about reverse engineering your guardian instincts."

"Yes."

"It's similar to that. Even a dark hybrid will find himself in the right place to save someone in danger, if that person was one of his father's guardian subjects. That's how strong a guardian angel's connection is to the ones he is to protect. It extends even to generations that were never supposed to exist, like hybrids."

Daniel's eyes fell as others scrambled around him to sedate the waking vampire. Jonathan emerged from the lake with chains and, along with three other angels, overtook Anthony before he could charge at Daniel. Daniel slowly raised his head and made eye contact with Anthony who snarled and reached for him just inches away.

"Take him below," Uriel said and Jonathan along with

the others walked Anthony to the water's edge and dove in. The weight of the chains that circled Anthony's arms combined with the pushing of the angels made it impossible for him to do anything but stay under the water as they took him to the cave.

Uriel turned back to Daniel and noted his distant gaze. "Something on your mind?"

Daniel raised his eyes to Uriel. "Something just occurred to me. Something private."

"Daniel, I can't help you if you keep secrets from me."

Daniel nodded as he took a few steps backward. "I know." He held eye contact with Uriel and backed away a few steps before turning to open the car door. He started the car. "I'm taking you girls home now."

He drove in a silence that the girls knew not to interrupt. Once back at their dorm, he stopped near the front doors. "Goodnight."

Hannah and Erika got out of the car and stood on the sidewalk as he drove away.

Minutes later, Daniel stopped half way up the hill to his house and parked the car. He walked toward the house and peered through the windows. Moonlight revealed an empty house, the movers having already done the job to ready the house for demolishing. He looked toward the guest house on the back hill and saw a light on. Further focusing of his eyes confirmed his mother sitting in a chair reading.

Daniel walked to the shed and ripped the padlock off the door. He reached behind a rusted filing cabinet and picked up cans of gasoline that he carried to the front door of the house. He walked in and doused the floor in the living room before emptying the can on the kitchen counters. He slung the gas from the remaining cans around the outside walls of the house and in a single leap jumped to the roof. His first step broke through the rotted wood and he angrily pulled back his leg. He emptied the final can on the roof and dropped to the ground.

He reached out to the wood and closed his eyes. Seconds of silence were followed by Daniel angrily punching holes in the wall, until he finally rested his hand upon the timber. He closed his eyes and took a deep breath. The wood that pressed against his palm blazed into fire and within seconds the entire house raged in flames.

Daniel stood back and took in the sight. He breathed deeply, watching parts of his childhood home fall to the ground under the ravages of the fire.

He turned, focusing intently on the tree line across the field as he walked toward the guest house. He knocked on the door until Marie answered, her hand on her chest and gasping at the sight of her home nearly burned to the ground.

"Mom, it's okay. It was going to be demolished anyway."

"Why?" She pressed her face to his shoulder and he hugged her, but looked back to the tree line.

"Mom, go back inside."

"What is it? I don't understand."

"I see something I expected to see. A shadow. I have to know whose it is."

Marie opened her mouth, preparing to speak, but didn't know what to say.

Daniel pointed inside. "Just stay in the house, no matter what."

She nodded and closed the door. Daniel walked to the side of the house and crouched down. He leaned close enough to the edge that he could hear, but not be seen. Seconds passed and he heard footsteps coming. Daniel lowered himself near the ground and positioned his head to see around the corner. He saw the figure move closer and then stop with the flames from the house down the hill illuminating his face.

Daniel whirled behind the wall and leaned back against it. He closed his eyes and breathed slowly in disbelief.

Minutes passed before Daniel looked back around the corner of the house. He watched the shadow disappear into the distant tree line then, Daniel stood to go into the house. When the door opened, Marie stood on the other side, pale and perplexed. "Daniel, what was that all about?"

"What if I just kept it a secret from you? Because maybe I just assumed you couldn't deal with the truth."

"What are you talking about?"

"I'm talking about my father!"

He walked past her, ignoring her requests for him to come back. He slammed and locked his door. He stopped short of the bed and stared at a picture of him with his mother that hung on the wall to the bathroom. He stepped closer and leaned his forehead beside it as his breathing quickened. One of his fists and then another in a riot of punches smashed through the paneling wall revealing pipes and wiring. He turned away from his destruction and listened as his mother yelled from the other side of the door, "What's wrong? What's happening? Daniel?"

He looked toward the door as though it would be next to feel the wrath of his knuckles, but instead, he took a deep breath and fell back on his bed. "Nothing, Mom. Go to bed please. I just want to be alone."

Chapter 20

WATER TO WINE

HANNAH WOKE UP hungry and dressed to go to the cafeteria. She turned on the local weather and saw scrolling text at the bottom of the screen: *Severe thunderstorm and tornado warnings for the following Tennessee counties.*

"Great," she said before walking out the door.

Once in the cafeteria, she took her tray and saw Daniel sequestered away at a table in a back corner.

She stopped by. "Hey."

"Hey."

"You mind if I sit with you?" Hannah asked, feeling awkward.

"No, but I won't be here long."

She sat down and watched Daniel's eyes as they remained fixed on his coffee. She looked left and then right to ensure that she couldn't be heard by anyone else. "Are you going to see Anthony today?"

Daniel didn't react right away, which made Hannah wonder if he'd heard her. Then he looked up as though her question annoyed him. "Maybe."

She took his hand in hers and waited until he made

eye contact. "You need to tell Uriel if you're going to join the Council. He said there's a lot to do and—"

"I'm not that concerned about the Council right now," he answered curtly.

Hannah hesitated briefly. "Then what's on your mind? What could be more important?"

"Natalie is carrying my child. I don't want my kid to grow up without a dad, like I had to. I've got to talk to her and find a way to get her away from the dark angels."

Hannah leaned back in the booth as Daniel's eyes returned to his coffee. The words Lucas had said to her echoed in her mind. Obviously, having a child with Daniel was another advantage for Natalie.

She leaned in so Daniel could hear her speak quietly. "You need to consider that there are other people who can be hurt by you not acting. I need to go, but please just talk to Uriel today."

He nodded his head. "I'll think about it."

Hannah stood. "I'll talk to you soon. Do you want to have supper with me tonight?"

"I'll think about that one, too."

Hannah forced a smile and headed out of the cafeteria. Rather than going to class, she went to her car. Digging the keys from her purse, she tossed her backpack in the back seat. Seconds later, the engine started and Hannah drove past the exit gates of campus.

She put the car in park at the edge of the high school parking lot and walked toward the woods, passing a couple of students who had ditched class in favor of making out behind a maintenance shed. After walking across the field and into the trees, she had the feeling of being watched by something more than human, a feeling that had become like a sixth sense during the past several months. She stopped and turned a circle without seeing anyone, but she had learned to trust her instincts.

"I'm here to speak to Lucas," she said in a raised voice.

The wind blew through the trees and the sky had grown dull: the foreshadowing of an incoming storm. Hannah's eyes darted to every crackling leaf or snapping stick, but she could only see trees swaying in the strengthening wind.

She started walking deeper into the woods and her pace quickened into a near run at the feeling of being followed. Someone stepped from behind a tree and caught her, putting a hand over her mouth to muffle her scream.

"I knew you couldn't stay away." Lucas removed his hand and held it up in front of her. "This better be good or Daniel won't even find pieces of you."

Hannah caught her breath. "Is your offer still good?"

Lucas cocked his head. "But you seemed so certain that I offered nothing of interest to you in our last little get together."

"I had time to think and this is what I want."

"I see. If I may ask, what changed your mind?"

"I thought about the two of them... together. One day, Daniel and Natalie will be some happy immortal family with their child. And I'll be dead. They're connected even if she's on your side and he isn't. I have to even things out."

"I see." He paused, twisting a lock of her hair around his black-nailed finger. "It certainly sounds like you've thought things through."

Seconds passed and Hannah shrugged. "So, now what?"

"I can fulfill my end of our agreement today. Yours will take some more time, of course. Need I remind you of the repercussions if you fail to provide my compensation?"

Hannah shook her head, pulling back from him a little.

Lucas smiled darkly. "Ready then?"

She closed her eyes. "Let's just get it over with."

Lucas smiled and leaned close to her. Hannah tilted her head, exposing her neck as he hovered his mouth over her skin. He whispered, "It's almost like you've done this before."

A stick snapped beneath a footstep and both Lucas and Hannah turned to see Daniel.

"Lucas, stop!"

Lucas raised his hands. "Daniel, I'm afraid this is none of your business. The lady and I are both consenting adults. She wants it."

Daniel's eyes asked Hannah if it was true.

"Daniel, I don't want a happy ending. I want a happy forever." Her gaze begged him.

Daniel's expression turned to shock.

Lucas stepped in front of Hannah. "I guess you have the lady's answer. Now if you'll excuse me." Lucas moved quickly and bit into Hannah's neck. The penetration of the venom through his fangs took her breath away, and pain pulsated throughout her body.

Daniel raced toward them and pushed Lucas away from her. Hannah fell to the ground, her eyes staring into the distance as she reached a state of near unconsciousness.

Daniel threw a fist into the side of Lucas' face, hurling him into a large rock that shattered upon impact. Thunder sounded and lightning flashed through the woods. Lucas stood and opened his mouth to speak, but both he and Daniel turned toward a high-pitched, freight-train sound that seemed to be coming right toward them. The massive funnel cloud broke the tops of trees and threw branches and debris as it neared them. Daniel and Lucas stood untouched by the circling wind as it grew closer. Daniel leapt toward Lucas and kicked him in the ribs. Lucas countered with several punches before Daniel blocked one and his elbow smashed into the dark angel's stomach.

The two exchanged fierce punches as the tornado neared. Lucas fell backwards after receiving a potent blow and Daniel pounced on him to deliver more. Lucas appeared overmatched and stunned by the beating he was receiving. He seemed to have given up. Just as Daniel reached for his neck, the trees around them uprooted and soared away as the tornado was nearly on top of them. Daniel yelled through the uproar. "I know who you are!"

Lucas was expressionless as he contemplated Daniel's words. "Surely you wouldn't kill dear ole daddy. And what about her?" he sneered, glancing weakly in Hannah's direction.

Daniel turned to see her barely conscious body rise as the dark air squalled around her. He vaulted toward her, just missing her outreached hand as the circling wind pulled her up past low-hanging branches and toward the tree tops.

Daniel sprinted through the labyrinth of flying tree trunks and debris. He watched Hannah as he positioned himself in front of her path and jumped. Grabbing her hips, he wrapped his arms around her stomach before locking his legs around a tree branch. He held on tightly as the wind pulled, suspending them high above the forest floor.

Daniel endured until the air slowed. As he felt gravity regain control, he braced himself and landed on his feet with Hannah safely in his arms.

Her eyes were closed and her body was limp. Daniel lowered his ear to her chest and could hear a slow heartbeat. He ran out of the woods with her and laid her gently in the passenger seat of his car. He started the Mustang and sped away as the tornado continued its path of ruin.

Once in front of the lake, Daniel stopped the car and carried Hannah toward the bridge. Uriel came hurriedly from the other side and Daniel laid her at his feet. "She was—"

"Bitten by a vampire. I can smell the venom." Uriel kneeled and examined the bite. Standing again, he turned back to the lake, raised one arm over the still, dark water, palm down, closed his eyes and uttered something indecipherable under his breath.

Daniel looked on, awestruck, as the water rippled and swirled, growing wilder by the second. Finally the waves parted and a hollow formed with walls of water, and Daniel could see the earth beneath. A rock at the base of the lake rumbled and moved aside, revealing a stone staircase leading downwards.

"Take her inside," said Uriel.

Once in the cave, Uriel directed Daniel to a room down a long corridor. Daniel laid her down on a bed in the room and Uriel followed with another angel.

"Daniel, this is Amilgol. He has specialized in vampire bites for thousands of years, even this type of bite."

Daniel nodded to Amilgol and turned back to Uriel. "What do you mean, this 'type of bite'? It's a vampire bite, right?"

Amilgol examined Hannah's neck. "There are different types of vampire bites," he said.

"Right, from different types of vampires."

"That's not what I'm talking about here. I'm talking about the bite specifically. This was a partial injection."

Daniel shook his head. "I don't understand."

"It looks as though the vampire was interrupted before enough venom got into her blood stream to completely turn her."

"That's a good thing, right?"

"Usually. However, there can be problems. It's likely she will still be part vampire, but mostly human. The blending of both species is not an exact science, so her traits might be slower to develop, if she actually has any."

"Is she going to be okay?"

"I believe so. But she'll sleep for a long while. I'll know more when she wakes up. You're welcome to wait with her." Uriel and Amilgol left the room, shutting the door behind them.

Daniel leaned near Hannah and tucked her hair behind her ear. He kissed her forehead and caressed her cheek with the back of his hand. "I should've never gotten involved with a human, but I just couldn't help myself.

Then I tried to pull back because I didn't want to put you in danger. But they went after you to get to me anyway. I'll make this right. I swear I'll…" Daniel tenderly kissed her lips and walked out, pushing the door closed.

He saw Uriel at the end of the hall and walked to him. "I want to talk to Anthony."

He nodded. "This way." Uriel took Daniel down a hall that led deeper into the ground. He stopped in front of a door that had an opening near the top, with bars stretching horizontally across. An angel stood guard at the door. Daniel turned back to Uriel. "What is this? A dungeon?"

Uriel opened the door. "Go on in, he's in chains. I'll be back in ten minutes."

Daniel walked through the door and saw Anthony sitting on the stone floor, his eyes closed and his arms chained to the wall.

"You don't have to open your eyes, but you'd better listen to me."

Anthony's eyes shot open. "What do you want?"

"Well if the human tick isn't awake after all. I came here to tell you that you can't go back to Lucas and company."

"You think I can't find a way out of these chains eventually?"

"I doubt it, but that's not what I'm talking about. You weren't conscious when he killed Kore."

Anthony's smirk fell. "Kore's dead?"

"Lucas broke his neck. He's convinced the two of you were planning mutiny, which means if he saw you, he'd kill you before you had a chance to speak."

Anthony took a deep breath. "I see. How's Erika?"

Daniel raised his eyes, surprised at the question. "She was okay the last I saw her. That's more than I can say for Hannah."

"Why? What's wrong with Hannah?"

"Lucas bit her. But he didn't get enough venom in her, so she's in some kind of limbo. She's asleep now." Daniel stepped closer to Anthony and crouched down to meet him eye to eye. "Look, the way I see it, you can't go at it alone. One of Lucas' thugs will hunt you down and kill you, or he'll eventually find and kill you himself. You're a wanted vampire."

Anthony blanched, eyes widening. "What am I supposed to do?"

"Uriel can change you back. And then you'll be less noticeable to the dark angels and can get protection from the Council. And from me."

Anthony shook his head, fear spreading across his face. "You really think Lucas won't be able to get to me just because I do what you say?"

Daniel sighed, uncertain. "I think the Council can protect you. And I'll be here."

"So you're with the Council now?"

"No. I'm still sorting through some things."

"Like what?"

"That's not a conversation I'm going to have with you right now."

Anthony looked down at the chains on his hands and nodded. "Fine. So I can still be changed back?"

"I think so, you'll need to talk to Uriel."

"Okay, I'm ready to talk. I don't have a choice."

Daniel walked out and the guard slammed three

latches closed to lock the door. Uriel saw him and headed down the hall. "How did it go?"

"He wants to be changed back, so I'd say it went well. He *can* still be changed back, right?"

"Probably. It's unusual for them to want to be turned back. What did you say to him?"

"I told him that Lucas would kill him if he came back."

"Why is that?"

Daniel explained how Lucas had killed Kore, as a result of Daniel's words to the girls.

"Clever. So you see how valuable a hybrid can be, since dark angels can't read your thoughts. Good work, but too risky with the lives of those you care about."

"I agree. But I know something else about Lucas now. Something that's been kept from me. He's my father."

Uriel crossed his arms in silence, his eyes glinting at Daniel. "What makes you think that?"

"He showed up when my house was burning down."

"And why do you think that makes him your father?"

"What you said about hybrids and guardian angels who turned dark still showing up when their guardian subjects were in danger. I've been wondering how my mom fell in love with an angel and it occurred to me that he would have to be her guardian angel, or else her real guardian angel probably wouldn't have allowed it."

Uriel nodded knowingly. "Again, clever. We should've known you would work it out. What are you going to do now that you know?"

Daniel held eye contact with Uriel and tensed his jaw. "I don't know."

Chapter 21

ENEMY OF AN ENEMY

Uriel entered the chamber where Anthony was chained and Daniel waited outside Hannah's room. He watched her through the window in the door, looking for signs that she might be waking.

Several minutes later, he turned to the sound of footsteps as Uriel approached. "I'm finished talking with him."

Daniel looked back at Hannah and then started to walk toward the exit with Uriel at his side. "And?"

"We're offering him protection and help in restoring his humanity, if he'll provide us with information on their strategies."

"There's something else that might be valuable," Daniel replied. "The last thing I heard before I realized Lucas was going to bite Hannah was that they had some type of deal. She was supposed to give him something in exchange for being turned."

"She *wanted* him to bite her? Why?"

"So she could be… with me."

Uriel slowly nodded. "I've seen this before. And what was she supposed to give him in exchange?"

"I don't know yet, but that'll be one of the first things I ask her when she wakes up."

"How did you know to be there when she met with him?"

"With other people it's still instinctive, but when she's in danger, I know that something isn't right with her specifically. I felt it a few seconds after she walked away from me that day."

"Good. You'll find that your abilities will continue to be fine-tuned now that you're aware of them. I'll send someone for you as soon as she wakes."

Daniel nodded and left the cave. Minutes later he drove up the driveway and sat in his car staring at the pile of blackness that used to be his house. He called Erika, but only got her voice mail, so he left a message asking her to call.

As he walked toward the house on the hill the smell of smoke lingered in the air. He unlocked the front door and entered to the sound of Marie's voice.

"Daniel, we need to talk."

"Okay, about what?"

"You burned our house down! That should be enough, but then you wouldn't even talk to me about it. You weren't making any sense with what little you said. Did you know that I've had to answer calls from the fire department and the police this morning?"

"What did they want?"

"What do you think they wanted?"

"The house was uninsured and going to be demolished anyway! Besides, it was a controlled fire on private property. It's not like I didn't think it through."

"Yes and that's what will keep you out of jail. So what's going on?"

Daniel shook his head, warily.

Marie threw her hands up. "Tell me!"

"I wanted to know who my father was! I figured he was your guardian angel because he wouldn't allow another angel to have a relationship with you like that. So even if he was a dark angel, he'd show up because your house was on fire. Now I know who he is."

"Daniel I—"

"You kept it from me my entire life!"

"I was protecting you!"

"Protecting me from what? He was with the Council until recently, so how could you have known he was dangerous?"

"Daniel, it's not that simple. But I don't have to tell you that. I know you're involved with them so you know angels can fall."

"But you didn't know he *would*!"

"You're right, I didn't! But I saw it in him. I knew he could go to either side. He couldn't resist power and it looks like I was right since he isn't with the Council anymore."

"I had a right to know!"

Marie picked up a cup of cold coffee from the counter and poured it down the sink. "Yes, you did. I made the difficult decision to risk your anger rather than your safety. But I guess it's too late now. I have to worry about both."

Daniel's jaw relaxed and his fists slowly unclenched. He put his arms around Marie. "I'm sorry you worry so much."

Marie couldn't swallow back the tears and pressed her face into Daniel's shoulder. "You were my baby… my little boy. How could I not worry?"

"I know, Mom. It's okay."

Daniel held her for several minutes until he felt her embrace weaken. "I've got a lot to do the next few days. A lot of people are in danger. But I'll be as careful as I can, I promise."

Marie nodded her head. "That's all I can ask."

Daniel took a glass from a kitchen cabinet and filled it with water from the sink. He took a long drink and held the glass in his hand as he thought. "Mom, have you seen Zeb lately?"

"Not for a couple days, actually," she said. "I guess dogs can go out on their little adventures and be gone for days at a time though. I'm sure he'll show up soon."

Daniel glanced out the kitchen window. "He's pretty old to be going out on adventures." His eyes traced the field and trees as he thought. "Well I have enough to worry with right now. Zeb, you're on your own."

In bed that night, Daniel tossed and turned amid dreams of women running away from unseen predators until they were too exhausted, or fell. He usually woke just before the fleeing person was attacked.

At sunrise, Daniel made himself a quick breakfast and drove to the lake.

Amilgol came from the bridge to meet him. "Uriel said you'd be here. She just woke up a few minutes ago."

Daniel and Amilgol hurried to Hannah's room. Her face pale and fallen, she reached for Daniel and they embraced as she sobbed.

"I thought I was dying. It was like I couldn't wake up from a dream and I kept thinking that if I died, I would have lost you completely." She raised a listless hand to Daniel's face. "Please don't leave me," she hummed softly before her eyes fell closed.

Daniel kissed her lips, feeling her softness. "Never." He felt her body go limp and laid her head back on the pillow.

Amilgol stepped from the doorway. "Because she didn't get enough venom to turn her, she's suffering from its poison. If she had fully turned, it would be a like a fuel. Instead, it's drawing the life out of her."

Daniel's eyes widened as Amilgol continued.

"I'm not saying she's going to die. She's undergoing what all vampires do, except that they don't feel most of it because of the conversion. It goes on in the background. She's experiencing something similar to dying, but without the superhuman concealment." He paused, brow creased with a frown. "Daniel, I'm not going to lie to you… she could become a lot sicker. There are times when the victim descends into a coma and never wakes up, even after they have seemed to improve. Sometimes, their transformation continues, until they are not just vampire, but more like rabid beast. I don't think any of that's the case here, but I can't say for sure. Hopefully she'll wake again in a few hours. So I wouldn't go too far away, if I were you."

Daniel dropped his head, a sigh escaping his lips. "She can't die," he whispered.

Amilgol accompanied Daniel toward the main hall when Uriel turned the corner and faced them. "How is she?"

"Not good. Still in the beginning stages."

Uriel nodded and turned to Daniel. "While you're waiting, I'd like for you to come with me to speak with Anthony. He's supposed to divulge some useful information about Lucas and his angels today."

"I'll keep an eye on Hannah and come get you if anything changes," Amilgol added.

Daniel followed Uriel to the stone door that imprisoned Anthony. They went into the chamber without a word and sat in chairs looking down on the defeated vampire, still chained and seated on the floor.

Anthony looked curiously back at them. "So you want me to talk, but you keep me in this hell hole?"

Uriel seemed unbothered by Anthony's complaint. "We keep you here because you're a monster. After you're turned back, we'll make other arrangements."

"A monster? Is that any way to talk to someone who's going to help you fight your enemy?"

"I feel no need to sugar coat it. For now, you're a monster. The faster you provide the information you promised, the faster you'll be human again and treated respectfully."

Anthony slammed his fist against the wall, triggering a commotion of chains scraping the floor and bashing into the stone. Uriel's expression remained neutral as he waited for Anthony to speak. Seconds passed as Anthony searched the room with his eyes for something to complain about or to destroy to further express his fury. Minutes passed before he surrendered, and sighed. "What do you want to know?"

"What has become of Zachery?"

"Vampire."

"By whom?"

"Tabitha."

"By his own free will or is he still entranced?"

"I don't know," Anthony admitted. "He looked pretty danged entranced to me."

Uriel stood and paced the room before turning back to Anthony. "What's next?"

Anthony's eyes drifted and he smirked slightly. "They're trying to make new hybrids to raise their numbers, since they can't make new angels."

"Are they succeeding?"

"No. Natalie is the only person I know who's pregnant with a hybrid. Lucas, Kore, none of them could get anyone pregnant anymore. It's like they're sterile or something. And now I'm told Kore's dead." Anthony glanced at Daniel.

Uriel raised his eyes to the ceiling and grinned in amusement. "So the prophecies are coming true."

Daniel lifted his chin. "What prophecies?"

Uriel slowly exhaled. "Angels have books just like humans. There are some in physical form for when we're on Earth and many in other forms in the spiritual realm.

There are books about heroes like Michael and Gabriel. We also have books of prophecy."

Daniel furrowed his brow. "Angels need prophecy?"

"We don't know the future, Daniel. There's only one who knows all of that. But some of us have the gift of prophecy to see bits and pieces and over the eons, we've made sense of some it."

"What was prophesied about Lucas?"

"It wasn't just about Lucas; it was about all fallen angels. Even when the Earth was young, rebel angels were sleeping with women and the offspring that followed was the dawn of the Nephilim or hybrid. Most hybrids were destroyed in the great flood. It wasn't until recently that dark angels started seeking human women again, and now I know why. It's to build an army of hybrids. But the prophecy said that a day would come when the fallen ones would no longer be able to procreate with humans. Yet one of their own offspring, the chosen one, would have a son who would be the last hybrid."

Anthony twisted toward Daniel, blinking in astonishment. "There were prophecies about Daniel? He's a 'chosen one'?" Anthony pounded the floor and laughed hysterically, but inhaled to silence himself upon seeing Uriel's furious expression.

"*The* chosen one," Uriel corrected.

Daniel's face remained expressionless. "So what does that mean? Chosen for what?"

Uriel's eyes drifted down from Daniel's. "The book is called 'Vision' in English and I suppose it's anyone's guess what 'chosen one' truly means. The prophecy wasn't clear. Many things are needed on Earth and elsewhere and I can only hope I'm interpreting it correctly by pointing the passages to you."

Daniel's jaw clinched and he nodded as he turned his face toward the wall. "Now that you believe I'm the 'chosen one,' what's next?"

Uriel stood and left the room, waiting until Daniel followed before he closed the door.

The two walked down the hall toward Hannah's room.

"Daniel, there are at least two things that need to happen: Zachery must be brought back to us, and Lucas must die."

"What about Natalie and the baby?"

"When Lucas is dead, I think she'll be far more open minded. I need your answer now. Will you join the Council or not? I'll need to plan differently if you're still on the fence."

"Yes, I'm in. I'll join the Council."

They both stopped in front of Hannah's door and Daniel went in alone. He stopped at her bed, crouched to his knees and began caressing her face with his fingertips. Her eyes flicked open and Daniel was unable to hide his astonishment at seeing that her eyes had turned to metallic silver that shone like pewter, sprinkled with emerald glints.

She smiled weakly at him, but her eyes glowed. "Daniel... I've missed you."

"I will *always* be here for you." Daniel leaned down to meet her mouth with his. Despite her weakness, he couldn't help his increasing fervency as he kissed her. But he pulled back suddenly when he felt his bottom lip sting. Hannah stared up at him, wondering why he had stopped. She reached a trembling hand to her mouth and her eyes widened as she traced a finger over her small, newly formed fangs. Her mouth fell open in shock and her head dropped back into the pillow as she peered into the bright blue of Daniel's eyes.

"It makes no difference to me," Daniel said softly, smoothing her hair.

From the doorway, Amilgol spoke. "I don't mean to interrupt, but I'm sure you have questions."

Hannah nodded, willing herself to find the energy to speak. "Am I," she fought back her tears, "a vampire?"

Amilgol's look was stern and unmerciful. "Isn't that what you wanted, Hannah?"

Her eyes darted from Amilgol to Daniel, and then to Uriel standing just outside the door. She slammed a clinched fist against the mattress and released a groan that transitioned ungracefully into a raspy screech.

She gasped before yelling, "This is not what I wanted!" Hannah twisted against the mattress, unable to find a comfortable position. "I wanted to prove myself, to have something stable again. But now I'm…" She'd used up most of her energy and could now only summon a few final words before descending back into unconsciousness. "I'm sick."

Daniel leaned down and kissed her forehead, and stroked her cheek with his hand.

She battled to keep her eyes open as Amilgol stood over her and spoke rapidly. "There could be some upsides to your ailment, Hannah. At this point, you're still mostly human. Vampires and dark angels won't be able tell that you're part vampire, and if they bite you, they'll die." His eyes traced her face before he continued. "You should sleep now."

Hannah's eyelids drooped until they were completely shut. Amilgol now spoke for Daniel's benefit. "This is just part of the process. Some take longer than others. If she comes through this all right, when the process is complete the vampire part of her can't increase, no matter how many times she's bitten. It's like she's received a vampire immunization, so to speak." He nodded encouragement toward Daniel and left the room.

Uriel lifted a ragged wooden chair from the hall and sat it next to Hannah's bed. "You shouldn't go into combat when your heart is here. Watch over her until she wakes for good and then we'll send Lucas to hell."

Daniel nodded grimly as he sat. "What did Amilgol mean when he said a vampire would die from biting Hannah?"

Uriel peered through the doorway, hesitating before turning to answer Daniel's question. "There can be a poison response to biting another vampire because a vampire's blood is void of life force; it's dead. That's why they seek blood from the living. If they drink too much dead blood, before they realize what it is, it will kill them since they're conditional immortals."

Daniel's eyes were slack and distant. "There's a lot to remember."

Uriel neared Hannah and leaned over her. "Any creature's anatomy takes learning." He felt her forehead and pressed a finger beside her throat. "She's progressing. I'm going now to meet with the Council about your decision. Amilgol will check in on her again shortly." He put a hand on Daniel's shoulder as he turned to leave the room. "Don't blame yourself for this happening to her. You can't guard everyone you love every passing second. We're all responsible for our own decisions."

Daniel nodded, his eyes returning to Hannah, but he spoke as Uriel stepped under the doorframe. "I saw something when I snatched Anthony. Something that didn't seem important at the time."

Uriel walked back into the room again, his eyes fixed on Daniel's. "Yes?"

"I saw an empty bag from the plasma and blood clinic. It was dried up lying in the mud against a tree. When Amilgol said that Hannah's blood would kill a vampire, it made me think that—"

"Don't finish. We can't risk anyone overhearing. Stay with her until I come back from meeting with the Council, and then we'll talk to Anthony to get the details we need."

After Uriel had left, Daniel leaned over Hannah, watching the slow rise and fall of her chest. He pressed his lips gently to hers, and whispered, "I love you, Hannah Sawyer. Vampire or not."

Chapter 22

FEAST OF BLOOD

THE SOUND OF the door creaking opened Anthony's eyes. "Can't you two just leave me alone? I told you what I know."

Uriel waited just inside the door while Daniel walked close to the chained vampire. "The day I rescued you I saw an empty bag from the clinic on the ground. How did it get there?"

Anthony chuckled. "What do I look like, a secretary?"

Daniel cut his eyes to Uriel who nodded back at him. Before Anthony could react, Daniel back fisted him across his face, slamming his upper body against the stone wall. "You think this is a game? You think I'm going to allow my child be raised by an army of—"

"What do you think the bags were for?" Anthony spit a tooth at Daniel's feet as a red stream trickled from his lips down the front of his neck. "We drink blood, for God's sake! The army's too big now and there aren't enough people to kill in this town, so Lucas came up with a plan that would keep us fed for good. A live person can give a lot more blood over a lifetime than one we kill and feed on only once. So we supplemented some." Anthony's snarl turned to a grin. "That doesn't mean I didn't enjoy a good killin' though."

Daniel shook his head and glanced back at Uriel.

"Lucas had a contact at the clinic," Anthony continued. "A year or so ago they started keeping some of the blood for us instead of sending it all to hospitals. That's so Lucas will let them and their families live. On Thursday nights, nobody works late."

"So on Thursday nights when Lucas decides it's feeding time," Uriel began, "he just goes to the clinic and brings the bags back to the others?"

"No," Anthony answered. "He goes with a group and they drink there. No vampire has the patience to bring it back to the group first. Lucas usually takes the higher ranks with him and when we're full, we bring back what's left. Those who don't get enough have to go hunting."

Daniel stomped the tooth into the ground, crushing it to powder beneath his shoe. "So you're a 'higher rank'?"

"As far as Kore was concerned, I was. So he took me with him."

Daniel glanced back at Uriel and his eyes sent an unspoken message before they walked toward the door.

Anthony slammed his arms into the stone floor, rattling the chains. "You're just leaving me again? Am I going to rot in here?!"

Uriel turned his head in Anthony's direction. "The day will come when you'll make good on your promises to help. But first, we'll see if what you said is true."

Daniel headed toward the exit, with Uriel, for the second time that day.

"Go and get some rest, I'll call when she stirs."

"I won't be gone long. I need to be with her, so if she wakes in the meantime, please call me right away." Daniel hesitated as he began to turn away. "What about what Anthony said?"

Uriel looked left down a hall and then right before answering. "We'll send someone to see if it really happens."

"And if it does?"

"Then Hannah will be able to enter the war in a much more direct way than any of us could have predicted."

Daniel walked across the parking lot and dropped into the driver's seat. During the drive to his house, his phone vibrated from his pocket and he answered to Erika's voice.

"Hey, you alright? How's Hannah?"

"She's not good. She has some vampire traits and we don't know what's going to happen. Right now, she's unconscious again."

"That doesn't sound good. I'm sorry, Daniel. Do you think you could come by today? I'd like for you to tell me everything that's going on with her. And Anthony, too. I'm worried out of my mind. Not to mention I'm lonely."

"I'm heading that way, so I'll be there in ten minutes. I can't stay long though, I have to go home for a bit and then I need to get back to Hannah."

Erika met him in the dorm lobby. "Come up to my room?"

When they got there, she held a plate of cookies up to Daniel. "I've really started liking chocolate chip with a glass of wine. Or two." She poured two glasses of wine and sat one down in front of Daniel.

Daniel picked up his glass and they each sat at the desk as a roll of thunder rattled the window. Daniel bit into the cookie and took a sip of wine.

"You're right. It brings the chocolate out."

"I know, right?"

The two sat quietly and listened to the rain splash as it filled a puddle outside.

Erika noticed Daniel's empty plate. "You want more?"

Daniel shook his head.

"Training for something?"

"Maybe."

Erika sighed. "I never could've imagined we'd both be in love with vampires."

Daniel raised an eyebrow. "I never could've imagined they even existed."

"Who? Vampires? Or someone you would fall in love with?"

Daniel lifted the glass to his lips and took a hefty mouthful of what remained. "Either."

As he placed his glass on the desk, his cell phone vibrated in his pocket. It showed no number.

"Yes?"

"Daniel, it's Uriel." His voice held urgency. "It's not good Daniel, she's not stirring; she grows paler and weaker by the minute. Her heart rate is decreasing. Amilgol says it could go either way."

"What?" His breath caught in his throat. "What can

we do? I'm heading there now." Daniel stood as Erika moved closer, frantically trying to hear.

"There is one thing… Amilgol has seen one thing work."

"What is it? We've got to try anything." Daniel struggled to repress his panic.

"If she drinks the blood of a vampire who's been changed back to human, it can halt the process."

Daniel paused briefly. "But that's—" He glanced at Erika as realization struck. "Anthony…"

Erika looked on intently, worry saturating her brown eyes.

"Yes."

"I don't get it, I thought that was a long process. Hannah needs this now!"

"There is a way, a single way it can be done faster. It's risky, and sometimes doesn't work. It's to do with a vampire drinking another vampire's blood. As we talked about, too much dead blood and it can kill the vampire. However, if a vampire drinks the blood of the fallen angel who bit him in the first place, it can revert him to human. It's a rare event, so we don't know a lot about it. But we're out of time."

Daniel's eyes grew wide as he turned to Erika. "Lucas," he whispered into the phone.

"Yes, Lucas. It was he who turned Anthony. You must capture him, alive, and bring him back to the Council."

Daniel closed his eyes and gathered himself. "Right."

"And Daniel, you'll have to do it fast."

"I'm on it." He hung up and turned to Erika, his heart racing.

"I have to go."

"Not without me, you're not." She quickly bent to tie her shoes and grabbed her jacket.

"Erika, it's not safe."

"I don't care, I'm coming."

He sighed, frustrated. "I don't have time to argue." He turned, went out the door, and began to jog down the hall. "You'd better be able to keep up," he yelled over his shoulder as he heard her footsteps pounding behind him.

To be continued…

Lee Wilson is an author and actor who has been seen in film and television. He has spoken at the Pepperdine University Lectureships and has ghost written for major national publications.

Photo: © Lee Wilson

You can follow him at Facebook.com/LeeWilsonFanPage and at Twitter.com/LeeWilsonTalks. For information on more titles by Lee and to register for book giveaways, visit LeeWilson.org.

The Saga Continues!

The Last Hybrid saga continues in the sequel to *The Last Hybrid: Bloodline of Angels* (at this time, the title has yet to be revealed). For updates, author interviews, book-group material, sample chapters, cover reveals and discussion visit **TheLastHybrid.com**.

Follow *The Last Hybrid* on Facebook at **Facebook.com/LastHybrid** and on Twitter at **Twitter.com/TheLastHybrid**.

Scan this code with your phone to be notified of sequels and other titles by Lee Wilson.